HOMEGROWN KILLER

I0547134

By Ivan Bering

Copyright 2018 Ivan Bering

A Charlie Taylor Novel

ISBN

978-1-7753266-0-1

AUTHOR'S NOTE

This story took place about six years after we caught the Irish home invaders. Ok. Ok. We only nailed two out of the three killers, but the slaughtering stopped. I say 'about six years' because there never was an exact start or end time for this account.

My psychologist no longer demands I write; instead, it has become a habit. As well, it helps to be with the History Unit, now known as the Cold Squad, and more structured working hours.

This was an emotional and devastating ride, with a number of friends directly affected. Unfortunately, I had to bypass a few regulations to get answers. I hope you can forgive the improper behavior; but, if you've read my other stories, you already know how much I care.

Charlie Taylor,

Currently: Head Investigator, Cold Squad

Previously: Senior Detective, Homicide Squad

PROLOGUE

THREE WEEKS AFTER THE RECORDING: SEPTEMBER 25, 2028

Profanity, in thought or speech, was a rare occurrence for the President. But at this moment one thought filled in his mind, and it was difficult for him not to scream: *what a fucking mess!*

Dr. Max Armstrong, a Nobel Prizing winning scientist, was the only other occupant in the ornate, impressive office. The President's urgent summons for this meeting had arrived 24 hours earlier. This brilliant researcher who had conquered his wilder youthful sexual exploits still struggled with his temper and impatience.

Dr. Max, as the news media often referred to him, had movie star good looks to accompany his scientific genius; this combination of nature's legacy regularly trigged jealousy in the scientific community. Most of the brilliant academics accepted the fact that this handsome man had earned his reputation, but some made the mistake of challenging him in a public setting. Max understood their intent, and his sarcastic response was brutal, provoking doubts about the questioner's intelligence. His verbal outbursts knew no bounds. The President had been warned.

Although the President spoke slowly and quietly, there was a tremor in his voice. "Dr. Max, what I am about to show you has, so far, been treated as top secret; in fact, only a handful of people know what happened. Unfortunately, this will change very soon."

None of Max's colleagues would have recognized his current demeanor: humble and mouth shut. The oval office with all the flags, the big oil paints, and other perks of the position were overwhelming. The President continued. "Since you are directly involved, and are the key individual, we have to talk. Alright?"

Max responded with a nod. "Yes, fine by me." But thought: *What the hell is this all about?*

The President, an excellent communicator, maintained eye contact and continued. "I want you to watch this recording which was sent to me by Judge Doug Brewster from your Sector 14."

As the President studied the unit and tried to remember how to run the video playback machine, Max thought about his Sector 14: *the great Judge Brewster, prick number one and Chief Kisashton, prick number two…….what a great combination of ass kissers……they are pulling something………..two idiots.*

The President finally had the device ready. "In the recording are Judge Doug Brewster, Chief Kisashton, Professor Tyler Carson, and the ex-con, really a recently arrested killer. The ex-con is making the accusation; Professor Carson is only an observer and has no official capacity. The killer requested the scientist's presence."

The video displayed the killer: a man of average appearance, with long blond hair tied in a single ponytail and large orange plastic glass frames; he knew he was being recorded and stared directly into the camera, rarely blinking, composed and articulate. As the recording played, Max felt his hands tremble and his heart race; he was watching a disaster. Twice he mumbled profanities, disregarding his earlier instructions to avoid swearing in the President's company.

The President halted the recording. "I'll stop here; the remainder consists of the Judge and Chief challenging his accusation. If we continued watching, we'd see more of the same: both men vigorously challenged the accuser but were unable to have the killer recant.

At the end of the recording, Professor Carson is adamant and states: we have to treat this as a plausible occurrence: this is a feasible event."

The President stopped, giving Max time to absorb the shattering accusation. The scientist remained silent but didn't have to wait long. "Dr. Armstrong, before you respond allow me to continue. The Judge agreed with Professor Carson and has recommended the formation of an Assessment Team: to include Professor Carson, who is a neurologist, and Dr. Wiek, a biochemist, both well-respected scientists. Your comments, please."

Max thought: *sure the two well-known scientists who have been trying to discredit my work for the last 15 years.....shitheads both of them ......mediocre at best...son of a bitch.*

The Nobel Prize winner exploded. "This is fucking bullshit. That killer, that son of a bitch is running a scam, and you have a few halfwits running their agenda to destroy my work ...goddammit..."

The President cringed with the outburst of vulgarity. "Calm down Dr. Max. I understand these two scientists are not your best friends. So here is what will happen. First, I will select two more scientists to add to the Assessment Team, and this full panel of experts will review the situation and this accusation.

The scope will include your original research plus they will interview many of the convicts who have been subject to your innovations. Unfortunately, they will be unable to conduct any autopsies because all those found guilty have been cremated. Next, until this incident is resolved, our system of justice will have to proceed without your scientific advances. The big issue is how do we keep this secret or can we? Once this becomes public knowledge, every convict found guilty because of your science will be launching an appeal. And of course, others will be trying to sue.

Both Judge Doug and Chief Kisashton have recommended we make this public and live with consequences. I agree with their recommendation, and this evening I will make the incident and our Assessment Team public knowledge. Is there anything you want to add?"

Dr. Armstrong's breathing became rapid, and his thoughts jumped ...*that fucking Doug and that asshole buddy of his, the Chief.* He finally composed himself and responded. "I assume I will not be included in the scientific review."

"Correct. It has to be completely independent. You will be able to challenge their findings but not be part of their work team."

Max, a genius by any standards, immediately understood the situation, and he understood the resolution would have to be fast, and the investigation would require a ruthless no holds barred approach. "Since my reputation is about to be destroyed and my science career ruined, I'd ask you delay your announcement for 24 hours."

"I agree. Is there anything else you want?"

"I want detective Charlie Taylor with a generous operating budget."

CHAPTER 1: THE TROLL

BEFORE THE RECORDING: JULY 2, 2028

"Come on Griffin tell us how many of your students do you screw each semester? Do you have a quota?" As he leaned over the desk, Wes didn't scream but was inches away from the man's face.

Two homicide detectives and Griffin were crowded into the small office. The workplace had a stereotypical academic ambience, disparate piles of paper scattered in different locations, books of various sizes and shapes populated the floor to ceiling bookcases. One large window almost filled the back wall; a multitude of stick-em notes plastered the large computer desk monitor and a variety of framed pictures in random locations added to the chaos of his office.

Professor Lewis Griffin smirked, not concerned with this in-your-face approach. "I assume you are here about Cara Gonzales; she was taking my course, and that is all I know about her death. To repeat I know nothing about her disappearance."

Senior homicide detective Wes Krause and his young partner, Jeff Hutton, were trying to intimidate the university professor; they suspected he was the serial killer the newspapers had baptized: the Troll. The baptism occurred shortly after young adolescent girls, with mental disabilities, started showing up dead; a reporter, who was born in Norway, came up with the name for the killer: TROLL. A creature with scary elements which the reporter hoped would get the publicity needed and maybe make parents and teenagers more cautious.

Griffin was a handsome man, little over 30 years old, just over six feet, with dark curly hair; his neat appearance was a sharp contrast to the two detectives who, in comparison, looked unkempt. "My relationship with female students is not your business. I do admit I do have a fetish for junior high school girls in their school uniforms with pleated skirts and knee socks. But it is under control, and I have not abused my privileges."

Wes exploded. "Jesus! Fetish! Detective Hutton, help me what the hell does that mean?"

As Wes played the caveman, Young Jeff played the cool intellectual. "He is trying to explain his interest in the younger set. It's a euphemism."

"Goddamnit! Euphemism! Damn it, Jeff you're supposed to help me understand."

Jeff was ready. "It means: when he sees the young girls he gets excited. The times he talks to his colleagues, he says 'fetish' because it sounds loftier, more poetic and harmless. You know compared to saying: they make him horny."

Griffin was getting upset. "You two have the manners of an angry wasp and are almost as smart."

Wes was relentless. "Are we starting to reach the well-educated superior man? You getting worried? You should be because: the words are 'horny as hell', and if it sounds mean or dangerous, it is. So listen asshole: stow the 'fetish' and tell us about the first-year student who was taking your class and has now been found raped and murdered."

The detective knew it wasn't working and knew when he started it was a long shot; his only hope had been that Griffin, in his anger, would let something slip. Wes didn't need much, just a minor admission which might allow an interrogation with a truth serum, the S1; this homicide investigator was normally systematic and thorough, but the killings had shaken him and resulted in this uncharacteristic yelling match. Griffin rocked his head from side to side, like scolding a young child. "You're on a fishing trip because of one charge which happened many years ago, and that complaint was dropped."

"The student dropped the complaint because she needed your course for her degree, but privately she, and some others claim, you are lecherous and horny, always standing too close, always ready for an accidental rub or an unintended feel."

"As I said you are on a fishing expedition. Unless you have more, I'm leaving."

He got up and walked to the door and into the hall. Wes yelled after him "Doc we are only one clue away from an S1 interrogation, and you know if we get clearance for a formal interrogation your entire history will be revealed. Best to talk now and restrict the damage."

"Goodbye, I was going to say 'gentlemen', but that is obviously a mistake."

####

The parking lot was on the far side of the Campus. The two detectives maintained a brisk pace as they followed the paved paths which wove around the perimeter of a vast expanse of grass and some old elm trees. The open space was filled with students, some playing catch, some devouring lunch and others just relaxing on the grass. Jeff thought: it must be a sweet life.

Wes towered over Jeff who was a small man and with a poor diet was developing a chubby exterior. Although at times his rookie naivety had to be endured, Wes liked him as a partner and felt he would mature into an excellent detective.

Before they reached the car, Wes started up. "Jeff, I'm convinced he is our man. Look at the video of Cara; she is 18 but looks and dresses like she is 13. That smart academic's fetish rules him"

The smaller man responded. "Cara is not his regular pattern, but I agree. Unfortunately, Legal will never sanction an S1 truth serum with what we have."

Wes handed Jeff his tablet; he'd retrieved the reporter's write up about the name. Jeff read: **The Troll is part of the Scandinavian folklore, an ugly creature who loves dark places and snatches away small children. This Norse myth attributed different characteristics to the creatures, but often the kids were left with an image of some who devoured humans, with large stew pot.**

Ugly, hard to catch or see, lived in caves or under a bridge, and hunted from those spots.

###

The senior Cold Squad detective, Charlie Taylor, ran up the stairs to the front entrance to the Hall of Justice. This was not a morning to be rushing about, but he'd promised Wes he would see him before heading to the Disciplinary Panel. Wes had pleaded with his former supervisor to get in early and interrogate a witness; he knew Charlie had a successful record in getting witnesses and suspects to reveal more than they intended.

Detective Taylor didn't want to rush this morning, but he had committed to Wes, before the Disciplinary Panel had set a meeting time and date. Contrasting thoughts swirled around his mind; he was unable to control his thinking: *after six years in the Cold Squad*.....

the Disciplinary Panel will have little choice…first I get thrown out of Homicide now this…. Emma is furious …..what a mess…..if they hadn't hurt Emma….doesn't matter…it was bloody stupid….to get caught was even stupider.

Within a few minutes, he was through the main doors, up the elevator, down the hall and listening to his former homicide partner outline the Troll case. It didn't sound good. Charlie wanted to help his friend but was not optimistic. "Come on Wes you must have more. Come on. One more time give me a summary version."

They were the only two men in the room; Wes because it was his office, and Detective Taylor because of his Disciplinary Panel review was to take place, on the first floor in 90 minutes.

Ordinarily his relationship with Chief Kisashton didn't allow him a friendly visit to the Hall of Justice. All staff in the Hall knew even a friendly greeting to Charlie could draw a reprimand. The Chief was convinced Charlie was responsible for how the staff labeled him: Chief Kissass. The title stuck and now was universal across the Sector, of course never uttered in his presence.

Wes wanted to take advantage of Charlie's presence. "This prof has a rep for screwing students, particularly the ones who look very young; second, for years he has been associated with institutes which care for the mentally challenged; he knows the staff, their routines, and the student body. And every time I talk to him I get the feeling he is ducking and weaving; he is the one constant at every institution where the girls were taken.

Numerous young mentally challenged girls have been raped and killed over the past 10 years …in three different Sectors from six different residences, and this Griffin has been associated with all six residences in one way or the other….he has a Ph.D. in education and helps develop training programs....all programs are tailored to the audience and very targeted ....he would know the students and the physical layout, including any full-time students in residence.

Now I admit Cara is a change...not the normal routine; she was a clever student, enrolled in Griffin's class, but her downfall was she looked like a teenager."

An impatient Charlie: "Jesus that is ridiculously thin. His education specialty means he should be working with these institutions. Griffin's domain is teenagers with an IQ of less than 80. He develops social programs and special classes. The man has a solid academic record. What else you got?"

Wes continued, "The other night two junior high kids launched a homemade drone out in a heavily wood area where one of them lives. Earlier in the day, an exciting rumor flew around: a mountain lion was in the area. These two wanted to see if they could get a picture. The kids were good and hooked up some infra-red night vision camera and started flying. No cougar but near the end of the flight the drone picks up a guy carrying a body into the woods. This is how we found Cara's body.

The kids panicked and ran home before calling 911. By the time a car got there, the man was gone. Unfortunately, they had the drone flying high, and it didn't produce a good sharp picture. Didn't matter, the guy was well covered, no identification was possible, but the body profile, height, and shape match the prof. Plus based on the kid's video, we know our suspect needs an alibi for 11:30 pm to 2:00 am."

"Shit, I repeat: you have nothing. You know his secretary provides an alibi for the night that young Cara disappeared. What the hell is going on?"

Wes tried to be patient, "His secretary, Elaine Lute, is a young woman deeply in love with our Professor Griffin, and she would say anything for him. Let me try again. I get so many bad vibes from this guy. I know how wild this sounds, but look he is smart as hell, knows his way around all the care facilities in the Sector ...... every girl who has disappeared he has been at that care facility."

"You and Jeff have been at this young lady for an hour, and she won't change her story. So I'm to come in play nice and see if she folds. Right? And don't ask: I have no black market S1 truth serum to medicate her drink for an easy confession."

Wes knew it was not going as planned. "I know it is a long shot. Sure I'm desperate. This guy is so confident and such a good liar; we can't crack him. I'm hoping if Elaine starts talking something will surface to allow us to apply the S1 interrogation. I just need one small inconsistency."

The S1 Interrogation made use of, what was known as, a truth sermon, part of the scientific work that earned Dr. Max Armstrong the Nobel Prize. Police required significant justification and the concurrence of Legal Division before using it. Without this tight restriction, there was the danger Police would use the tool in a random fashion, picking up any suspicious characters off the street and hear involuntary confessions.

Charlie could sense the desperation and came to one those "what the hell" decisions.

"Alright, first get the Garden clear of any staff and then make sure the camera and audio are active on the large waterfall set. I'll go at her up there.

Wait a minute ...wait.....just a minute. What else can you tell me about this Elaine Lute?"

Wes went back to his screen, scrolled for a few minutes and then began a series of verbal bursts to explain her history. "Here we are…..almost graduated with a Fine Arts degree but is a few classes short ……looks like a below average student………has a couple more years to complete the missing courses……..no disciplinary issues…."

Charlie interrupted. "What was her major?"

"She focused on music…the classics."

"Good. Load the sound system with Mozart, Beethoven …the whole classic package.

I'll talk to her in the Garden. Not for too long. You'll know when I have finished. Then I have to run to my Disciplinary hearing. Let's go. I'll go get the young lady."

Charlie walked into the small interrogation room and saw a young woman, who was very tense and upset. "Hi Elaine, my name is Charlie Taylor; I don't work for Wes or homicide. I'm just here to make sure you understand your situation."

Before she could respond, he continued. "Come on let's get out of here there is a better spot to chat…on the top floor of this building."

Elaine was a small woman, model thin, looked much younger than her 23 years, more like a teenager. Her coal-black hair was pulled straight back into a single large ponytail; her dress, to Charlie, seemed rather informal for a senior assistant to a full Professor: worn black jeans, a simple long-sleeved white sweater, no jewelry except for small diamond studs for her ears. Charlie thought: a bloody kid.

They walked out of the room, down the hall and to the elevator, up to the top floor without a word spoken. As soon as they stepped out of the elevator on the top floor, Elaine was shocked. "God this fantastic!"

Charlie laughed. "It's known as the Garden…it fills the entire floor. A grateful billionaire had it designed and paid for the construction and pays for the upkeep. If the place depended on the police for feeding and watering, all the plants would be dead within two weeks. It is normally restricted to police personnel who want some quiet time to relax and get reenergized. It is early, so the place is normally vacant at this time of day."

The sun shone through an ingenious plastic dome which controlled the amount of sunlight allowed to filter in the Garden. There were numerous paths and benches surrounded by a multitude of green plants and boulders of various sizes and colors. Here and there a bed of bright flowers and a selection of shrubs. Numerous small waterfalls were located along the perimeter, with a large area of falling water at the center of the Garden. In the background soft classical music played continuously. The entire complex was unoccupied.

"Stop here Elaine and have a cup. It is all free; many different coffees, teas and hot chocolate. Let's fill up." She was surprised to see a small but very modern kitchen with many varieties of coffee, tea, chocolate, and herbal mixes. Her hands trembled as she prepared a large mug of herbal tea. Charlie didn't stare but watched closely, knowing he had little time to assess her as she surveyed her new surroundings and listened to the piped-in music. Charlie guessed: she is impressed with the grandeur and possibly with his unstated role.

Once both cups were filled, Charlie led her to the largest waterfall. "I apologize for Wes. He is under tremendous pressure to find the Troll. I can help you, but to do a better job, I need to understand your situation. Tell me how long have you been working for the professor?"

"I've been at the U for three years. I started in the general office, was there for two years and then Grif spotted me, and I've been with him for a year. I'm delighted and lucky to get the job."

"Boy, that was a fast promotion from the pool to a senior position with a department head."

"He said: as soon as he saw me, he knew I was the one for his office."

"Elaine, I understand your loyalty, but I have to make sure you understand your position: not a warning just clarification. OK?"

"Well, these gardens certainly make talking easier."

"Good, here is the situation. The police are after the Troll, and the public is terrified. The detectives will not stop. If there is anything in your story no matter how small or insignificant that they find doesn't match the facts, they will charge you."

"I'm not afraid. I'm not lying."

At that moment the music changed: the four famous notes of Beethoven's Fifth Symphony filled the air. It was the pause he wanted. As she closed her eyes and swayed with the music, Charlie thought: maybe she was ready. "Here is where it gets ugly for you. Let's suppose he didn't spend the entire night with you but came in late. Suppose he did kill someone; you could be treated as an accomplice, and that means the death penalty, there will be no appeal. You are taking a chance by even supporting a small inconsistency.

As I said all the police need is one small discrepancy in your sworn statement, and they will be after you. Now I don't believe he killed anyone, let me repeat: I don't think he killed anyone. But you are still in a vulnerable position. The ironic part for you rests in the new amended criminal code, Section 16.48. The new law is unambiguous: to lie to the police is now considered the same as being on the witness stand, that is, perjury. And the penalty is jail time.

There is something you have to consider: I don't think the situation is as bad as everyone appears to believe it is. Maybe it was just an embarrassing moment for Professor Griffin, and you're risking jail time to save him some embarrassment. Eventually, the truth will surface, and even if he is innocent, your lie will mean you're out of a job and will end up with a criminal record, after a few months at Sector Farm."

A few floors down, two men sat before a video screen and a recording device. Young Jeff was impressed. "Thank god, Charlie is current. I never can keep up with all the amendments."

Wes smiled. "There is no amendment to Section 16.48 and, in any case, the section deals with authorization for the use of interrogation techniques, such as S1."

"The shifty bastard!"

Elaine stared at Charlie. "I don't understand."

Charlie knew he had arrived at the critical point in the interrogation. "I'll share this with you because I hate to see you get caught in this mess. But we have to have an understanding: this stays just between us. OK? Yes? Good. Ok, here it is.

My wife works in the university administration, and the most recent gossip is about Professor Griffin; he has been given a warning to stay out of gambling casinos. I don't have any details about what happened, but the U is trying to protect its name. Even with tenure, the professor has to be careful."

Charlie paused, waiting for this new revelation to have its impact. Then he continued. "My guess: he was at a casino that night and doesn't want anyone to know. It's too big a risk for him; I doubt his tenure might be in danger. The worst? He'll get slapped with another warning. Not fatal but embarrassing for this proud man."

Again he paused, not wanting to throw too much at the young woman. He started again, pushing his support for the professor. "No, I don't think he is guilty of killing any girls. No way. A good looking guy like that doesn't need to rape women.

However, I have to tell Wes about the gambling issue. Later this afternoon, Detective Wes and his team will start a canvas of the casinos in the city.

To repeat the danger for you: if they confirm he was gambling that night and this confirmation happens before you tell us the truth, they will go at you with Section 16.48. This means your job is gone, and you get a record and all for nothing. I'm sure he is not a guilty man".

In the observation room, young Jeff reacted. "He is lucky his wife works at the University Amin; otherwise he'd never known about the gambling issue."

"His wife doesn't work at the University, and there is no gambling issue."

"Bugger got me again!"

This time she set down her mug and bent over at the waist, face pointed at her shoes. She whined and sounded like an animal in distress. The stress was too much for the young woman, not accustom to telling lies. A few minutes later she straightened, wiped the tears from her face and said. "You have to promise the U doesn't hear about this; he doesn't need that aggravation, and I know he has fought with them."

"Elaine, I guarantee you no one in the police department will mention the casinos. They'll capture his image in the place to clear him of this killing."

"Thanks, I trust you. You are right. Professor Griffin did not spend the night; he came in early, around 5:00 am in the morning, very tired, looked wasted and only spoke long enough to tell me: he loved me, and I had to swear he arrived at six pm, and we spent the night together."

"Thanks, that was a good decision; Wes will not tell the University about the casino. Now is there anything else you want to share with me; I don't pass on everything to Wes. We often don't agree. I have a more sympathetic nature; I understand people can and will make mistakes which they later regret."

Elaine smiled, relieved that she had stopped lying and felt very comfortable with a detective who could explain the issues. And he indeed was sympathetic. He understood the problems of life and would protect her.

Charlie recognized they had turned a corner and pressed: "So is there anything else which might help me understand the two of you? It is important that I understand Professor Griffin; I mean: given some of the gossip about him and his students, it may not be that easy to get the Homicide squad to leave him alone. That homicide detective doesn't like academics and can be a real pit-bull, looking for anything as a charge. I can pressure Wes to leave him alone. I'm prepared to help you both, but I need a better understanding of your relationship. How long have you been together?"

After blurting out the truth, she was more relaxed and for the first time in many hours could smile; she was not used to being dishonest, and now the tension had drained. She didn't understand why Detective Taylor wanted more, but Charlie seemed to be the protector for her and Griffin. As the Fifth Symphony played and the sprinkling of water from the falls hit her face, she was ready and proud to be able to share her romantic life finally. A life which Griffin had insisted be kept secret. Elaine was proud of their love and wanted to share; she started by describing their initial meeting and the hot relationship. "He so much more experienced than me. Still, we do have fantastic sex…our fantasies are well..."

The detective supported her. "Nothing to be ashamed of; sex is a part of life, and many partners develop fantasies which are normal."

After a short hesitation, Charlie took a leap, the type of move which his instinct told him was right; he lowered his voice, like sharing a personal secret. "When we were first married, I bought the Kuma Sutra book."

"God! Do you mean the ancient Indian Hindu text about sexual positions?"

"You got it. There are around 100 different sexual positions fully illustrated. We spent a couple of years working our way through the book."

Elaine was impressed and pleased with Charlie's openness and frank discussion about sex. "Boy, we never went that far but did a lot of role-playing."

"Do the two of you have favorite roles?"

He was pushing, but now that she had started, it appeared she was thrilled with her relationship with a full Prof and want the world to know. It was time to talk, and the ambience and a sudden a break in the cloud cover flooded the Gardens with a soft, warm shelter, all making it easier to finally tell someone about her love and her mature bond. No one else knew, and she did want to brag. "We have a number of costumes and makeup; it is fun to dress up. My favorite well it...." She hesitated, sensing maybe she has gone too far.

He had to press. "Go ahead this is not abnormal behavior." Would she continue?

At that moment the Fifth Symphony abruptly stopped, and Mozart's Eine Kleine Nacht took over. Elaine closed her eyes and started humming, her favorite classical piece. In the last few minutes, it all came together: Grif was safe, no more lies, an understanding detective, and Mozart. She felt secure and pleased to be able to freely talk about her adventures.

"Our favorite is: I play a 13-year-old school-girl; in my closet are four different outfits some different school uniforms, jackets, school crests on the jackets, short skirts, knee socks, the works; then I often fix my hair into pigtails. He dresses like a school teacher, often as a chem teacher with a large white smock."

"Boy, that sounds exciting."

"Oh god! It is, and Grif almost goes crazy, and this gets me going. Sometimes I wonder how we don't hurt each other… but he does hit me …not hard…. well once he broke my glasses but it was an accident…he was so sorry, and I healed fast. Also exciting is the noise, he sounds like a train locomotive coming down the tracks. I guess this all sounds weird."

"No, not at all…..I'm a strong believer in individual freedom, and you are both intelligent adults…. nothing is wrong ….a solid relationship…good for you."

"There is one thing that, at first I didn't like but have come to accept it, and I got very good at the acting part."

"Elaine, don't stop this sounds good."

By now she believed in Charlie, and there was no holding back. "Very often he wants me to act as if I'm not very smart….you know like really dumb. I couldn't do it right until he showed me some pictures. I kept them, and I practiced, got some thick lens glasses and even do a little drooling. I'm good at it. I have all the pictures of the girls he wants me to play; all the images are in my closet with the costumes.

Here let me show you. It took a lot of practice."

With that, she undid the ponytail, ruffled her hair, took some glasses out of her purse, started breathing through her open mouth, squinted her eyes to a cross-eyed position, and within seconds some saliva dribbled down her chin. Charlie was shocked and impressed.

"Yes, you are good! Very good."

###

Two floors down, Jeff, Wes's junior partner screamed. "Got the son of a bitch."

Wes relaxed, his hunch justified. "Yes, we do. Take some help and pick him up at the U. I'll do the paperwork and all the prep we need for an S1 interrogation; my guess is when the truth serum cruises through his body he'll brag about every girl he raped and killed. He will share everything."

Jeff continued to be impressed with the ex-homicide detective. "That damn Charlie is unbelievable. But his wife will be pissed off to hear his comments about their sex live played for all to hear."

Wes laughed. "Not to worry. That was not his sex life. When Detective Webster's first wife divorced him, he sounded off for the entire station to hear.

When he was first married, his wife bought the Kuma Sutra book and even forced him to take special stretching exercises so he could perform. He was so pissed off because they only got to page 24 when she left. He tells a great story about his struggles with the various positions and the contortions he had to stretch into. At any party after a few drinks ask him to tell you the story; it is hilarious. If he is drunk enough, he will even demonstrate some the more elaborate positions. All the wives and girlfriends have heard the stories. So Charlie's wife will know and so will Webster."

"Damn it! Does Charlie ever tell the truth?"

"Yes but I admit the man likes to tell stories."

##

It took Charlie 20 minutes to get Elaine back to the original interview room. Once she was back and seated, he ran down the stairs; the crowds around the elevators meant he couldn't wait. The

Disciplinary Panel inquiry room was in the building but on the first floor. A late arrival would add more fuel to the already simmering funeral pyre. He knew it would be bad; the only question was: would they kick him off the force? Would he be forced to resign?

While Charlie ran the stairs and young Jeff left to pick up Professor Griffin, Wes finalized the formal request for an S1 Interrogation.

At last, he had a few minutes to himself, and all the stress of his position resurfaced. This leadership role, as head of Homicide, was not a natural position for him; he'd preferred a back-seat role, able to take direction rather than determine the path to take. He often wished Charlie was back as head man.

Wes more closely resembled a 1960's hippie than a homicide detective. He had a dark complexion, tall, with a long dark brown ponytail, a beard which was occasionally trimmed, black plastic framed glasses because corrective surgery was not possible, a relaxed persona. In reality, he was an excellent athlete, with strength and speed, who played on the same recreational basketball team with Charlie and their mutual friend a Roman Catholic priest, known as the Monk.

Homicide's troubles were not over. With Griffin, they had one man, which would bring some relief. A second killer was still active and dangerous: THOR. This man's notoriety spread fast once the news media printed his letters. Within days after his Troll story got national coverage, the same young reporter received an email from this second killer; the one using the hammer. The reporter's Scandinavian heritage attracted another killer:

"I write this to someone who has the background to appreciate my position. I am Thor and use Mjollnir (my hammer) to protect mankind and get rid of the scum. I'm sure you can provide your readers with the details of my origin as a loyal and honorable god; my lightning hammer will strike all who transgress.

All men who lust for their own sex will soon feel the weight of my wrath. They are not safe and soon will fear the streets."

The reporter, of course, knew Thor was, again, from Norse Mythology and was the hammer-wielding god associated with thunder and lightning. It was too good to resist, so he named and publicized his second killer story. It was with some reluctance because this might be construed as his viewing the killer as a vengeful protector of society.

But he used the name, and it stuck; a second Norse character for the public to fear. The LGBT community was furious with the reporter; they believed the news media was making him into some type of folk hero: a vigilante cleaning up the streets.

At this point, there was no way the detectives would have been able to guess what the future would bring. But soon after the conviction of Troll and the eventual capture of Thor, the homicide world would revert to bedlam, with the public screaming for answers.

These two psychopaths would become the biggest nightmare the justice system ever encountered. The fame and praise Homicide gained with captured of the Troll vanished in an instance when Thor was finally arrested and in custody.

CHAPTER 2: DISCIPLINARY PANEL

BEFORE THE RECORDING: JULY 2, 2028

It was bad luck, unbelievable bad luck.

The episode, too stupid to be called a plan, was exposed by two elderly women. Rather than walk back to a regular shopping mall exit, they forced their way past numerous construction barriers and under barrier ropes, then used a set of doors which were labeled 'for contractors only.' They exited into a section of the shopping center's parking lot which was roped for, and reserved for, contractors. Since it was past the Mall's closing time and the construction workers had left for the day, this section of the parking lot was deserted; at least it was until the show started.

One woman said they had been shopping all day; their feet ached; the women knew they were taking a chance going through the construction zone but were too tired to walk back to a regular exit.

Once they exited out on to the isolated parking area, the second woman explained she had never seen anything like this in her lifetime. Someone had driven his SUV onto the contractor's lot and was trying to run over a thin, short man running across the pavement. The runner kept screaming obscenities, some of which they'd only heard for the first time, and the driver seemed to be teasing him by coming close and blasting his horn.

The Disciplinary Panel had reviewed the women's statements, and now they were ready for the Detective.

As the Chairman of the Disciplinary Panel read out the detective's record, accomplishments and prior incidents; Charlie

Taylor, a senior detective, thought back about the event which brought him back in front of the Panel.

Two idiots had been randomly attacking people, mainly seniors, and single women, in the parking lots of the shopping malls, both large and small malls. There was no pattern except: it was always late in the day when the crowd was light. They were a sadistic pair, and when in the mood, they would deliver a beating and or rape a woman, again not every time, it didn't matter if the victim gave them money or not. Stakeouts proved useless because the couple were dormant for long stretches, then hit different malls at different times.

Charlie only became interested when Emma was mugged in the same parking lot; she was fortunate not to be raped, but the beating was harsh: a black eye, some bruised ribs, and a severely sprained ankle. The only reason she escaped the rape was because the mall had hired a new security guard who was making extra rounds with his dog.

"Since the time your wife was mugged, it is our understanding that you have become a frequent late night shopper at that mall. Detective, are you paying attention? Have I missed anything?"

"No sir. Your summary is complete, and I am ready to give you my version of the incident."

"Go ahead Detective Taylor. I assure you we have placed into the record the fact that your wife was attacked in this same lot. Therefore there are mediating issues to be recognized. So there is no need for you to cover her situation."

The most recent member of the Panel, although she had a distinguished legal career, was new to the Sector interrupted. "Is it true many of your colleagues refer to you as Crazy Charlie?"

"Unfortunately that was attached to me ages ago. Since I joined the Cold Squad, other than this Mall incident, I've cleaned up my act and kept my temper under control. If you review my last six years with the Squad, you'll see this is true."

The Chairman knew all about Charlie's record and wasn't about to allow a presentation about his excellent police work; he was abrupt, "Today we are here for one reason. Best you tell us about the incident, from your perspective."

Charlie thought: *screw you*. Then began.

"I'd wrenched my ankle earlier in the week. At first, I used the cane my wife bought for her injury; then because of my size and weight the guys in rehab decided to reinforce the cane; it was exceptional heavy but would not buckle.

Anyway. It was late in the afternoon but still not dark. At the mall, I was limping with my cane back to my SUV. I was parked at the far end of the lot just behind some of the small huts used to collect the shopping carts.......adjacent to the area roped off and reserved for contractors .....even the main lot was almost deserted .... a slows shopping evening."

Charlie drank from a water glass and thought: might as well let it all hang out; no point getting caught in a lie.

"I had just opened my door and was ready to get in when these two idiots appeared. They'd been lurking behind the shopping cart hut. One was directly in front of me and the other on the side, both had knives..........I can't remember the exact words of the threat, but it was along the lines 'get on your knees and hand over your wallet'.......same words used on my wife."

He stopped again; the rest was going to get ugly.

"The man in front was very close and bent over in a wide stance ready to pounce on me; I pretended to look at his partner, and when he stepped closer, I wheeled and delivered a full karate kick to his groin. He went down, holding his groin and screaming...... I was able to follow through with a kick to the face."

The Chairman, couldn't resist. "I suppose you were wearing your heavy shoes with the extra support for your sore ankle."

Some panel members smirked, but Charlie never acknowledged the sarcasm. "His wailing distracted the other one long enough for me to use the reinforced cane on his head and with a simple kick to the back of his knee, I had him face down on the pavement. He was a small man and not strong. I pressed the cane on the back of his neck and made him an offer; I told him I was going to get in my car and start the motor, when I honked the horn he was to get up and run to the far end of the lot, across the contractor's piece of pavement. At the end was a large section of green lawn. If he made it before I ran over him, he was free to go.

He started swearing and yelling; I tore down the rope barricading the contractors' parking lot area.......this gave him a large section to start his run. I got in and started the car. Opened the window and told him after I blew the horn he would have a five-second head start; if he didn't move I would drive forward and run over both legs......by now he was in panic mode......I pressed the horn, and he was off...I'd slowly drive up behind him, occasionally use the bumper to nudge his butt.....then blast the horn....every blast was a great incentive, and he found more energy."

The Chairman interrupted, "The witness said the man was weaving from side to side like a running back on a football field trying to avoid a tackle; then your horn would blast, and he would scream words like 'crazy bastard'."

"That's true. At other times he would look back and yell 'fucking son of a bitch'....especially when I got too close and nudged his butt. And of course, there was the trail he left."

"The trail?"

"Yes he'd wet himself and there was a steady trail of urine marking his path across the lot. I didn't intend to run over him. I just drive up real close and hit the horn for encouragement.

When he got the grass median he collapsed.... I got out to see how he was.......he was gasping for air, unable to get up; he'd lost control of his sphincter muscle and was sitting in a load of feces."

"Is it at this point you played with him and offered him a 100 dollars if he wanted to try and make it back to his partner?"

"Yes, I did. I admit it was a cheap shot, but all in all, I think I did him a favor."

"Care to explain?"

"His little run was better than months of rehab; the next time he thinks about mugging someone, he will remember the run across the parking lot. But I also admit it will be some time before he can hear a car horn without some trauma."

One of the Panel members didn't appreciate his humor. "Your flippant attitude is not shared by the two wives. One is now at the hospital waiting for her husband to come out of surgery; we don't know the details but at minimum one testicle will be gone. It seems to have disappeared into the man's interior and can't be retrieved. Plus he lost a half dozen front teeth.

The second woman testified earlier today. Her husband has not been physically damaged. However he is undergoing treatment with a psychologist; his nerves are shot, and he has to wear diapers. If they walk on a street, the blowing of a horn appears to be a signal, and he will automatically void and at times his sphincter releases.

This is compounded by some of your colleagues' antics. On a slow day, it appears they monitor his movements. If he and his wife try to take a walk, it is not unusual for a car to cruise behind and blast a horn, of course, he begins running and filling his diapers. His wife says it is an unmarked car, but she is sure it's a police vehicle; with the windows down she can hear them howling with laughter.

I am not sure you appreciate the consequences of your actions."

Charlie never smiled or commented. He knew it was Detective Webster or one of Vice Squad crew that blasted their horns. They viewed the two criminals as mean and ugly. It appeared the Panel had forgotten the many victims and their anguish.

"Detective we reviewed the incident before you arrived, and there is nothing you have said which changes our conclusion: you are now suspended for six months without pay and will have to do 100 hours of community service.

The only reason we have not requested your resignation is the unusually strong support you received from Stephen Miller, former Judge for our Sector and Duncan Stirling, former Chief of Police, Bill Thompson former Warden of our Sector prison and our Nobel Prize winner Dr. Max Armstrong. Is there any more you would like to say?"

"That little guy who was doing all the zigging and zagging….I think we should consider him for our Olympic team …..that son of a bitch could run!"

"Detective, that smart ass comment is going to cost you another $500. Good day."

Of course, his last comment was soon over the Internet and played in every police station across the world. Charlie became a folk hero; there was not a bar in the city where he had to buy.

Later that afternoon, former Chief of Police, Duncan Stirling saw the clip "that son of a bitch could run". Somehow the audio clip of the Disciplinary Panel hearing was leaked along with the story of Charlie's actions and suspension. The Chief smiled and thought: that crazy bastard did it again.

Around the world an unusual phenomenon developed; sometimes occurring in police bars but most often in a police locker room where staff were changing and getting ready for their shift. In a quiet interval, someone would shout "that son of a bitch could run" and then the entire room participated in a stomping of feet, simulating a running man, followed by an outbreak of hysterical laughter. For men and women of the force, the black humor was a welcome relief; the scope of the event astonished the more formal legal community.

The Tokyo Metropolitan Police Department had more than 40,000 police officers. Out of that large number, it was not surprising to find a joker who knew how to handle video recording equipment. The joker's objective was to use Charlie's words and the incident to create a YouTube film which captured a small group of officers mimicking a running criminal. He spent some time selecting the men he wanted in the video, the time of day, and the room to use. The result was a quality production.

The Japanese police encountered many of the same problems as the rest of the world's law enforcement. So Charlie's attitude and remarks played to a captured audience. The video from Tokyo was voted the best. An entire uniformed locker room stamping their feet, followed by gales of laughter told the story.

The whole world understood the trigger was a tall Japanese officer who screamed the words 'that son of a bitch could run.' No translation was necessary.

CHAPTER 3: THOR ARRESTED

THE RECORDING: SEPTEMBER 4, 2028

"Monk, your new ears look great. I gather there is no frustration like you suffered from the first set."

After a brisk five-mile run, two men, wet from heavy perspiration, walked down towards the side entrance of the Abbey, occasionally stopping to stretch. Since Charlie's suspension, he had time, and Monk was excellent company. This giant of a man, a Roman Catholic priest, had been his friend from elementary school through university and into adulthood.

Even his gentle smile could not subdue his menacing appearance, a tall man at 6"8", just a fraction over 300 pounds, a shaved head, and hands each the size of a small computer monitor. He got the 'monk' label at University when he was the only regular church attendee on the team. Now Father Ed but still Monk to many in the community.

Some years ago the Robin Hood killer had sliced off both of Monk's ears. Almost immediately after the priest's rescue, a plastic surgeon had attached a set of artificial ears to his head.

"Charlie, you're right. The new technology is a significant improvement; it fools almost everyone. I no longer get the long stares or dumb questions. However, there is one rather weird feature of the new prosthesis. Here let me show you a photo, with the Bishop."

As Monk searched his phone for the photo, Charlie smiled at his friend's, unexpected, vanity. Monk had the picture he wanted: "Here look close at both of us. Do you see?"

"No. You both look normal to me."

"I know it is rather subtle but concentrate on my new ears. Compare them to the rest of my face. Look closely. Try harder."

Charlie was about to brush it aside but saw how important it was, so gave it another more thorough scan. "Well, well. I see it now. Your ears are darker than your face. Not much but enough to look almost like a suntan. But the difference is so minor; I'd forget it. Anyone able to tell you why?"

"No one has figured it. I don't think it's on anyone's priority list. It's just a fluke that the new plastics, or whatever they use, shows up darker on photos. I can live with it. Most people never study a photo that closely to pick up on the prosthesis color difference. And I no longer have any skin irritation.

So forget my ears and look at you. Charlie, you look like hell. What happened?"

Their close friendship allowed for frank conversations, not many holds barred, both men excellent athletes and continually challenging each other, whether on the basketball floor or running tracks. Monk was still recovering from an unprofessional period in his life but loved his new assignment as an instructor at the Abbey.

The Abbey was a seventeenth-century edifice built by a sect of monks whose origin no one could remember. It was a series of interconnected buildings of various sizes and shapes. Since the buildings and the grounds are diligently maintained, the result was a magnificent piece of architecture and a perfect setting for someone seeking peace or just a quiet environment to walk and reflect. Five years ago the Abbey was designated a historical site; today it was a multi-functional facility, with many different buildings: a residence for novice priests, a retreat, lecture hall, and a conference facility for rent. With a multitude of jogging and walking trails, it was an excellent spot for Charlie to work out and keep from getting bored with an exercise routine.

The detective didn't hesitate in responding. "Emma is on the warpath and has frozen our conversation…. she's mad as hell."

Charlie couldn't believe the difference the twins made to his home life. Emma was constantly scolding in a loving way, but she was an extremely happy wife and mother, and Charlie could make her laugh and dance with ease; it was a home filled with love and energy.

The twins were a few months short of five years. Ella (which mostly became Ellie) looked like Emma with rust-colored hair, long legs and slim build. But her temperament was all Charlie: athletic, a quick hot temper, fast to laugh and quick to cry. Paul (who refused Paulie) was almost the polar opposite personality, quiet, smart, slow to respond, tall, thin, but not resembling either one of his parents.

Monk pushed. "What did you do?"

"Breakfast was finished…. Emma was in the bathroom doing her morning routine, and the kids were coloring at the kitchen table. I was standing by the patio door trying to drink coffee and talk on the phone. Well the phone slipped; I went to grab it and spilled coffee on my pants, at which time I muttered the F word……muttered is not the correct word ….it was more like a yell of disgust.

A new word is what both kids loved so when Emma came back into the kitchen the both of them were running and screaming."

"Doesn't sound too bad."

"Oh…..picture this ……they started running around the kitchen table accusing each other of being a fucker. Both kids think it's hilarious maybe because of my reaction…this isn't the first vocabulary enhancement they got from me. Of course, walking into a room where a couple of five-year-olds are screaming "fucker" and laughing hysterically, has to be a shock to the system."

"Charlie, you idiot!"

"Well then began the campaign to get them to forget the word and not use it. Emma refused to send them to preschool today. She's afraid they'll dirty up the conversation for the young ones."

"Emma seems to have reacted rather harshly."

"Didn't I say this wasn't the first time I added to their vocabulary?"

##

Detective Wes Krause and his partner Jeff Hutton found themselves back at the university; this time at a crime scene at the favorite gay bar: OPEN HOUSE. The bar sat at the top of a small grassy hill.

At this moment, students from across campus flooded the area, watching all the action: ambulances, police, white-smocked technicians, and police trying to keep order. The flashing lights, sirens and a multitude of rumors made it the place to be, certainly better than a stuffy lecture hall.

Wes found the situation hard to accept; after weeks of fruitless police efforts, this maniac gets trapped in the washroom of this small exclusive club, a favorite spot for the young campus LGBT crowd. Thor, homicide's elusive and brutal quarry had made an incredibly stupid and clumsy error.

The narrow hall and small washroom made it difficult for the Forensic team to finish its work. One thing was sure they knew the killer. The weapon, wounds, and blood made it easy: they knew they had captured Thor and his hammer. The other big surprise: the killer never offered any resistance, no denials and made only one statement.

He insisted: there was no need for an S1 Interrogation, the truth serum was not required; he would provide a full confession, but he wanted Judge Doug Brewster and Chief Kisashton present. Plus he demanded the neurologist from the University staff, Dr. Carson, be allowed to sit in on his confession.

A few days flew by, and no one seemed interested or in a hurry to hear Thor's confession; Wes knew better than to try and press the Chief.

Heavy cloud cover and the early onset of the autumn temperatures provided some relief to the overheated city. In the Halls of Justice, Chief Kisashton was buried in paperwork and was completely oblivious to the weather. The man reveled in ensuring documentation was completed, although he flirted with accuracy; his personal contributions always enhanced the official release. He knew Thor was waiting but felt no obligation to rush. His attitude abruptly changed when the Judge burst into his office.

Although the capture had occurred days ago, either he or the Chief had been forced to reschedule the pending confession of Thor. Judge Doug was not happy: "Delay after delay. Chief this is not good. We have to go down now and hear this confession. Professor Carson is waiting. Come on, drop that damn paper."

He waved his arms, and the Chief followed. When they entered the interrogation room, everything was ready: Wes and Thor waited on the other side of a large table.

Professor Carson, standing against the far wall, knew the Chief and there was no small talk; the academic was also a close friend of the Judge; this fact and the fact that he was an active and vocal enemy of Dr. Max allowed him to be present at this confession. Most people didn't understand: Carson's animosity for Max was not a question of jealousy for the Nobel Prize but originated from a public debate in which Max brutally destroyed Carson's arguments against the S3 mind probe.

Wes started the official recording by entering the date and attendance. He nodded for Thor to start. The killer didn't hesitate:

"My named is Chris Evans, and I did all the killings as Thor; in my apartment, you will find all the evidence you need. Years ago when the justice system changed and prisons were decommissioned, I was on death row sentenced for first-degree murder. I became the first convict at Fort Green prison to undergo an S3 brain probe which declared me innocent. Since the new technology declared me 'not guilty,' I was released and my criminal record expunged.

What you have to understand, I wasn't born a killer. My life all changed after you people bombarded my brain during the S3 memory probe, the memory retrieval technology. Brain cells were destroyed, and God knows what else happened during that interrogation. You used untrained staff, and the examination exceeded the 45-minute time constraint. I was in bad shape after the interrogation, and Dr. Kate and her team kept me for days until I appeared to recover."

The man stopped and started smoking his cigarette. The rest of the confession came out as a series of broken segments as the man's emotions appeared to require brief recovery periods.

"After I was released there were recurring headaches..............real pain and it forced me to rest in bed......knocked me off my feet...........then all was good...the pain stopped...........until about a few years ago, when the urges started.............I've always hated the gay crowd ....watching two men kiss on TV almost made me puke, but this was different...........the drive or urge was overwhelming..............first I was arrested a few times for fights at gay bars......then the police arrested a teacher for an affair with a young male student but his case was thrown out .... I was at his hearing, and I knew he was a first-class fucker, and I knew he would be my first.

It wasn't hard.....just had to be patient.......he was an arrogant bugger and thought he was free.....I actually caught him hiding behind a large bush in a LGBT playground...caved his skull in... in broad daylight..............I slept like a baby that night ....there was no turning back......the high was better than the sex. I started my research on the gay community ...where they congregated, best clubs and hook up sites ...... I did lots before they caught me.... I love to sink my hammer into a skull.........I'm shaking now just thinking about another one.

But you have to understand that S3 brain probe is what did it...............I was never the same after they scanned me and released me ....it changed me and made me a killer...........a fucking maniac ....that is what I am now.............all thanks to how the state destroyed parts of my mind....I..."

The rant continued with the Judge challenging the allegation and the Chief pressing and accusing the man of lying. Nothing they said made a difference; he could not be shaken, and his version of the cause and effect gained credibility with each question and explanation. The State had made him a killer; he wasn't born a killer, was never a violent man.

Professor Carson smiled, finally, he had the proof he had been waiting for all these years. This killer was all the evidence he needed; the maniac was the fruits of a reckless scientist. He looked at the Judge and, with a nod, quickly affirmed his support. And with Carson's stamp of approval, the recording was sent to Regional Board, and within another hour it was sent to the President, and within another hour Dr. Max got a summons to see the President immediately.

This time the two friends, the Chief and the Judge, relaxed in the Judge's chambers.

Doug Brewster was medium height, slightly overweight, sporting a full auburn beard, and regularly had a mouth full of pipe, which he chewed relentlessly, particularly when under stress. He could develop a compelling legal argument but at times was viewed as a disingenuous team member. An ambitious man, Brewster had been surprised and disappointed when he had not landed a Judge's position on the first round of Sector appointments. And now as the successor to Judge Stephen Miller, he was in a commanding position to address any perceived slights. And Charlie Taylor was high on his list.

Immediately after Thor's confession, Judge Doug Brewster grabbed the initiative and started an Assessment Team (as he called it) but knew the final confirmation would have to come from Regional and the President. He knew what he wanted: Professor Tyler Carson a neurologist with private practice and a tenured academic; Dr. Ryan Wiek a biochemist employed by a firm with global sales and a prolific research commentary. Both men well respected but known opponents to Justice Reborn and Dr. Max. The Judge wanted to be sure they were part of the team.

Neither he nor the Chief were overly concerned about leaks to the public, and within hours the President and Max's meeting exploded across the globe. The entire system of justice about to be destroyed because of some sloppy scientific work by a Nobel Prize winner at least that is the slant the Chief was careful to give to his favorite reporter: the man, grateful for the biggest story of the year, was not likely to challenge the Chief's interpretation of events.

The Police Chief and the Judge almost glowed. Both men enjoyed brandy and strong coffee. The Judge had been smiling hard for the last few hours. "I hope our mad scientist calls in Charlie Taylor to get him out of this mess. This is a no win; both will be smeared when this over.

I'll make sure no S1 interrogation, that damn truth serum, is used on Chris Evans; and I know both scientists will back me, no more interrogations with Dr. Max's chemical cocktails. And here is a plus:

I know they screwed up this guy's S3 brain probe. I've done a bit of homework. There is a woman, Marcie Callay, who conducted the interrogation. They fired her; now she is ready to throw some gasoline on the fire.

We can also single out Judge Stephen's wife, Dr. Kate, and maybe Charlie's wife, Emma. They were all part of this."

The Chief tried not to cheer, but his hate for Charlie was intense. "Shit this is like Xmas, Thanksgiving and the Easter bunny all wrapped up together. All we need is for Charlie Taylor to try and bail horny Max out of this!"

CHAPTER 4: THE RESEARCH CENTER

CURRENT TIME: SEPTEMBER 26, 2028

Today the President was succinct and impressively calm, but his message caused an uproar across the world: *Dr. Max Armstrong's S3 memory scan, or brain probe, has been seriously challenged. The assertion is: it can damage the brain and lead to undesirable aggressive behavior. The allegation is: one extended memory scan has turned a man into a serial killer. All Dr. Armstrong's innovations will no longer be used until this issue is resolved.*

There was talk of stripping Dr. Max of his Nobel Prize, but no one understood how this could be accomplished; his enemies seemed to dominate the news screens and kept up a relentless stream of criticism.

Rick, a theoretical physicist, reflected the worries of most of the scientists at the Research Center. His friend Gary unbundled his lunch, while Rick complained. "Here we are the men and women at the top of their field, best in the world, and we are about to be painted with the same stupid brush as Max; next, they'll probably shut down the Center and ship us out the door. All because that bastard was too fast and too sloppy. He refused to follow up, too arrogant to believe he could be wrong."

Both Rick and Gary, two renowned physicists, loved the outdoors; every noon hour they scrambled outside to one of the kiosks for lunch. The Research Center only had the one main building but maintained extensive landscaped grounds for the staff. Gary started picking at his lunch and then voiced his concerns. "We're ok for the moment; the Assessment Team hasn't started their work to see if Chris Evans, the killer, is speaking the truth. However, you can see how stressed out that bastard is, running from floor to floor."

The bastard, Dr. Max, created and ran the Central Research Center; he was an international superstar. The research facility had one mission: solve the environmental problem. Global warming and pole reversal remained the dual threats to the extinction of the human race. Max recruited his team from across the world. His team was often compared to the 1940's crew used to develop the A-bomb.

The difference being the A-bomb development was based on solid theoretical data. Dr. Max's team had to deal with many more unknowns and a global disaster as the penalty for failure. He became known as 24/7 Max, and that was an accurate reflection of his work habits, a demanding, driven, brilliant scientist.

Rick was more in touch with the grapevine. "Of course adding to his stress is the fact that his young wife wants a divorce. I'm surprised it lasted this long. She is just a bad as he is; last weekend she was picked up…the charge was DUI, and he had to bail her out."

"No, I don't believe that one. I think that's some dirty gossip. Better one? I heard she might be pregnant."

"Could be. Well for once, Max is keeping it in his pants. Even with all her wild antics, the young wife, Sally, seems to be keeping him in line. But I sometimes think, because of the hours he works, his original skirt-chasing reputation was an overblown character assassination by the press."

Dr. Max Armstrong received the Nobel Prize for his discoveries: the truth serum, colloquially known as S1, and the memory scan or brain probe, known as S3.

His work took place when global warming and north/south pole switching forced a doomsday scenario on the world. Society developed a new psyche which demanded certainty: no tolerance for the legal politics of obfuscation, time too short for the continued coddling of those who refused to cooperate and play the game.

The solution appeared in the form of Dr. Max Armstrong's innovations. The advances meant there was no longer any doubt about guilt or innocence. His discoveries allowed the radical changes to the justice system, soon branded as Justice Reborn.

The novel interrogation techniques, from S1 to S3, were liberally applied, and the accused convicted by his own words or his memory of the crime.

Politicians amended legislation at record speeds. Justice Reborn, demanded consequences for all actions, with mercy reserved for the victims. The universal acceptance of the death penalty even applied to repeat offenders: the fourth criminal charge became your last, the third for a sexual offense with a minor.

Rehabilitation Farms replaced prisons. The first step of prison reform, clear death row, used S3 memory scans to release or execute convicts waiting on death row.

The second step of prison reform meant processing all remaining prisoners. Every prisoner was interrogated with the S1 truth serum and, if required, S3. In the end, each convict faced

one of three alternatives: outright release, transfer to a Sector Farm, or execution if a murder surfaced.

Rick laughed. "To change the subject: how was your experience with the S1 and the S3 Interrogations? I think you were right to experience the procedures. There is no way by just reading the literature you would have been able to understand the impact."

Gary didn't hesitate. "You're right. It was somewhat disconcerting, but I am glad I did.

The S1 was, as everyone says, like a truth serum. I was fully conscious, aware of what I was saying .....even realized I was incriminating myself but couldn't stop .....it was like I opened a facet, the words tumbled out .....and I want the world to like me ...I had to cooperate. I'll bet I only consumed a teaspoon full of the damn mixture."

Rick smiled. "I told you it is impossible to beat that drug cocktail. For the S3 Interrogation: you want to share that experience?"

"Why not? You were open with yours." Gary hesitated for a moment, not due to reluctance but he needed to swallow his food. "There was an incident in junior high: a friend was getting a beating, and I ran away; this is a guilt trip I have been carrying. I've always had a problem remembering the details; my psychologist constantly wants to hypnotize me. He believes a detailed review will rid me of the guilt. I have always refused.

Last week I decided to try with an S3 .....sort of kill two birds with one shot: experience an S3 and get to see my embarrassment. I gave the technicians the year, and my father came in as a Watcher; I had confessed to him, years ago. Still, I was worried because once they started, I would not be able to control what they saw; but the Watcher team were all men, and so wild masturbation would not shock them.

Like your session, they kept the S3 down to a maximum of 25 minutes well within the range of 'no damage.' Other than that there was nothing unique about mine. They strapped on the helmet with all the inlet cables and one large outlet cable. Here I started to tense up, not for long; I was fed some meds to make me relax. From there on: no tension and never felt a thing.

As you know each accessed memory pocket gets displayed on the big screen and a Watcher has to decide if the technician has to probe back in time or ahead to a future event. A Historian and my father were the only members of the Watcher group. My father has an excellent memory and often beat the Historian in recognizing a memory segment. Mind you I did feel a strange sensation each time the probe reached a different location, but felt no pain as the unit retrieved and displayed the contents of my memory. That is, as they bombarded a separate section of my brain, it never hurt.

When they retrieved and displayed a new segment of my memory, I could hear my father saying either 'ahead' or 'back'; the Historian was mainly saying 'agree' ……. a real cool character, smart as hell this Historian.

The jumps ahead or backward in time are difficult to control, and a leap back may suddenly retrieve your history as a toddler, in other words too far back. It is during the new placement of the probe where the skill of the technician comes into play. I think this is the source of the problem with Thor's original brain probe; a poorly trained technician who couldn't zero in on the time frame they were searching. As a result of too many minutes of brain shelling.

In my relaxed state I had no idea how long it was taking, only heard one warning announcement: ten minutes have elapsed; after the warning, it didn't take too long before I heard my father and the Historian confirm: "We have it. Shut down."

And before you ask: yes I saw the segment. I forced myself to watch the beating from start to finish. I squarely faced the incident, with no turning away. Will it help with any psychological or guilt issues I'm carrying? I don't know, but I never want to see it again. Although I will admit my performance at the fight was not as weak as I remembered....so it might help."

Under Justice Reborn there were no longer any prosecutors, defense attorneys or juries; there was no need———the truth was on the table, and no debate was necessary. A Judge who was assigned a designated territory (a Sector) was the key player, and he was provided with a large staff; there were four divisions of specialization: Legal where lawyers ensured the legislation was applied correctly; Investigative which was the police department; Forensic which worked at crime scenes and monitored the interrogation processes; Prison which managed the Farms and the halfway houses.

They continued with lunch, both men ordinarily soft-spoken and introspective. Both men knew the sun flare activity had ceased, the world average temperature had dropped, and weather patterns were normal. Most attributed the changes to two factors. First, unbelievable global cooperation resulted in a massive tree planting program; trees of every variety now dominated the landscape. Once people understood the carbon dioxide absorbing properties of trees, the planting activity occurred at all levels of society and across the world.

Second, energy storing technology resulted in a variety of options from using modified fuel cells to molten salt; this along with the innovations in the solar panels now made electrical power more attractive as a replacement for petroleum fuel.

The magnetic pole reversal has stopped, with the scientific community unable to provide a reason. But many of the experts were predicting a stable situation for a least the next decade. So in addition to Thor's accusation, this stability also threatened the Center. Why spend all this money if the world is safe.

Gary stopped chewing and asked, "Rick what is your best guess? Is this Thor's accusation valid?"

Rick was fast. "There is no reason not to believe there was some brain damage. Look they still have, hidden away, some of the first convicts who exceeded the 45-minute duration of the brain probe; they are the classic vegetables, but no one mentions them anymore.

And remember no one has ever examined in detail the brain of a dead convict. I mean someone who underwent an S3 scan and died of natural causes or was executed after a memory scan found him guilty. No one knows what an autopsy of one of those brains might reveal. Our Dr. Max wasn't interested. Too busy rubbing his body against any willing female."

Gary had the last word. "I agree. How can you not continue to irritate the brain for more than 45 minutes and not cause permanent brain damage? Not just 45 minutes. I hear they went closer to 55 for the Chris Evan scan, so Thor could have been created. What a screw up that first scan

CHAPTER 5: A STAY OF EXECUTION

CURRENT TIME: SEPTEMBER 26, 2028

Charlie wasn't yelling, but his anger was palpable. "How can you work with that creature? Even the other convicts loath him."

The detective and his brother had finished their weekly breakfast, sitting on stools around the small kitchen island, hot coffee steaming off both cups. Sam Taylor, the psychologist, heard his brother's complaint and wondered how much of Charlie's irritation was due to his suspension and how much by his real hate for this type of killer. As the older brother, Dr. Taylor continued to worry about his younger passionate brother, knowing at times emotions drove the detective.

Although the brothers were close, almost the same age, both tall and lean, their temperaments, attitudes, and interests were far apart. Sam, in the right light even looked like Charlie, was a student in every sense of the word; his academic record was outstanding, and his calm and sympathetic demeanor resulted in a large practice. Plus his regular contributions to scholarly publications won him more accolades.

A recently government-funded research project included three people: Sam with years of practical experience in working with deviants; second, a genetics professor who made a strong case for mother nature's hand in determining behavior; and a psychiatrist whose academic qualifications were outstanding; the sanctioned research project focus was serial killers. Among the issues being addressed was the universal question: born a killer or nurtured into the state. It went beyond this, and the group hope to ferret out what nurturing might have changed the evolving character of a young child.

Individual researchers, with each convict, analyzed one aspect of the case. Although there were no restrictions, each man was to emphasize one particular facet. Sam was to focus on the start of the killings and in particular the first murder. What drove this man to go beyond the boundaries? All the experts believed breaking the barrier with the first slaying would have been the most traumatic.

Any killer, agreeing to participate, got a three-month delay in his execution and was guaranteed no more new S1 or S3 interrogations; three more months of life were too good to pass up, and most agree to tell all, with nothing held back. Sam was the last one to interview the man, known as the Troll; the killer had over a 20-year span killed a number of young teenagers; most bodies had been recovered, but a few remained missing.

"Charlie, I can barely stand the man but.."

Charlie didn't let his brother finish. "The guy is such a pig. Can't keep his mouth shut. Any convict who shares his supper table is going to hear the details of how he tricked and murdered the girls. He revels in the telling. I don't know why he hasn't been executed. You guys will learn nothing from him except..... he is the worst kind of nut case."

Sam was thoroughly familiar with the man's history and knew what he was dealing with: a brilliant but twisted mind which, although he projected many false faces, had a profound contempt for all humanity.

"Sam, how can you even stay in the same room with that scum?"

"Listen brother; the human decision process is not as straightforward as you think."

"Enlighten me."

"The scary thing is when we are in a highly emotional state, our decision making process is not the same as when we are cool or normal. And the worst is when we are in a state of high sexual arousal. Research has shown, time and again, in this state, you will take risks, engage in activity which you would reject in normal circumstances...."

Again Charlie interrupted. "Wait a minute are you justifying these killings?"

"Here is what some academic research finds: a decent, reasonable, kind man whose frontal lobes are fully functional and controlling his behavior will change. I mean, in a state of sexual arousal, his reptilian brain takes over, and he could become unrecognizable to himself."

"Best to provide some proof and second, how the hell do you test anyone when he is sexually aroused?"

"Listen and learn. First, the researchers gave the test study group a series of questions with yes or no answers; this was under no stress, no time limit situation. All were direct questions like: would you have sex with a 70-year-old woman? Would you like to see a naked 12-year-old girl?

You get the idea. And the results showed standard behavior patterns and no wild deviants. Next came the same questions, later in the week, but under sexual arousal and the results were startling different, standards went away done, men had changed their attitudes and showed a marked sexual aggressive behavior. The striking change even shook up the researchers. They had anticipated some changes but these results were frightening."

"Son of a bitch. But how in the hell did they get them into this state?'

"First, they were in isolated rooms with on-going porno showing on the walls, with intermittent gigantic nude photos flashing on the walls. The men were told to masturbate but hold the climax; each man had a tablet, and the questions flashed on the screen for a touch response. So before they climaxed, they answered the same questions, one at a time. As I said, the results were scary, not related to the first round in any way."

"I understand part of this, but we know he was Mr. Cool when he was selecting his victims and planning his attack."

Sam understood Charlie's observation and had studied the killer. "I know and agree, but I also know he is very quick to get to the aroused state. And at this point he is unbelievably vicious. I'm not sure what my point is ......except I think it is easier to avoid the state than try to control it once you are in it.

So maybe parents were on the right track when they encouraged kids to avoid wild parties. I see a teenager better able to deal with sex in a controlled state. But once they are in an aroused state, life becomes more difficult and they may make a decision they will later regret. Best if they try to avoid getting worked up."

"I still don't know what your point is."

"Maybe I'm saying there is no such thing as a fully integrated human being and that one of your multiple selves may surface under the right conditions; and, the boundaries between right and wrong can blur."

"Sam, I sometimes wonder if you are strong enough for your work. Let this go. You could never have saved this guy."

"Brother, I have to leave and thanks for breakfast. And remember just because I talk to him doesn't make me a fan."

Before Charlie could do more venting, Sam was out the front door and walking to his car.

Sam's interviews took place at the Farm 114 where a unique room existed for confidential sessions. Once prisons had been decommissioned, Farms were used for the new approach of short sentences, with strenuous physical work and extensive rehab programs. The Troll was on a couch; he wasn't able to fully stretch out like a bed but was comfortable sitting with his upper body upright.

The recording equipment had been set up and would add to the total research record on this man. Sam decided to come across as someone who had not done his homework, sloppy and a time waster; he wanted to see the Troll's reaction. So he started with a weak question:

"Professor Griffin, do you remember the first one?"

Lewis Griffin stared at Sam wondering: *how dumb is this one.* And he couldn't control the sneer. "For Christ sake, Doc, stop playing games; you fucking know I remember; let's play this way: I'll go back to the beginning and tell how it all unfolded. That's really what you want. Right?"

"Lewis, you're right. Sorry for the stupid opening; yes, I'd like to hear about the first one in as much detail as you care to share." Sam hoped his attitude of 'humble servant' played to the Troll's need for dominance.

"Here we go, and I'd appreciate a minimum of questions until I finish. I do enjoy reliving this one.

It began in the late summer after grade seven and before we started grade eight. Stan claimed he could fuck Bev anytime he wanted and bet my friend and me five bucks each. It was a bright and boring Sunday afternoon, so we took him up on the bet.

He took us to the deserted stockyards, next to the railway station, on the very edge of our small city. There were no cattle in the holding pens, and there was one small covered enclosure with piles of straw in different parts of the compound. The place was deserted, no cattle and no workers. He positioned us on the outside of the enclosure: I mean the holding pen, with a roof and a fully fenced perimeter. We crouched on the outside of the west wall or fencing where there was a narrow gap between boards; this was to our viewing platform; then he ran over to the front of the yard to wait.

Shortly Bev came down the street and over to the primary enclosure, there was one opening, a big cattle gate. Stan was waiting for her. The stockyards were about three blocks away from the city streets and a few hundred yards from the main train terminal building.

Now a word about Bev: she is the key to my 20-year journey. I don't know what her IQ was, but she was slow, occasionally drooling, speech slurred, even her walking was weird, like a pigeon-toed stagger; today she would never have been in a regular school, but at that time there was a different theory about how best to work with disadvantaged kids. One of the problems: she physically had matured, meaning we had an early matured 16-year-old in a group of 12-13 years old boys.

Stan took her hand and led her deeper into the enclosure. They must have done this before because she started undressing immediately and soon was just in bra and panties. Stan didn't waste any time and was soon standing naked beside her; then he went to the far corner and dug out a large piece of cardboard from the piles of straw. More proof that this was not the first time.

She lay down on the cardboard and Stan started playing with her tits. Soon he had them out of the bra and began kissing them with big lip smacks.......the bastard made sure he was not blocking our view. We couldn't hear what he said to her, but next, she took off her panties and turned over. What a look! She presented her big white ass to him and of course to us.

By this time my buddy and I were breathing hard and were so stiff, neither of us could say a word. When he mounted her, my partner gave out a small moan. Then Stan went at it, and the two of us were nearly out of control, each had unbuttoned our flies and were stroking the meat. I can still feel the tension; I'd never seen anything like it. And then my friend lost control and screamed as he climaxed. I let out, *'oh fuck.'*

Bev heard us and looked in our directions; we both panicked and ran like hell through the high grass and damn thistles ....we wanted to get to the sidewalk and the residential streets. Didn't even bother putting our peckers back into our pants; for about four blocks we must have been a hilarious viewing, scared shitless, out of control running and dicks banging away in front of our pants, slamming from side to side like a limp sausage."

"Did she become your first?"

"Relax Doc, let me tell it. For the rest of the summer, I couldn't get her out of my mind. It was her large bare white ass that kept recurring. I masturbated so much I'm surprised I didn't do permanent damage."

Sam persisted. "Was she your first?"

"Yes, but you have to wait until session two; but this is how it started, and Bev was my ideal. Next session I'll blow you away. There is the guard, bye doc."

###

Terry Paterson was driving to the Research Center with Charlie in the passenger's seat and Manuel Moreno in the back. All three men used to be homicide detectives until a political move had them demoted, moved out of homicide, and forced to develop the Cold Squad.

This Squad came into existence because Dr. Kate petitioned the Sector to follow up on all the criminals who were identified during an S1 or an S3 memory scan. She uncovered a series of men and women linked with violent crimes; this all occurred as prisons were decommissioned and convicts either released or executed. As crimes were confessed and crime scenes displayed, accomplices surfaced; many of these were offenders who had never been charged.

Although it was apparent there was a large population of guilty men, establishing a proper name and identity was the challenge. Often only a nickname was heard during a memory playback, sometimes just a face was seen and no name: this was their starting point. The Sector's Archivist, Dr. Kate, although not an official member of the Cold Squad, did an excellent job of finding cases which appeared to warrant attention. The resulting irony was, under Charlie's leadership, the Squad achieved outstanding and speculator results.

The team members, Charlie, Terry and Manuel, all came with unique skills and one prevailing attitude: when they smelt the ending, the clock did not exist; this was not an issue for Terry who was not married. And Emma tolerated Charlie's absences, but Manuel's marriage was rocky from the start and this added to the stress.

On a regular basis, they cornered a criminal who thought he was safe and forgotten. Dr. Kate selected cases from the archival tapes she was classifying and storing; video recordings from mind scans used to assess death row convicts and then S1 interrogations. If these accomplices had never been charged, then they were prime candidates for the Cold Squad to find and arrest. The big surprise: rather than the demotion Chief Kisashton anticipated, the Cold Squad exploded into the success story of the year.

Charlie insisted the work be prioritized, and he didn't want to waste time on petty criminals; the result was their arrests often made the front page: their first case arrested a serial killer of young men, the hitchhikers on the Highway of Death. Shortly followed by the conviction of a team of financial swindlers who had taken millions but had never been convicted. And so it went.

There was a TV crime documentary which ran for 36 episodes; the high profile success of the Cold Squad meant many of their cases became part of the documentary series and then the TV special started including some of their earlier homicide cases; the original title was to be CRAZY CHARLIE but Emma threaten to sue, and the producers agreed it was not appropriate: besides, no one could prove he bent the rules to get confessions.

The team was a tight-knit unit, and outsiders often wondered how they seemed to communicate with so few words. Being on the same wavelength was one thing, but this group was a mixture of complementary skills: Terry was the street person. He knew the bars and alleys, and once he has a scent, he was a pure bloodhound. Manuel completed numerous computer courses and spent countless hours on the Internet; his natural talents flourished. He had even traveled to Hackers' Conventions and was accepted, with his true identity only known by a handful of hackers. Charlie relied on instinct and picked up signals and clues others missed; and, he was able to turn his thinking in a direction that no one else considered. They all missed Wes, who had been with them in Homicide, but they understood; Kisashton never gave him a choice: either take Charlie's old position as head of homicide or he would put them all through a Disciplinary Panel review which they would never pass.

As they traveled in silence, Charlie scanned various pages of a book his brother had given him. Most of the paragraphs made him shake his head; most it was almost incomprehensible. Finally, he reached a couple of paragraphs: "Guys listen to this:

.......a deep cognitive illusion that's been fostered in the field for a generation and more. People say: whenever we have a physiological causal account, we don't hold somebody responsible. Well, might that be because whenever people give a physiological causal account, these are always cases of disability or pathology?

You never see a physiological account of somebody getting something right. Supposing we went into Andrew Wiles' brain and got a perfect physiological account of how he proved Fermat's Last Theorem. Would that show that he's not responsible for his proof? Of course not. It's just that we never give causal physiological-level accounts of psychological events when they go right.

Manuel was first. "What the hell does that mean?'

Charlie thought for a moment. "Let me try. Let's suppose we arrest a thief, and it is discovered that he has a brain lesion. Now the argument begins that he is not responsible; it was the fault of the lesion. But this argument always runs one way. So if a scientist discovers a cure for cancer, but then we discover he has a brain lesion. No one says he didn't do it; the lesion did it!"

Terry laughed. "Don't be bitter. We now have the brain probes which force the public to see the crime. Ok, guys here we are.....front door of the Research Center. I assume you'll only be a few minutes."

Charlie responded. "Not sure Terry. All I know is Max said it is urgent, drop everything and come. My guess: he'll want some help, but his current shit storm needs a scientist and not a detective."

This was of those rare times when Charlie's intuition was wrong.

Former Sector 14 Judge Stephen surveyed the chambers where he spent many hours; the upgrades were as luxurious as gossip reported. He slowly drank his coffee and wondered why he had been summoned. The well-tailored young assistant had ushered him into the chambers rather than have him sitting the standard waiting room, a courtesy not offered most visitors.

Finally, the new Sector 14 judge burst into his chambers: "Sorry Stephen but some issues can't be delayed."

"No problem Doug. The coffee is excellent, and I've always enjoyed the view. My guess: this has something to do about Justice Reborn being put on hold."

"Right. Let me fill you in with some current concerns. First, Chief Kisashton informs me: we have the start of a small crime wave; some criminals believe we will not be able to process them. And the Chief thinks they are right.

Justice Reborn has been fully operational for at least eight years and due to the success of S1 and S3 his police manpower has been operating with minimum staff. Not only are there fewer detectives and patrol staff but many senior staff have retired or resigned; the result is the current force has little experience in conducting penetrating interrogations. The Chief is worried he will soon have overflowing holding cells as his staff get up to speed.

With prisons decommissioned and turned into trade schools, we are only left with our medium security Farms which are also filled. The President wants us to hold all accused until this Thor issue is resolved. This is turning into a mess."

"Doug, I think you are going to have accept the early release of many in the Farms; otherwise you won't have room."

"I agree and have already started an analysis of the Farm population; we still only have five Farms. But I didn't get you here to cry on your shoulder. We have to think ahead. If we have to revert to the old system of justice, how long would it take us to get operational?"

Stephen was impressed; no one had thought about this possibility or the size of the job to turn back. "Doug that will be a helluva job. Not only are the police inexperienced: Legal has a young staff; none of them have ever served as prosecutors, none understand the role of a trial judge.

We no longer have courtrooms; I think most were sold and turned into everything from downtown apartments to coffee shops. There is an entire infrastructure, if I'm allowed to use that word, which doesn't exist. Think about it: clerks, stenos, security, etc all the people who knew how to make the trial process run …most of these people were pensioned off."

Judge Doug smiled and knew he had the right man. "Stephen I would like you to assess our current state and devise a plan which would allow us to revert; I mean evaluate all aspects.... from retraining staff, searching for office and prison space..... the entire gambit. We have to know how much this will cost and how long it would take to get off the ground.

Within a very short time, the conclusion might be: Dr. Max made some errors in his haste to get the Nobel Prize. If that happens, we have to be ready. If we can't immediately revert to the old system, then I need a practical alternative.

You, more than me, have had extensive experience in the old system, as a prosecutor, as a defense lawyer and then as a courtroom judge."

Stephen didn't like what he was hearing; his bent head gently swayed from side to side. Neither man spoke for some time; then it was Stephen: "I agree it has to be done; it is even more complicated. S3 and S1 allowed us to use the death penalty and to implement a four-strike policy.

If we are forced to revert to the old system, there will be defense lawyers arguing about any inconsistencies, police errors, and psychological factors associated with a deprived childhood and on it will go. I can't see the public accepting the death penalty when there is the smallest element of doubt. This means we turn back to elected officials and if necessary legislative changes."

Doug gave Stephen a few minutes then started. "I know, but we will be overwhelmed if we try a complete reversion all at once. I think the first step will be to get a process in place so we can charge and prosecute those charged, regardless of how inefficient it might be.

The legislative changes will have to come afterward. So will you do it?"

"Yes, I will. There is one condition: this has to be treated as top secret. If it is leaked, some of the press will turn it into a story that we have prejudged Max. The President will be furious; he still deems Max a national treasure. If you accept my condition, I'll get to work this afternoon."

"Stephen I agree: top-level security. And call me if there are roadblocks."

As if on cue Doug's assistant was at the door. Stephen understood the demands of this office and quietly left with a small nagging doubt. He wondered about Doug's commitment to secrecy; the new Judge agreed too quickly.

CHAPTER 6: AT THE LAB

"Max, in case you haven't heard: I'm suspended, screwed, out of action, finished for many weeks, not available. Plus, I have to go; Terry and Manuel are down in the car waiting for me. They just gave me a ride to allow me to turn over my current workload."

The men were never friends in the conventional sense, but through a series of shared experiences a bond and an understanding had forged. The laboratory on the top floor was vacant except for the two: a Nobel Prize winner and a senior politically insensitive detective.

The world-renowned scientist was upset. "Charlie where the hell have you been? I had the President delay his announcement, to give me a chance to work on a strategy with you. To get a head start. But you were impossible to contact. Now the whole world knows, and we haven't even started our investigation to prove this Evans character is a liar."

"Our investigation? I can't help you. No one will cooperate with me; I'll not get access to files, nor get calls returned and on it goes. I'm sorry."

Dr. Max Armstrong didn't appear to be listening. "Screw that. At this moment the President's office is talking first to that asshole Judge Doug and then to asshole number two, Chief Kissass. Within the next ten minutes, you will be reinstated, given a generous budget, and have Terry and Manuel to assist."

Charlie thought: *Jesus, he's done it. Got his way. This will be interesting.*

Max didn't slow down. "First we talk, and then you go collect your badge and gun."

"Alright. Alright Max. I believe you but slow down. I need some details. I gather there is a tight timeline. If the Assessment Team's report comes out first, it will be a difficult recovery. So tell me: what do you have for me to work with, files, and interviews.......everything you have."

Max jumped right in. "Our contact will be minimized. My time will be eaten up by appearance before science committees; also, they don't want me influencing your investigation. So once you kick off, I'll have to stay away; you will be on your own for most of the time."

Charlie couldn't resist taking a shot: "I gather with all the friends you've made over the years, I can count on support from many of the academic community."

Dr. Max ignored the sarcasm. "Listen you have to play this like some of your other famous cases; fast, reckless, and no holds barred. You may have to break more rules than you normally seem to do. I'm a dead man, ruined if that biased Assessment Team starts delivering ponderous scientific jargon. You know those two bastards have been waiting for years for this kind of opportunity."

Charlie, with the recent suspension still fresh, didn't like those comments. "Goddammit! I told you I was finished with those tricks. Besides with all the rumors out there, it would be impossible for me to feed anyone the S1 interrogation drugs; they are all too suspicious. If I offered someone a drink, they would probably think it had been modified and dump it! Plus you keep forgetting it is against the law to use the S1 truth serum, unless authorized by Legal."

They both knew the law; this conversation was just a walk around. They both knew what was going to happen. Max continued. "You know my situation. You also know I went out on a long limb to assist you in the capture of the Leprechaun. That's at least one debt to be repaid. Best I show you some new toys. After a quick look, you can decide what and how to use them."

The former senior homicide detective remembered his last case with the Irish maniacs, led by the Leprechaun, butchering all occupants of a household. There was no doubt without Max's risky participation he would never have solved the case. Max had covertly prepared the dosages of the S1 truth serum; it was this mixture Charlie used to doctor his main suspect's drink.

Shit, he owed more than that; Max also helped with the Robin Hood case and the interview with the disorganized schizophrenic; then there was his intervention in Monk's distressing session. No more. He knew he had debts to pay. He already had the scent; the hunt was on; there would be no rules; best not discuss this with Emma.

As Max searched for his material, Charlie continued to think: *Max, for the first time in his life, was terrified. The entire community seemed prepared to crucify him, except for me......Max is the smartest man in the world and all his innovations had proven to be accurate; the S3 memory scan proved the executed convicts were guilty.*

And certainly, each time he had used the S1 interrogation, it had resulted in a valid clue. Problem: the damn S3 memory scan was a severe intervention on the brain. Going over 45 minutes had always been a known dangerous side effect. Shit. Max never denied that fact and always warned about the excess time, but, it appeared, everyone had forgotten his caveat. Or maybe Max's fear of rejection meant his warnings were always too low key and never a persistent high profile communication.

Regardless, Charlie owed him, and that was all that mattered. He would play as he always had; the difference this time: a ruined career, if caught, meant the twins and Emma would suffer; also the Chief and the Judge would be watching every move. The Chief, in particular, guessed he had conducted an illegal interrogation that is why he no longer was Senior Homicide Detective.

Max held two small spray bottles and started. "Here is my latest: not published work, and it stays under wraps until this is all clear. In fact, I may just keep it a secret between the two of us. Here you are: S1 developed as a spray. I'll give you two bottles.

It dissolves in or on almost anything. You can spray onto coffee, drinks, or food. The good news there is no drowsiness, no loss of memory. The best: it is easy to use: for a person under 200 lbs one spray in a cup of coffee; if over 200 lbs, best to use two sprays. I said it dissolves, but really it sits on top of the surface. With the first sip your subject is getting full force, and if food or gum it's just as fast, doesn't matter.

I save the best part to the last: it is impossible to detect afterwards…can't detect…no odor…..no longer any sleepiness……and no longer any significant memory loss. Problem is: it has limits. It is not that powerful; it will only work if you have someone who doesn't have to incriminate himself. A guilty person will fight and probably be able to resist.

It will be most effective on someone who wants to gossip but is reluctant because he might screw a friend. The new spray will get him talking and fast. But as I said, most useful on a person who won't hurt himself by telling you the truth. If you have a hard nose bastard, guilty and familiar with police interrogation, this is not going to work."

"Jesus, Max are you sure? If this gets out, it will all be over for you and me."

"Goddammit. If this isn't solved fast, it is over in any case. I wanted you on the case because, besides your intelligence, I know you will be prepared to use it and anything else I have. But I understand if you don't want to use the S1 spray."

Charlie knew it was time to speak up. "Ok, ok ....you know I will ....I don't believe that little bastard."

Max grinned; he knew he had the right man. "Hold on before you go. I have some more for your arsenal. Come to the back, and I'll explain."

The two men retreated to Max's office where he explained. This last innovation was extraordinary. The detective was impressed, not only with what he was hearing but the fact that the breakthrough had never been published; but then he understood this improvement had significant implications. Maybe it would never reach the public arena. Never get published. Would he be the only person in the world who would know about its existence?

The fact that Max was sharing the breakthrough with him was another sign of how frightened Dr. Armstrong was. Had he made an error in his first Nobel Prize innovations? No matter. Max had taken off the gloves and was prepared to break the law to find the truth and expected Charlie to do the same.

Charlie cradled two small bottles of the S1 truth spray. As he walked down the street, he never doubted the rest of the team would support him. First, he had to see the Chief and hoped the President's office had made the call.

###

An hour later his session with the Chief was over: reinstated, badge and gun back. But as Charlie walked down the hall he thought: *that was too easy, no anger, no scowls, no harsh words............it was almost like he wanted me reinstated... he wants me to head up this investigation......wonder what the bugger has in mind...he wants me to fail.........thinks I will!*

Before Charlie got to the exit, Detective Webster grabbed his elbow and steered him to the back entrance. He forced him out to the lot where the afternoon shift was getting organized, picking up their vehicles and their assigned partners. The news Charlie had been reinstated had become public knowledge; Webster not only knew everything, he also spread the news. He pushed him through the back entrance, then forced Charlie to stop on the concrete pad overlooking the back assembly yard.

The yard was filled with all men and women going on their shifts, plus every detective not out on call, plus many of the office staff. The patrol cars were lined up on a 45-degree angle with an alleyway in between. The police personnel filled the assembly yard, men and women standing in-between the cars and behind vehicles.

Webster had a microphone and began his presentation for the entire yard. "Charlie on behave of all the working men and women of the Sector we salute you. All of us wish we had the balls to kick ass like you do; your video will live forever. Now I need you to march down between the rows." A cheer exploded from the crowd.

Webster didn't hesitate; he pulled Charlie off the pad and onto the yard's pavement. As soon as Charlie got to the first car, it started: everyone jumped to attention and saluted, the horns played a seven note musical couplet **SHAVE AND A HAIRCUT---- TWO BITS** and the force shouted out the words, the entire refrain was repeated and repeated as Charlie walked the gauntlet.

The loud tribute was heard inside the building, and all the windows were filled with the remaining administrative staff, a building of onlookers, including Chief Kisashton. The almost spontaneous tribute made it obvious where the hearts and minds of the staff resided.

Charlie hit the end of the line he turned and returned the salute. Hats flew in the air, and the shouting filled the yard. He turned and marched to the front street where Terry and Manuel waited in the car; he bowed his head, didn't want anyone to see the tears he couldn't control.

All he thought was: *Jesus it was good to be back.*

Kisashton continued to stare down at the courtyard as his patrol team rushed out to their day's assignments, and the detectives wandered back into the building. His jealousy had evolved to where it had become borderline pathological, harboring all the dangers with this type of obsession, distorting judgment and rationalizing inappropriate activities. He could not understand Charlie's appeal. A popularity which covered all the ranks in the department, support for a detective that he saw as reckless and insubordinate, a man who three times had been within inches of being thrown off the force.

What the Chief failed to understand was that his own behavior, and the working environment he established was toxic. The unspoken rebellion to his control was growing by the day. Charlie's insolence and success was now the rallying point.

He thought he had buried him under the bureaucracy of the Cold Squad. But that fucking Dr. Kate had fed the Squad high profile unsolved cases and then promoted their success, when all they had done was pick the low hanging fruit.

Now rumor has it: the President wants to meet with Charlie Taylor. Judge Doug is furious with the new celebrity, of course forgetting that he had pushed for the Cold Squad demotion.

He was smart enough to recognize his obsession, and his current mantra was: patience. Unfortunately, neither intelligence nor Judge Doug's instructions were enough to control his behavior.

The reporters were fast. So fast had anyone who thought about it, they would have concluded: someone leaked the news; Chief Kisashton didn't worry about being found out; his source had never failed him. The noon news blared the issue:

"......we now have two teams: first the Assessment Team comprised of world recognized scientists; they will apply all their scientific knowledge to the S3 memory interrogation. Were the scientific methods employed or were there some sloppy procedures involved in the Nobel Prize-winning discoveries?

Second, we now have the Detective Team headed by our famous detective, Charlie Brown, oops sorry, that is Charlie Taylor; this group is on a fool's mission. Detective Taylor, regardless of his success in homicide, is a close friend of Dr. Max Armstrong who is the accused in this case. Not sure what this second team hopes to accomplish, except try to diminish the testimony of Chris Evans. One can assume this team will accumulate all Evan's criminal activity, augment his criminal record were possible and try to convince us that this ex-con is a liar.

This unfortunate mess has been compounded. Yesterday our investigating group uncovered another of Dr. Max's proposals; this was presented to the Regional Board. The basics of his recommendation: he recommended a project to test the entire population between 14 and 30 years old. He is convinced he can identify individuals who will, in the future, commit serious crimes. Once we recognize them, he then proposed they be locked up and be subjected to modern psychotherapy until his tests show they have changed. Yes. I am serious; he wants to lock up individuals who might commit a crime.....haven't done it yet but might!

The question is: has this genius gone off the rails? What else has he tried and never revealed?

Our system of justice, Justice Reborn, depends on Dr. Max's innovations; the accusations of the confessed killer, Thor or Chris Evans, could destroy this system. We need the truth, and not a warped defense of Dr. Max as the Detective Team may try and provide......."

In another city, a tall, attractive woman listened to the news. After a few minutes considering the alternatives, she decided. She would act: best to have the inside track, best to know what is going on in all the camps, best to be safe. It was time to get an old debt repaid; she picked up the phone and made contact with an old friend who fortunately was in a position to help.

As she spoke to her old friend she thought: *she had waited a long time for this debt to be repaid, but today the woman couldn't wait; she needed inside information.*

CHAPTER 7: COSMIC JUSTICE

The President, pushed for time, chewed vigorously on a roast beef sandwich, as he watched Charlie load his plate and pour a coffee. After Charlie was settled, the President started. "First, let me thank you for adjusting your schedule for the flight up here; there will only be the two of at this meeting."

The detective found it challenging to eat and keep up a conversation, so put down his sandwich. "No problem sir. As you can guess, I am confused as to why I am here."

Although he had rehearsed his words, the President took some time responding. His problem was: he could not afford any hint of prejudice or favor in this case. He still deemed Dr. Max a national icon, a national treasure; he wanted this scientist cleared, found not guilty. The thought of reverting to the old system of justice filled him with horror. Justice Reborn had reduced crime rates, reduced costs and reduced repeat offenders; his political opponents knew his stance and would jump on any hint of his interference.

He gave Charlie his winning smile and light-hearted chuckle: "Detective, I am not stupid enough to think I can direct your investigation. My concern is that you understand some critical ground rules; my experience tells me that in these cases it is not unusual for instructions to be misunderstood. I'm sure you understand; the more layers, the easier for a breakdown."

Charlie replied. "Sure I understand." But thought: why not a conference call?

The gifted politician never took his eyes off him. He had all the details on Charlie's career, even knowing about the 'crazy

Charlie' moniker; he had enjoyed the Cold Squad TV series, stunned by the Squad's spectacular success.

Many of his staff were recommending a more senior, and conventional detective take over the case. The President wouldn't decide until he had a face to face; he considered himself a connoisseur when it came to judging men or women, a task undertaken many times.

He began. "Charlie, for all sorts of reasons, it is critical, as your investigation progresses that your contact with Dr. Max is minimized. We all understand you may have questions of him, issues requiring more detail, that sort of thing. But you or both of you must exercise a great deal of common sense and discretion. First, minimize the number of times the two of you have a solo meeting; second, keep all meeting short, maybe under 15 minutes.

You see this is a political minefield: Max has many enemies and you, also, appear to have irritated some men and women in the upper echelons. You look confused.

The issue is: we have to avoid any hint that the two of you cooked the books that you both developed a plan that destroyed this Thor's creditability but didn't solve the problem.

Charlie thought: *this sounds like bullshit. Why am I here?*

But he said. "Yes sir. Max already told me that…not in so much detail but understood."

The President tried to lighten the mood. "I am curious. I understand you regularly establish a solid starting position and assess all the evidence in light of this supposition. My question is: what is your starting position."

The detective didn't hesitate: "I see Max as the smartest guy in the room, in any fucking room. I don't see him as trying to bullshit his way to a Nobel Peace Prize; he is fast, not stupid."

This time the President's smile was genuine. Charlie's cursing in his presence when he had been instructed to curb it, was the convincing moment. The President saw loyalty, passion and strong commitment. This is the man, regardless of the Crazy Charlie signature, who might be able to save Max and Justice Reborn. "Good man. Good hunting. Unfortunately, I can do nothing about the time constraints."

"Thank you, sir." With that he got up and left the room; he finally understood he had just passed a test; he'd convinced the President; the job was his.

It was going to be a long flight back. It would not be possible to change his next meeting: Dr. Kate was too nervous and upset. He'd be exhausted, but he wouldn't make her wait.

When the smart ones screw up, they take it hard, and it appears to live with them forever.

At least that's what Charlie was thinking, and this was the behavior Dr. Kate was exhibiting. She was having trouble maintaining control; occasionally a small sob would escape. She looked at the floor and said, "Charlie.....the Chris Evans S3 interrogation, the brain probe, was a fiasco. I blame myself for allowing that technician, Marcie Callay, to tackle the first death row convict at Fort Green Prison. But she was connected. I even received a directive from Regional to use her. And remember it was all new, and we didn't have an abundance of trained people."

A small group sat on comfortable lawn chairs in Kate's backyard. She wanted full support and requested, her husband, Judge Stephen and ex-warden Bill Thompson to attend. Charlie didn't object to their presence, knew and trusted both men. They sat in the shade provided by the large overhang, but the atmosphere was tense. And Charlie was confused by her last comment: "Hold it Kate. Fort Green was the second prison, so I don't understand; there had to be some experienced staff."

"You're right...we were the second prison. The problem was the staff at the first prison, White Rock, executed 155 men in 90 days; everyone thought they had been through enough and warranted a break. They never came to Fort Green. This meant it was the first time around for my group. The first time on probing the brain of a possible killer. The pressure was intense. My god, we were going to decide if an execution was to take place. But I admit: we, although nervous, were confident."

Charlie had more questions. "I know about the extended interrogation of Evans, but thought the 45 minute time limit was only a guideline. That is, not everyone suffered if this time was exceeded."

"You're right in the sense: not everyone suffered brain damage with an extended memory probe. We weren't sure why. Some people lost a few IQ points but recovered within 24 hours; some never recovered. I mean they could still function and had you known them before the probe, you probably would never have noticed any change. The biggest impact was on those who were below average intelligence; losing IQ points could seriously damage their lifestyle."

Charlie wasn't convinced. "Kate I've been wondering: has there been too much made about an IQ score? Was the damage that severe? We often hear comments that the tests are not perfect or the results are only one facet of a personality. ...."

Kate understood he was trying to play down the results and interjected. "No the test results are significant; they do predict performance. If people routinely won Nobel Prizes with low IQ scores, or, for that matter, aced calculus exams but flunked IQ tests, we'd junk IQ tests. So we did damage to the convict and can't duck the issue.

Immediately after Evans, we introduced a 20-minute timer. Every 20 minutes a warning sounds and reminds you of the time remaining. The signal, a series of beeping sounds, becomes more severe the closer you come to the 45-minute time limit."

Kate's explanation set Charlie back. "Jesus Kate, I thought all this had been worked out and spelled out before you tackled the first interrogation. This sounds a little too much like a trial and error approach on live subjects! So what happened with Marcie?"

The Judge thought Charlie was too harsh and tried to signal him to tone it down. Kate didn't seem to mind, continued. "Marcie was smart enough but never developed, what we call, the 'feel.' As you know the S3 interrogation is both an art and a science; she knew the theory but once dealing with the life and death situation, she failed. She seemed to freeze and was too slow in responding to the Historian's commands. Marcie struggled trying to decide the direction to move the probe.

There were also incidents where she kept her finger on the switch too long and continued bombarding his brain. I mean this should not have been occurring during the repositioning of the probe. Shit.

In any case, Evan's interrogation went over not 45 minutes.....
but 55 minutes. It should never have happened. We had bombarded
his brain for almost an hour. I can't believe we did that, and I
supervised. Of course, he was found not guilty, but the result was
ugly; and, we were unsure as the best treatment to get him back on his
feet.

In the recovery bay, Evans was like someone rescued from a
car crash. He slurred words, rambled on with incoherent sentences
and couldn't respond to any questions. We had to put him in
diapers........he lost all control. Every couple of hours he would start
screeching, like a wild animal; the sound terrified the staff; it was
wild and crazy.

It went on for a few days and then slowly he started to
recover....back to normal. The memory probe proved his innocence,
but we kept him in the prison's small hospital for another week. The
psychiatrist staff kept him under scrutiny. The testing showed he'd
only lost a few IQ points, but given the margin of error in the testing
this means he could be back to where he started.

At the end of the week, we released him. The entire team felt
relieved; he looked and sounded good. Again remember the time
pressures. There was no way we could assess any long term problems.
We had to keep going. There was no plan to follow up and evaluate
him later. But honestly ..... I wasn't sure...shit."

She stopped and walked over to Judge Stephen; he hugged
her. Dr. Kate had requested this review meeting take place at her
home where her husband, Judge Stephen, would be present; at the
time he had been the Sector Judge and was still a highly respected
man. Kate also asked Bill Thompson, ex-Warden at Fort Green, to

attend; the prisoners had named him Uncle Willie, but this was a term of respect and not scorn.

Everyone remained silent as Kate continued: "At that point, I should have replaced her, but she was very aggressive, pulling on her political connections. Besides everything was happening so fast, and we had not completely assessed Evan's interrogation. The team voted to allow her one more S3 brain probe; I could have overruled the vote but didn't. The results of the second interrogation were even worse; the convict was found to be guilty and wheeled to the execution chamber. If he had not been found guilty, he would still be residing in one of our institutions as the classic vegetable.

The Region Executive decided: none of this was to be reported to the news media; the news reporting made it sound like we were an efficient assembly line. Well after, your wife, Emma started on the S3 interrogations, we did achieve this degree of success.

So here we are: one goddamn mistake, and we have completely overturned our new system of justice."

That was all she could take and buried her face in Stephen's chest. He tried to calm her down. "Kate, please relax. This was not your fault. We all thought we had the perfect solution. We also knew we were far out on the edge of science, a vulnerable position, most of us were willing to ignore the risk." With a quick nod to Charlie, the Judge walked her out of the room.

Uncle Willie started, "Charlie, it was chaos, and everyone was nervous, convicts, guards, admin staff, and technicians. I mean everyone. As Kate said, we all knew the theory, and there had been some practice or dry runs but remember we were instructed to decommission all prisons and the first step was to clear death row. This meant execute or release, depending on the S3 results; there were

175 prisoners on death row, and most of these convicts would be executed."

Willie stopped to drink from his hot coffee. Charlie started. "I remember when I served as a Watcher. Jesus, you had a traffic jam of hearses in your parking lot; you never knew how many were going to be executed on any given day, so there was always an excess of hearses waiting for their turn to haul a body away."

The ex-Warden began again. "On one floor we had set up the interrogation room with all the damn sophisticated connections and cables; down the hall was a smaller room where we housed three Watchers and the Historian. The Watchers had their screens to see the convict's memory displays as they were retrieved. And further down the hall, on the same floor, a large room where all that day's extra Watchers waited; again an excess of people, because we didn't know how many we eventually need. Each convict could name his own set of Watchers to help with his memory scan: hence there was always a crowd.

On the floor above was the execution chamber and an adjacent room where the Citizen Team sat and observed the man being strapped down. Each person on this Team had a release button, but only one switch or line contained the lethal dose. Again we had another room to house the extras waiting their turn as the Team. This Citizen Team was selected from the public, just like old-time jury members, but we didn't allow them to participate in multiple executions. So that was the reason for extras assembled in a waiting room.

On the floor above this was a medical team ready to assist with any convicts found to be innocent.

And all this was to be a smooth operation: convicts were wheeled from one room to the next, ordinary citizens moved from one place to the next, executed men stuffed into body bags, each piece of bulky baggage then wheeled down to the parking lot and the waiting limousines."

Charlie was impressed. "Jesus Willie that was a helluva workload and coordination issue."

"Better believe it and that first day was the worst. After all the hot sunny days we'd encountered, the weather turned: on this day the sky darkened, and few drops came down, but the worst was the thunder and lightning. A Hollywood script on execution day.

To top all this off: the convicts, even those not on death row, decided to make this special. They'd memorize three different spirituals and started singing …….finished one and started another …, I say singing, but it was closer to yelling. To this day, if I close my eyes, I can see the sky and hear the words **'swing low sweet chariot'**.

Again, remember we had 175 men sitting in cells wondering if this was to be there last day. At this time a rumor was circulating that the rest of the prison population would also be subjected to an S3 memory probe. In summary, the mood was ugly, the place dangerous and tension is too mild to describe the background Dr. Kate and her team were working under."

By this time Judge Stephen had returned but without Kate. "I got her to stay in the back garden; we can go there before you leave. Charlie, the bureaucrats at Regional ran it as a paper exercise, a big math problem, so many prisoners, so many body bags, etc. They failed to understand or accept the fact that these were real people and emotions would be high, mistakes would happen, and we would have to live with them.

Detective, I don't mean to put more pressure on you, but this accusation of Chris Evans is an utter disaster if true. And, the longer this remains unresolved, the more pressure for us to revert to Cosmic Justice."

"Judge, I have no idea what you are talking about."

"Traditional justice deals with where flesh-and-blood human beings interact. Cosmic Justice wants to rectify social inequities; the notion being some segments of society, through no fault of their own, lack things which others receive as windfall gains, through no effort of their own."

"Don't stop there."

"For example, in the mid-1900s various restrictions were placed on police in their arrest and interrogation of suspects in criminal cases, and in search of their property. The rationale for these restrictions included claims that inexperienced and amateurish criminals, ignorant of the law, were more likely to make admissions that would prove to be damaging to their legal defense, while sophisticated professional criminals were far less likely to trap themselves in this way.

This was viewed as an injustice from a cosmic perspective, and correcting this inequity among criminals became the explicit perspective of our criminal justice system."

"This doesn't sound all that bad"

"Well there are a couple of issues to consider: first, Cosmic Justice focuses on one segment of the population and disregards the interests of others who are not the immediate focus of the discussion but nevertheless pay the price for the decisions made. The cost to the third parties was primarily ignored, pretended not to exist or dismissed with loft phrases as 'that is the price we pay for freedom'.

Second, the great U. S. Supreme Court justice Oliver Wendell Holmes said: *some people may be born clumsy so that they inadvertently injure themselves or others, for which in the courts of heaven they will not be blamed. But in the courts of man, they should be held to the same standards or accountability as everyone else. We don't have the omniscience to know who these particular people are or to what extent they were capable of taking extra precautions against their natural tendencies. In other words, human courts should not presume to dispense Cosmic Justice.*

But, unfortunately that is what happened for a long time."

Charlie was still not sure he understood all of Stephen's concerns and asked. "And you're saying our friend Dr. Max shattered that tendency?"

"Yes, when his innovations put on public display the violence and brutal attacks of many crimes, it was impossible for politicians and lawyers to continue defending individuals who wailed about their unprivileged childhood or some other disadvantage. With the S3 memory probe, the offender's satisfaction with the crime and his complete disregard for his targets were obvious for all to see. The truth was overwhelming, and we went back to traditional justice with a vengeance."

Charlie stared at the Judge for a few minutes, not sure how to react. "Judge that will take me a few minutes to absorb."

The Judge smiled knowing Charlie understood more than he was willing to acknowledge. "Not a problem. You know where to find me if you want another lecture. I do have a package for you: Kate has assembled everything she has on Chris Evans, his preliminary interview, the actuals S3 memory scan, and his time after the interrogation. Do you have any special plans for the material?"

"I've hired Helen Tucker, the jury specialist; she had a thriving business back in the day when we had juries. Defense lawyers asked her to read potential jury members. She was excellent at spotting liars. I want to know all I can about this guy and would like to see how she reads him."

Willie put down his cup and offered his opinion. "Let me give you this: he was found guilty under the old system, before Justice Reborn; even the S1 interrogation, our truth serum, didn't exist, and Chris was on death row for some time with many appeals.

As you know, I tried to get to know the men and spent some time with Chris. I had a hard time visualizing him as a killer; he was still wearing the ponytail hairstyle but didn't have the body he now has; in fact, he was rather a soft chubby character, not too smart, passive and open to or the recipient of any of the jokes the convicts wanted to play. He never retaliated and never blew up. All in all, he never seemed to fit with others.

And the man I see on the TV interviews is a more aggressive version of the man I knew and also appears to be a lot smarter. Listen I know this is not a scientific analysis, but the guy has changed and not for the better. Sorry Charlie."

###

The Judge had taken Kate inside, and Charlie was gone; Uncle Willie stayed in the backyard, waiting for the Judge to return. In the silence of the large beautifully landscaped yard he thought back to those turbulent times: a little over eight years ago Justice Reborn came into existence with record-breaking legislative changes.

At that time the lack of definitive solutions to address climate change made the public a demanding force, unwilling to accept gray answers, everyone believed their death sentence, via a super-heated sun, was on the horizon. Since prisons were to be decommissioned and Dr. Max's technology to be used to free or execute criminals, the pressure fell on the Forensic and Prison Divisions to implement. Legal appeals no longer existed. If the Forensic team found you guilty, Prison staff would execute you.

Willie knew it would be impossible for most people to understand the stress and chaos of that time. Prisons were to be emptied under tight timelines which politicians kept trying to change, the faster the better.

A single execution had always been a challenging event, and suddenly they were conducting two or three a day, for day after day. The first decommissioned prison executed almost 200 convicts in less than 90 days. Even though the scientific world sanctioned all of Max's innovations, for Forensic and Prison staff there existed some lingering doubt. What if a flaw existed? Science always seemed to revise theories every few years. How many innocent men and women had been executed? It took a few years before all doubt vanished. Now this damn Thor.

Willie knew all staff, from the men wheeling gurneys, to the cremation officers, to the highly paid techies who declared the guilty sentence; he knew most had wrestled with sleepless nights. But now, years later there are those who wish to second guess, a universal habit made more appealing by the sensational aspects of the case. The ex-warden would do everything he could to support Dr. Kate but understood it would have to be a personal struggle for her.

###

Four hours later Charlie had another critical meeting on the second floor of one of the oldest buildings on campus: the Chemistry Building.

The men leading the Assessment Team, Dr. Carson and Dr. Wiek, each sat on tall stools in a large chemistry laboratory. The neurologist, Dr. Carson, started. "We apologize for the surroundings, but we just had this lab assigned to us and haven't cleared out the adjoining offices." He was a very tall, gaunt man who certainly seemed pleasant and not as Max had described.

Charlie smiled. "Professor Carson, no need to apologize I'm used to working in much more unpleasant surroundings."

"I assume you are here to find out about our team; I guess you know we are waiting for two more colleagues, one from Germany and the other from Japan. But the scientist from Japan has refused the invitation. Hence, there will only be three of us on the Team."

Charlie had one key question: "Yes I know that, but the burning question I have is: why don't just subject him to an S1 Interrogation? This truth serum has never produced any severe side effects."

This time Dr. Wiek, the biochemist, took the lead; he was average height and looked like he enjoyed rich deserts. "No….. we refuse to subject this man to any more of Dr. Max Armstrong's chemistry. We've been shouting for years: he has not followed up on any of his interrogated convicts………..didn't even have a proper starting medical history for these men.

We have no way of knowing if this chemical cocktail caused permanent erosion in the brain cell which doesn't show up immediately. How many convicts are now complaining of memory loss? Or have cancer? It goes on!"

His emphatic denouncement was interrupted by his partner, who tried to present a more balanced opinion. "Detective we know that Max is a genius, but he does have a reputation of brushing aside any questions or suggestions which he believes are immaterial or of no consequence. In the academic world, the rumor is that he bullied his team into the result he wanted. Not good."

Charlie now understood Max's concern. *This was not going to be an unbiased assessment; they wanted to bury a brilliant but arrogant colleague.*

"To repeat: we will not allow any more chemicals into this man's system. We have a series of tests which should allow seeing if there has been brain damage."

Charlie started to counter with: *but you have no way of knowing the starting point and what Evans was born with, if the damage was there for years before the probe.* Then decided the observation would not be accepted.

Dr. Wiek. "We will wait for the German scientist, but on this one point, we are firm: no more of Armstrong's chemistry. I hope this answers your questions."

They both got up from their stools which Charlie knew was the signal to leave; his interview was over.

As Charlie waited for an elevator he remembered some of his wife's comments; years ago, on another issue, Emma got one of Max's original team members to open up. The frank discussion stunned Emma. This old team member, a respected scientist, complained: Max forced them to accept his work. The man said Max maintained any more follow up was a waste of time.

Oh yes, Max used the argument: FAPP: meaning 'for all practical purposes.' Again saying they had enough data to satisfy their needs. No need to do any more testing.

Emma pointed out: at that point in time, the mind probes were not being used to decide a man's guilt or innocence. There was no plan for large scale testing of all convicts and determining if an execution was merited.

As the elevator descended Charlie, as the sole occupant, inadvertently voiced his thoughts: *"Jesus Christ what a mess!"*

###

On the top floor of the Research Center, Dr. Max Armstrong paced the entire level from north to south and back again, an endless process, the only noise in the vacant area was the slapping of his sandals on the bare tile floor. The uproar was unbelievable, and for the second time in his life, Max kept his mouth shut and stayed, or more accurately hid, in his lab.

There were more than a few academics at his throat; the general public, with its short memory span, was infuriated and many screamed for a recall of his Nobel Prize. It was not surprising: someone had gotten their hands on a sensitive and controversial research paper; Max was proud of his efforts and not careful about concealing the work. However, someone had gone a step further and carefully mentioned that it was under consideration by the Regional Board.

His mind raced. *Why and how had this been released to the press? Who was out to destroy him? He finally realized: he had very few friends. He was vulnerable. One man stood between him and total ruin. He gambled everything on a smart homicide detective, a man who regularly solved complex cases but also carried a reputation of recklessness and a hot temper.*

If Charlie was pushed would he disregard all boundaries, would he share the recent secrets Max had shared with him? One more secret piece of research revealed, and there would be no recovery for Max.

Judge Stephen, the former top man for Sector 14, sat back in his chair and drank deeply from an Irish coffee. His study was almost soundproof, and he had the quiet he enjoyed; the Judge tried to think of how he could defuse the situation. One wrong word or sentence and he could be a target as well.

The current explosion in the news centered on a research paper. Years ago, Max had presented the work to him; the scientist was looking for feedback or advice as how to proceed; Stephen recognized the explosive nature of the research and recommended that Max make significant changes before going to the Board.

He recommended Max publish the work as a theoretical study, a follow up on Lombroso's work but make it clear it was not for implementation and drop the lockup recommendations.

Stephen was furious; he knew that the Commit-Them Proposal, as it got recognized by the news media, had never been presented, as a recommendation, to the Regional Board. It was theoretical research Dr. Max conducted by following up on some earlier work by a pioneer scientist, a Cesare Lombroso. Lombroso thought certain humans were born criminals, a type of primitive man. And they could be identified through various characteristics, testing and measuring physical features; these evaluations would identify future criminals.

Kate quietly entered the study, watched and finally spoke, "Steve, I don't understand. I thought he did present to you a proposal to lock up teens who had not committed an offense."

"Yes, that's what makes this complicated. Max carried out extensive tests on over 500 young men, 18 years or younger. Every one he isolated did end up carrying out a violent crime. Now some might have slipped past him. A few became non-violent criminals, but the point is he was right every single time....all became criminals of one variety or the other.

His report did recommend massive testing and incarceration of all that were so identified; he was using me as a sounding board before he presented to the Regional Executive. I talked him out of lockup recommendation; we agreed he would publish his work as a research paper and not make any policy recommendations and definitely not propose locking up teens.

His original conclusion was to incarcerate all those who failed his testing. I mean a lock-up before a crime was committed. It was an impressive piece of work; damn it he got every single one, no exceptions. I mean each individual he identified did commit a violent crime within three years.

Max accepted my recommendation and dropped all reference to an early lock-up. He decided he would first make the Region aware of his work, before publishing, and I agreed with this approach. Dr. Max went under the guise of requesting their approval before he published. Of course, the Executive is not stupid, and they saw the apparent potential but also saw the obvious eruption which could result.

Since Max provided reference and backup for support, two of the Executive went so far as to read the original work of Lombroso; they knew Lombroso had recommended the incarceration of all who had been identified.

They asked Max not to publish any of his research and had the meeting minutes sealed. The Chairman stated they didn't want him to stop this work; the potential was too obvious, and in the future, it was a step the country might have to take: test all between 12 and 18, lock up those who fail and keep them in until remedial efforts could change them.

Max accepted their decision but was unhappy about the situation; in fact, he was steaming because he, wrongly, thought they had throttled his work."

Kate was still puzzled. "Then why don't you call a press conference and explain it was just a research study and no lockup recommendation was ever made to Regional?"

"Because this press release was brilliant. It appears someone got hold of Max's original report presented to me. As soon as I try to explain, the first question will probably be:

Judge Stephen isn't it correct that Dr. Max recommended, to you, nationwide testing and lock-up policy for all teens that failed his test?

If either of us, Max or I, try to explain, it will immediately surface that he did put that in writing. As I said a very clever release and one hard to refute."

"God Stephen, what the devil was Max thinking?"

"It wasn't his finest hour, but look he was so excited by his success he never thought about the social consequences."

"Can you do anything to help?"

"I'm thinking about an approach. As soon as I am satisfied with my strategy I'll contact two men who served as Regional Executive when the research paper was discussed. I'm not sure either one will be anxious to help Max. It is such a blistering topic, and they'll not want to get close to it."

"You have to try. You know we owe Max a lot more than many are prepared to admit."

Stephen realized he was afraid to call a news conference; and it appeared Max was also in hiding; both men would prefer it, if Charlie handled the accusation and tried to correct the erroneous reporting.

Stephen picked up the phone, trying to reach a former Regional Board executive; the correction could not come from Max, some Executive would have to speak up. Since the Executive never knew about Max's original recommendation to Stephen, he could honestly state that: there was no recommendation of that nature; it was a research report.

But the Judge knew the accusation had been released to further damage Max's reputation. Trying to correct the allegation was not likely to change many minds about the Nobel Prize winner. It appeared the academic jealousy and envy Max had fostered knew few limits.

This was a dirty game to destroy him, and it appeared there was little tolerance for any unorthodoxy from what had become a very conservative world.

CHAPTER 8: THE FIRST ONE

"Doc, is your profession able to answer this question: why do you always remember the first one: first screw or first kill? For me, both firsts happened at the same time, so it is burnt into my mind. I can still see her white ass. The big white ass was sticking in the air. God it was great.

Doc! ....Sam!........ You're going to have to work on professional detachment. I can see disapproval written all over your face."

This was Sam Taylor's third, and possibly last, session with the Troll; he had heard worse confessions, but this smirking maniac disgusted him. The killings revolted him, and this academic's unwillingness to control his emotions was a profound disappointment: the brilliant man had allowed wanton lust to direct his life. Sam tried to regain some control.

"Professor Griffin, you are a smart man and perceptive. I will try and listen more carefully and shut down the judgment unit."

"Good man. I knew I would be able to tell you the story. It is one I've always wanted to tell. You'll be the first to hear it.

After the stockyards, I started working on a plan: Bev was still in our class; except for a couple of girls, most kids avoided her; I began to follow her and learn her habits; when no one was around I took the time to talk to her; at first she was a bit leery of me. She warned up when I gave her the candy she loved, but I made sure it was always an isolated spot, and no one saw us.

On the way to her house, the street ran up against a park region. For about a six-block stretch, the east sidewalk butted up against the park perimeter; there were only houses on the west side of the street. On the east side, a heavy curtain of trees and tall bushes grew close to the sidewalk, over the sidewalk in places and narrowing the walk almost to back trail status. It was a dangerous stretch because if you carelessly pushed through this greener, you could tumble down a steep ravine; usually, no one tried to access the park this way because there was nothing at the bottom of the gorge. The fall leaves were still hanging on and the dense foliage, on the east side, was like a large dark blanket, impossible to see past. I'd found a spot which allowed me to hide behind the green curtain and not tumble down the ravine. It was late October when I hid in the high bushes and waited until she was the only one on the street.

Without showing myself, I whispered to her to come closer to the trees; she smiled when she saw me; even the slobbering didn't turn me off. I waved the candy bag, tricked her into coming into the thick foliage. I had a spot where I could move a few bushes aside for her to step into the shrubbery. I continued teasing her with the heavily sugared gumdrops, so she followed me down the slope. Once she stepped off the sidewalk, the bushed sprung back into position, and we were invisible from anyone on the sidewalk.

It was very steep; fallen branches littered the path, well really there was no path, just some of my original footprints to follow. I had to help her down; she giggled as she slipped her way around and some branches slapped her legs. It was about 30 yards to a small level opening where we stopped.

I gave her the candy bag, and we sat together on an old blanket I'd stolen from someone's backyard. While she nibbled away at the candies, I started to feel her oversized breasts, she never even acknowledged my feeling around, even when I loosened her bra."

He began speaking in bursts, pausing to enjoy the memory of his first kill; each recall segment appeared to have special significance for him. His voice was low; as he delivered, he stared at Sam hoping to trigger a reaction.

Sam turned away pretending to adjust the recording equipment, taking his time to ensure he had recovered neutrality. When he rotated back, he was shocked. A pantomime had started; the Troll was in his own world, completely reliving the incident, his hands grabbing the imaginary victim, his mouth kissing and biting. In the small room, no one else existed, with his eyes closed history was replayed.

"I was jacked up; I said: *time to take your pants off.* The bitch refused ...said only for Stan...........I exploded and slapped her face and kicked her......she started to cry but bent over and took them off...............I turned her over and looked at my dream: her big white ass.............I damn near screamed and bit her ass a couple of times ....she is crying, but we are so far into the woods no one heard......finally I was tired of licking and biting and mounted her."

Now the killer flipped on to his stomach and had his hip thrusting, moaning in pleasure, the couch rocked with his violent thrusting. At this point, Sam's thoughts were confirmed: *god he is mounting her. Oh Jesus! I think he'll climax.*

"I'll never forget ....I thought I would die it was so fucking delicious......finally I was spent, and she stopped crying and started to dress..............she looked at me and said her brother, who was a brute, would be at my house before supper...... the rock was just the right size for my small fist, and I smashed her head and face...well more than once...it felt good, and I gave her lots of hits."

Detective Charlie Taylor's brother had just witnessed the 90 seconds of desire which drove this man to kill again and again; Sam crossed his arms, each hand in an armpit, all this to conceal his trembling hands. *Charlie was right about his killer.*

Now the room was still and the veteran psychologist, although stunned by the performance, remained silent. The Troll flipped on to his back, completely ignoring his earlier performance, was now under control, cold and calculating; he started again.

"The ground was full of tree and bush roots, besides I never had a shovel, so I couldn't bury her. I wrapped her up in the old blanket, tore some branches of trees, gathered leaves and as much dirt as I could scrape up. Covered her body. Well, at least sort of camouflaged the burial mound. Of course, I mounted her one last time ……then the covering started…..not great, but that became my pattern. You know two fucks….one when they could scream and one when they never uttered a word." He laughed as he made the declaration, more of a howl than a laugh; a laugh that scared Sam and one that he would relive in a number of nightmares.

The Troll recovered quickly and continued. "Then lady luck came to my rescue. Before I got home, an early snow started to fall…. very heavy, a record snowstorm, and it stayed. There was so much snow the city was paralyzed, no cars moving, no buses, school canceled and people ordered to stay home unless it was urgent. Although they searched for her, this section of the woods, particularly my spot, was almost inaccessible and never part of regular hiking. Access was further hampered by mounds of snow and few days of melting and more snow. The weather meant the police priority turned to immediate issues, like traffic and collapsing roofs; the search was delayed continuously or disrupted. They never found her that year.

Dad got a new job, and we moved in early spring. It was almost ten years before some boy scouts practicing some woodcraft skills found her. I had been gone for years, and even my friend had moved. Remember my old pal? He was with me watching Stan do Bev in the stockyards. He had moved away, so not an issue.

Stan had been too crafty, he'd not bragged to anyone else, and even he was not a suspect. Of course, they were looking for a man and not a grade eight student."

Sam had maintained his composure but wanted to finish with this man. "How long did it take for the next one?"

"I never stopped looking for a target type: age, mental condition. I don't know why. I guess you might be able to help me understand that fixation. I wanted another Bev. I was meticulous, but finally did spy a couple of potentials from a different school. I was now in high school but was trolling the junior high and elementary grounds. I had a rotating paper route and got to know the city; one afternoon I had a late delivery and spotted her.

No more. You can get the details from the other two men on your study committee; you are only one who knows about the first one. And you all understand how my academic credentials got me into the specialty schools and boarding institutions. I had full access to all the students, their records, IQ, everything.

After a while, I was able to identify the ones who would cooperate. I admit: when I started I made a couple of mistakes, and the girls reported me. But with my credentials, I was able to wiggle out of the situation and slowly withdrew from that school. You know you learn from your mistakes, and soon I was rolling. God, it was so easy once I had the pattern; the most significant issue was getting them out without been seen. But enough. Now I have something else. Something better.

I can tell you who the con artist is, but it will cost you."

"What? I don't follow. Who is the con artist?"

"He is the guy in the news who claims the S3 Memory Scan, the brain probe, turned him into a killer. I know who is, and he is not who he claims. He is not Chris Evans.

To name him: I want three more months of life. And this is not negotiable. Go tell that pompous Judge Doug he only has one option.

I can tell the police who this guy really is!"

###

Dr. Kate spoke softly, and her image on the screen reflected a stressed lady, "Charlie, I want to apologize for my performance yesterday; I so want to help you and find out what is going on."

Dr. Kate's Mexican heritage reflected in a soft olive complexion, dark eyes, long, vivid black hair which now contained many randomly situated white streaks, the hair being pulled straight back, a no-nonsense approach. She was a healthy mature woman, a runner, not competitive, but she did maintain a regular schedule. People described her as slim, but she noticed over the last year the extra pounds had more tenacity. Her marriage, after her felony conviction, to her long-time lover Judge Stephen Miller had shocked many friends, but it was a stable relationship, and both parties flourished.

"And before you ask: there is almost nothing on file. Since Chris was found innocent everything was wiped: no fingerprints, no DNA, not even a picture. Remember he was one of the first we processed, and the general thinking was he should be treated as if he had never been accused and in prison.

All we have is the video of his mind scan, and even that is not great. Come over if you want more, and I will try and fill in any gaps."

Charlie smiled; Kate was one of his favorites. "Not a problem dear lady. Uncle Willie filled in some of the gaps, and the package you sent was excellent. I know people are howling for answers, but it is early, and you know it is going to be a bitch.

You should know that damn Judge Doug has been trying to set up a meeting. I've ducked every request but am running out of excuses. My spies tell he wants to set a time limit: we solve the case in five days, or he shuts us down and begins the process of reverting to the previous system before Justice Reborn and Max's innovations."

Kate knew about her husband's undercover assignment; she thought it was time to divert the discussion: "How is Max?"

"Horrible. I have never seen him like this. The man is not thinking straight. I'd appreciate it, if you would visit him. He needs support like he has never needed in his life and doesn't even understand his needs."

"It is good to see the two of you have become so close. I will go to his lab tomorrow. No phone call warning.....just to the Research Center and into the lab and drag him to lunch. Bye Charlie."

Charlie was worried about her. He knew she was a perfectionist and wholly dedicated to science. This accusation points at her: not able to control the process and allowing an inexperienced person to conduct the probe. Worse: some are whispering she withheld information about the degree of damage that the man sustained.

Of course, even if some of it is true, Judge Stephen will also be tainted, and his academic career could be ended.

For Detective Wes Krause, even acute embarrassment couldn't erase the memory; his thoughts had their own tenacity: his drunken uncontrolled desire and the woman's hot naked body continued to dominate his thoughts. All the valid excuses didn't help: he'd been ripe for this type of incident; his days with little sleep, weeks without female companionship, and too much alcohol. It didn't matter. Nothing could excuse what happened. He'd made a mistake and a bad one.

Charlie was surprised to see Wes walk into his office. Since the Cold Squad was housed in a different building than Homicide, this walk over was probably more than a social call.

Wes handed Charlie a drink, closed the door and dropped into the visitor chair. "There is your favorite hot chocolate. Careful it is damn hot."

Charlie knew his friend and immediately sensed something was wrong, big time wrong but decided to let Wes control the conversation. "Thanks, just what I need: a break from the paperwork. But you look like you had an accident on the way over."

"God I wish I could …oh shit I have to tell someone….. and I do need some advice …I really fell …"

Charlie stopped him. "Slow down Wes. Take your time. I have a full cup and not going anywhere. I thought you went to the big bash at the Polish Hall last night."

"I did, and it was as advertised …all the food you wanted and all the free beer included in the price of a ticket…if you wanted the hard stuff that cost you extra ….and a live band, you know the ones for the beer fests with tubas, horns, and fiddles……loud, fast and almost not stop music…..lots of great sausage."

"So far sounds like fun. Take a date?'

"No. I left it too late, and besides I've been out of circulation for too long. But I spied a big table with some people we both know: Detective Webster and big John from his squad. The tables were massive …seating at least 12 people. Webster called me over, and I sat at the table.

Webster's surprise date was Donna Smith, Chief Kisashton's admin assistant….with her hair down and casual clothes I almost didn't recognize her; she introduced me to her friend …

Alice …a tall brunette, a fitness instructor and it showed… name of Alice for Christ sake….. Alice like the kid in Alice in Wonderland. I should have followed my first instincts."

"Slow down friend. What do you mean your instincts and Alice? She say anything?"

"No she just smiled, and I thought: she smiles like a satisfied cat who owns the world and can get what she wants, regardless of the consequences."

"Jesus that is some assessment from a three-second smile. I gather Alice was built."

"Proverbial, not an ounce of fat, short tight dress…oh, goddam it Charlie."

Charlie set his mug down on his desk, sensed the turmoil and pushed his friend. "Keep going."

"Everyone at the table was introduced.....I didn't pay much attention ...I planned to have my supper and a beer and then beg my departure. Donna was with Webster and Alice was with a guy who must have started drinking earlier in the day. After supper, the band kicked it up a notch ...Alice's friend was already hammered and could barely keep his head off the table ...so she is after me to dance.............well I had enough beers and went for it.

Soon we had a routine, dance, run back to the table for a quick beer then again on to the dance floor....Alice's boyfriend decided to lie under the table to everyone's amusement. Our dancing got more uninhabited ...fuck it was absolutely wild ......by this time I even forgot about other people.....I held her by the buttocks, and she just laughed and pushed into me."

"Jesus Wes. Did Donna and Webster see all this?'

"I don't know... we rubbing each other so hard I'm surprised we didn't catch fire...then Webster and his dance partner bumped into us. Webster leaned over and said 'best to take it outside'..........it was like a slap and I knew I had to move. I told her I had to go to the bathroom She want to go too.... we walked off the floor.

The bathrooms were down a long hallway, really wide, almost 6 feet, with only a couple of dim lights in the long hallway; it was some distance from the dance floor. The ladies' door was first, the men's another 6 feet further on...then the damn hall extended another ten feet past the men's doorway but there were no lights in that segment of the hall, so it was dark....you could only make out the emergency exit door because of the red light mounted on the top of the exit sign."

Wes stopped and drank from his mug. Charlie understood they were coming to the worst part; he was silent and waited for his friend to restart.

"I rinsed my face in cold water and decided I would duck Alice and tell her friends I had to leave in a hurry. But when I stepped out, she was there and grabbed me and dragged me farther down the dark hallway into the shaded region, far from the toilet doors and the crowd.

She leaned against the wall and pulled me to her ....the kiss probably melted my belt buckle.....then she reached under my belt and said *'if you lift my skirt, you'll find I left my pants in the ladies room.'*

I was stunned....Jesus before I could react... her skirt hit the floor...she must have been holding it up and just let go....there she was naked from the waist down ....I grabbed her buttocks.... I'm drunk almost out of control.

I think it was her loud moaning that triggered the change...I didn't sober up, but I began to realize this was not good....I still had my hands on her ass, but instead of pulling, I started pushing .....I don't want to hurt her, but I was struggling to get free. At this point I hear a noise in the hall and turn my head; there is a bright light, and a camera is taking my picture."

Wes stopped to gather his resolve and Charlie thought: *another mess is coming.*

"It seems Donna worried about Alice and came looking for her. Webster followed her. Their timing was perfect. Webster heard me yelling at Alice...he tried to divert Donna, but she was too fast and had her camera. She ran from him, off the dance floor, farther down the hall and into the dark zone where we both were still holding on…Alice with her skirt on the floor, bare legs wrapped around me …….me with my hands on her bare ass… … I turned when I heard her and then she started snapping pictures ….. on the photo, you can't tell that I'm pushing away ……………..Donna never said a word, just turned around and left the hall. Alice grabbed her skirt and ran after her."

"Holy shit. It sounds like you had a good time!! Sorry, cheap shot, couldn't resist. And your concern?'

"Donna now has evidence of a senior police officer screwing in a public place; if she can't prove fornication, it will at least be indecent exposure and whatever Chief Kissass wants to make of it. He's still after you."

"Have you talked to Miss Donna Smith? Asked for the photo?"

"Yes this morning, and she gave met this superior smile and said she hadn't decided what to do with it."

"Son of a bitch. Wonder if she has her own agenda."

"Can you put Manuel on to her and friend Alice? I mean dig deep and look for dirt or weird behavior?"

"Sure I understand what you're asking. This is strange. If Donna wanted to help Chief Kissasas, why not give him the photos right away? What the hell is she after? And about her friend. Regardless of the situation, sounds like a helluva date."

"Charlie no more jokes. I can't sleep with this hanging over me."

"No worries. Get out of here, and I'll get Manuel on the search. I don't like any of this; it was a setup. But why? This is a diversion we don't need.

Something is now clear. We know where Webster is getting all his inside information. He and Donna....... would never have guessed."

Before Charlie could say anything more, Wes stood up, waved and left the office.

Alone at his desk Charlie sipped his hot chocolate and thought:

Wes had been struggling as head of Homicide.....hadn't been dating...even started skipping the informal sessions with the team....the man had been lonely and didn't recognize his situation.

This was a setup. But why? And why Wes? Even stranger...Donna as an instigator!

The President who in a few short months would begin a re-election campaign leaned forward with his head resting on his left arm; every once in a while he muttered an obscenity. This unusual behavior reinforced the seriousness of the situation.

Only the Attorney General was speaking, and he had the undivided attention of the entire Cabinet. "As you all know, or have guessed, the situation is rapidly becoming completely unmanageable. Let me summarize:

• First, the relatives of every executed convict have hired a lawyer, with only one objective: prove a faulty verdict.

• Second, a multitude of civil rights organizations is organizing protest marches in all the large cities.

• Third, a small but vocal academic set is starting to hog the news channels, and they are not the friends of our Dr. Max.

Well no point in continuing you understand. Right?"

The Secretary of State a tall, thin woman who rarely displayed any strong emotions, followed with her comments. "I am flooded by requests from every country that followed our lead. Most want scientists on the Assessment Team. They have concerns that we will try and prove the killer's accusation as false and save Dr. Max.

Shit! A couple even threatening to sue us. Not sure where this came from but does again reflect the seriousness of the mess. Smart people aren't thinking. Each country is facing the same turmoil we are.

Mr. President concerning the criminal investigation team: can we consider replacing Charlie Taylor? I know he has been very successful, but he also has a reputation."

The Attorney General, Carl Brewster, interrupted, "I would strongly support any move to appoint a more senior law enforcement officer. Taylor's work in Sector 14 although successful has been tainted with controversy; his attitude and behavior are, by some, considered a disgrace to the Sector."

What the cabinet minister failed to reveal is that Charlie humiliated his brother, now Judge Doug Brewster, to a point where his staff gossiped about their encounters. Years ago when Doug a pipe smoking polymath and senior on a legal team tried to coerce a detective team, Charlie asked if he shoved the pipe up his ass if that would clear his mind. To this day the incident lives in the Legal Division of Sector 14. The Brewsters were a close family and insults were not forgotten.

The President allowed the remark to sit on the table before he replied. "I understand your concerns. Unfortunately, I made Dr. Max a promise, and he wants Taylor. I have thought about opening another team but gave that up. Time is the big issue. And I doubt more scientists or detectives will help.

The scientific men on the Assessment Team have been slow getting organized but remember they are among the best we have. So please remain calm and no unsanctioned press conferences."

With that, he abruptly stood up and left the room. This uncharacteristic move left a few wondering if the pressure was too much for the mild-mannered man.

CHAPTER 9:   TOO DEVIOUS

Terry nearly exploded. "It's simple: Wes got horny."

The small team of detectives, known as the Cold Squad, occupied an insignificant office space. It had been easy for Chief Kisashton to allocate the least office space available, with only three team members it should be adequate; he then used budget constraints to force them to take old furniture dragged out of storage. Not many understood: the group's focus and drive meant these deprivations meant little to them, minor bumps in the road of life.

In this room, the Cold Squad was in a heated disagreement. The three detectives were arguing about a potential diversion. Terry continued. "There is no time to waste. We're risking a lot because Wes got horny. I don't understand. Why spend time on this? Charlie, why has this got you so interested?"

Manuel stayed silent; he'd been thinking the same thing. Charlie explained his concerns. "I know what is bothering you. I'll run this past you. There are a number of alarms; some on their own may not be that much, but when I look at the total I can't help feeling this was a setup. And why a setup?"

Terry would do the talking for himself and Manuel. "Alright let's hear it."

"First, if you review the security tape you'll notice most women are wearing jeans or some type of long pants; this was advertised as a harvest time beer fest, with bales of straw and lots of cowboy boots. But our Alice arrives with a skirt so short she doesn't dare bend over.

After she and Wes leave for the bathroom break. Miss Donna Smith waits for her chance, gives them time and then chases them down and knows they are at the back of that long hallway. How did she know their location?"

"Come on Charlie, even Wes said he and Alice were a raucous couple; all she had do was follow the noise."

"Maybe but remember the band was blaring so loud, it was hard to hear your friends across the table. Then why did she go looking? Worried about her friend? She didn't care the entire night, during the lurid dancing. Last, and most puzzling, why was her camera in the ready position?"

Now Terry hesitated. "You're starting to interest me."

Charlie never stopped. "Look at the three photos she gave Wes. Wes turned to face her when he heard her; so we can identify him. But look at Alice in all three photos, she has turned her head away. We are left with a full view of his hands on her bare ass and her legs wrapped around him. If Alice was surprised, why not turn to the noise?

The way it is now you could publish the photos and the only one embarrassed is Wes. The woman remains unidentified. Last, why hasn't Donna Smith told Wes what she wants? My guess she wants him to sweat and be more receptive when she makes her pitch.

Again most puzzling.....Jesus, we only have one active case. How can this be related to Max's problems?"

Terry was still reluctant. "I see what made you suspicious, but it seems a rather elaborate plan just to see him sweat. Do you think Donna wanted to get something on Wes rather than our case? What is unique about him?"

"That's what's bothering me. It's an elaborate trap. For what? Donna had to involve a second person, this Alice, which makes more difficult to execute. And how does she know how Wes might react? I guess as long he kept drinking, and the dancing was hot, the ladies probably thought they had him."

Manuel made an addition. "What both of you have failed to question: if it was all legit and an unfortunate accident, why did Alice not use her correct name?"

It was the proverbial show stopper. Both stopped and looked at him. "So you did find something."

Manuel started to reveal the results of his searches. "Yes. Not a great deal, but I've only been at it for an hour. First, the Chief's admin assistant, Donna Smith: she was a brilliant student through elementary and the first years at high school…. then she drops off the radar ……returns to the records when she is 19 to complete grade 12 and enrolls in college …….top of the class or next to it …rather than U she selects a business option at college ……….top of the class …gets on with the force and within a few years she is with Kissass, as senior admin assistant ….also runs a small supply business with her mother…….hospital supplies…. online orders….making good money"

"What about Alice?"

Manuel is ready. "Wes got the security tapes from the Polish Hall, and we were able to isolate a good picture of his friend Alice as she came in the Hall. And I have to say: Wow she is a piece of work …….with that skirt, she is lucky someone didn't grab her in the parking lot."

"Got a picture her?"

"Yah here she is. I used our face recognition software and identified her: Adela Houston. She owns and runs a small business, about 50 miles northwest of the city. It's a medium-sized operation for boarding horses; she also trains horses, gives riding lessons and rents horses by the hour for riding around her ranch, a medium sized spread... and Donna Smith boards a horse with her; they call the place the Barn.

Here is where it gets interesting; there is also a gap in her life cycle ...between ages 15 and 16................ I can't find any records. My guess both of them got into the Juvenile System, and that is why all the info is blocked, it's standard protection for young offenders. Want me to break into that system? Faster than trying to get some authorization. Not likely anyone will notice."

Charlie never hesitated. "Yes do it." With that hasty command given and received, Terry and Charlie hurried down the hall and out of the building.

Charlie stopped, thought for a moment and then said, "Terry, I don't know what is going on, but there is too much for this to be an accidental encounter .... we have to go one level deeper.......Manuel won't get caught...we have to find out about these two ladies.... my bet it relates to our project and not to Wes."

"My assessment: this is a dangerous person, but I can't decide if he is telling the truth."

That was how Helen Tucker began. The two men and Helen sat on the tall stools which were part of the lab on the top floor of the Research Center. The entire floor was vacant except for the three of them. She was impressed by the thousands of dollars' worth of equipment and machines which crowded the space. Strange to see it all idle; even her voice almost echoed in the enormous room.

Helen used to make a living working with lawyers and helping in juror selection, identifying those potentials who may be lying or hiding a strong prejudice. She had been the best and charged top dollar. The S1 and S3 innovations had almost wrecked her business; however, today, she flourished: employed by large corporations who would never have access to the S1 truth serum. Companies called her in for clandestine evaluations of employee videos; the issues ranged from possible fraud to harassment rumors.

Helen always enjoyed explaining her specialty. "Gentlemen, research has found one set of characteristics useful in identifying a liar: micro-expressions, or incredibly fast facial movements, that on the average last between one-fifteenth and one-twentieth of a second and are exceedingly difficult to consciously control. The theory is that lying is more difficult than telling the truth and with the added pressure on our mind, we might show 'leakage' or those instantaneous facial tics which seep out despite our attempt to control them.

These micro-expressions are too fleeting for an untrained expert to spot. Even the best trained have admitted they can have problems detecting the good ones. But this is often my initial focus."

Although slightly heavyset, she was an attractive woman with a no-nonsense look and stared at Charlie, as if assessing his reliability. "I repeat: you and Max are going to have a hard time with this one."

Max was anxious. "I don't think I'm going to like what you have to say."

She smiled and continued. "Let me make some comments. The people who lie as part of who they are, the real masters of the game, these people are not an open book. They don't lie as amateurs;

they are craftsmen. For them lying isn't uncomfortable or cognitively draining, or anyway an anomaly from their daily routine. Charlie, you must have run across many of these characters."

Charlie responded. "Yes, and I know what you mean. They are so good we couldn't even get a room full of detectives to agree as to whether we were listening to crap or an honest statement. But now with S1 that is a thing of the past.

But here we are screwed; Chris's claim makes it impossible to use any of our new tools.

Too many experts are screaming a flaw in S3 also makes the S1 questionable. So until we prove Chris wrong or right we are stuck with the old method. So Helen, what can tell us?"

"Gentlemen, the smart, intelligent psychopath is a superior liar. Mr. Evans scares me and makes me uncomfortable. People like him seem to have the skills of a true wizard, plus they have no conscience. If you watch the interviews, he is cold to the core."

"Are you saying Evans is a liar and a psychopath?"

"That is what I'm telling you. But will I put it in my final report? No, I can't. I have to account for all my assessments; this means the written reports are carefully crafted. Getting sued is too expensive. What I told you is my best guess and my feelings. He is too good for me. I can't say if he is lying or not."

Charlie was frustrated. "Jesus, what do we make of that?"

"Sorry for rambling. My official report will be: I can't tell if he is telling the truth or not. But off the record, I'm saying he is a dangerous man, and I think he is up to something. I can't believe him, but I have no idea what he might be lying about or what part of his story is true. Sorry, I know this is not what you want to hear."

She made a few more observations about Chris's eyes; Charlie thought: *yes his eyes are weird but what the hell does that matter?* Then Helen was finished; she gathered her notes and without another word walked out of the room. Max was stunned by her comments and abrupt departure. Charlie smiled, accustom to her mannerisms and social interactions.

Charlie tried to be positive. "Well Max she has confirmed our assessment. This Chris Evans is not a straight forward person as he presents to the world. He has his own agenda. When will he reveal it? Or will he ever? How do we find out? Sorry, this time my excuse for rambling....shit."

Max, upset and silent, walked to the window and looked down at the yard. Finally, he spoke, "You know this will ruin me. All my work is gone. No one knows how hard I worked and the hours I put in every day. They keep talking as if I have this superior IQ and that it was all easy, no effort, just woke up one morning with all the answers. Sure I took some chances but only after hours of lab work and hours of cross-checking. God damn it Charlie ... I'm...."

He stopped and shuffled out of the lab. Charlie was shocked at his condition; it was the first time he'd ever seen Max defeated and depressed. He began to understand the amount of Max's life was invested in these two innovations. A brilliant career to be destroyed because one convict claimed these advances had turned him into a killer.

Unfortunately, it seemed the entire academic community had turned on Max. This attitude no doubt the result of his many arrogant put-downs and his frequent disregard of the feelings of any competitor, real or perceived. For Dr. Max it wasn't personal; he just hated inferior science and refused to allow for honest mistakes.

Charlie thought about the ancient shibboleth: *be nice to those on the way up because you will meet them on the way down.*

Up to this point, regardless of his strong declarations to the detectives and the President, Charlie had been ambivalent, not sure about how hard to press. Small lingering doubts often surfaced: *Had Max moved too fast? Pushed too hard? Did his arrogance result in brain damage?*

Now Max's depression triggered a shift, and Charlie made one of his 'the hell with it' decisions. He didn't understand science or Max's work and innovations, but he knew Max. His decision: he was going after this Chris Evans with all the resources he could muster, and if he had to cut corners he would. Max had not hesitated to help him in the past; now he would reciprocate. His starting position, and he always need one, now was entrenched in his mind: Max's science had proven his genius.

Somehow this convict, with or without outside help, had created a feasible scenario.

It appeared Charlie would have to throw the rule book away; he would not hesitate.

###

The detective thought this must be the story of my life: one disruption after the other. It's never a good time, but the teacher insisted that both parents should come to the school.

They sat in a classroom, now empty of all the students, surrounded by electronic whiteboards and samples of work assignments. Charlie and Emma sat on one side of the desk and the young teacher on the other side. The detective's mind was on the murder suspect; he even forgot the teacher's name which she provided moments ago. She was young and serious. Apparently, Ellie had disrupted her class.

"First let me tell the good news: Ellie is very smart, and I enjoy having her in the class; unfortunately she is quick to anger, and since she is faster and stronger than even the boys, the fights are all one-sided. Yesterday, out in the yard, she started by chocking a boy, I know he is a bully and often picks on the small kids, but all the same, we can't condone this behavior. Last, Ella threw him to the ground and slapped him."

Charlie woke up and interrupted, "I don't understand why we are here? Schoolyard fights must be a common occurrence."

"You never let me finish. While Ellie was slapping him, she screamed 'you fucker'. This was a continuous scream, loud and strong, until the yard supervisor was able to pull her off him."

Charlie had a hard time suppressing a grin.

"The result: for most of the class in the yard, a fun word entered their vocabulary. When I got there, the group was playing tag but instead to saying 'gotcha'.................they screamed 'gotcha fucker' whenever they made a tag. The entire yard was bedlam, obviously many already knew the word, but Ellie gave it the stature for everyday use."

This time Charlie started to laugh; all the tension of the week drained from his body. He couldn't stop. Emma grinned, fighting a losing battle to maintain her composure; she understood her husband's situation and temperament. The young teacher, who had interviewed many couples, stared in disbelief at the reaction of the parents.

CHAPTER 10: GETTING ORGANIZED

A secret was tormenting one member of this tight-knit group.

Manuel knew he should tell the others, but each time he started his resolve failed; it was too emotional for him. He intended to protect the group, not destroy it, but eventually, his silence would be devastating. He tried to clear his thoughts. He sat in the room with the group and waited for Charlie to take the lead.

Charlie had all members in the small Cold Squad conference room, ready for a review. Terry and Manuel had already dropped all their current Cold Squad initiatives, to entirely focus on Chris Evans; Wes was present but recognized as an associate only, homicide would remain his priority.

Charlie played Evan's interview tape and started. "You've all seen and heard what I've heard. Any comments?"

Manuel surprised the group. "This Chris Evans has dog eyes."

Everyone laughed, but Charlie was impressed. "Very good my friend. My jury specialist also picked this up; here I'll play her comments."

He adjusted his system to find the relevant comment. The juror expert, Helen Tucker was heard discussing Evans with Charlie; her voice filled the small space:

"Charlie, have you noticed his sclera?"

"What?"

"The whites of his eyes; they are extremely small, certainly not normal."

"I never noticed.......... thought he just had strange eyes, but now I do. Jesus, it is a bit weird ...more like a dog."

"Here is a curious piece for you to consider; in comparing the human anatomy with that of the 200 odd monkeys and ape species, an interesting fact emerged. In all our primate relatives the sclera is barely visible whereas for us it is very significant. One theory is: the whites of the eyes are the mark of a highly social and cooperative species whose success depends on sharing with others our thoughts and intent. The sclera so outstanding, like a beacon, signals to others the direction of our gaze and what thoughts might be in our minds."

"So you are saying according to the theory: this son of a bitch is shifty, not sociable and certainly not willing to share. And is good at hiding his intent ....and is probably a liar."

Charlie turned off the unit. Terry was impressed. "Manuel...great call detective....nice call."

Charlie came back. "Look you know we are pressed for time and have some very unusual barriers, so I am going to state my position: this Chris Evans looks solid, and everything he says has scientists concluding it is possible, in fact very likely; the Assessment Team so far has only two members, both enemies of Max: professor Tyler Carson and professor Ryan Wiek. Both have wanted to bury him for years.

My gut tells me Thor is a liar....about what and why I don't know, but he smells, and I believe in Max. Doc is a fucking genius and head and shoulders above most scientists on the planet. I know his reputation as a horny bugger, but I've never felt he lied about his work. In fact, he is meticulous about his work, spends more hours in his lab....more time than anyone...........Emma tells me no one can match his work ethic."

Wes smiled at his friend's emotion. "Jesus, Charlie I'm convinced!"

Charlie wasn't smiling. "I know you're aware of my past shortcuts so no need to go there. Today, as I see it, to solve this case I'll have to overlook official regulations which could mean a shortened career; today 'overlooking' is a massive understatement.

I mean there will be no rules. So this morning, I'm giving you a chance to keep away from the dirty stuff; you can stay on the team but will work in a limited fashion, not sure if that will work but no need to ruin a career unnecessarily. Let me know before the end of the day. I will not hold this against you; this includes you Wes."

Wes was not going to stand for this. "Charlie, you asshole. Don't you remember how many times you have already compromised us?"

Terry and Manuel broke out laughing. Manuel added. "Boss, we know you'll do whatever it takes other than shot the guy with your service revolver!" More laughter.

"Sorry. I had to ask. The time constraints are impossible, as you know we have to beat that damn Assessment Team full of academics. The first step is to walk through Evan's entire record. We'll start with the first murder conviction in a bar fight. Manuel let's hear his record."

Manuel projected Chris Evan's picture on the back wall and started his summary:

"This man was charged and convicted of first-degree murder in 2018; this was before we had the S1 Interrogation tool, our truth serum; so it was an old fashion jury which found him guilty.

While he was in Fort Green prison, all of Dr. Max's innovations were accepted, and Justice Reborn revolutionized our system of justice. Legal appeals were no longer used; the S3 Memory or Brain probe was used to clear death row cells: innocent and you walk; guilty and they wheeled you down the hall to the big sleep; he was the first convict interrogated at Fort Green.

There is no official written report about his S3 interrogation, except a note that it went over the 45-minute time limit. Forensic did discreetly move the young woman, a Marcie Callay, who conducted the interrogation, out of their Division into some remote location working under the Legal Division. Dr. Kate held Evans for over a week, then released him; he was innocent.

For a long time there is nothing; I mean there is no pattern of serial killings. He seemed to be going straight. But then a pattern starts to build; enough events occurred to prove there was a serial killer in our Sector and Sector 13; he targeted male gays, attacking mainly in public parks in the late afternoon or at night. His approach was simple: monitor, watch his targets and find out when they were alone and use a hammer to smash in the head. His first killing he used a ball-peen hammer, next standard claw hammer; he left each hammer at the scene. Third one: he killed a large man with a small sledge hammer.

This was when that big-time crime reporter started calling him 'Thor' and the name stuck. No police department came close to solving the cases, and there were more killings; sometimes he used the mountain climbing hammers with a modified head, just like a pick; in all cases, he left the killing hammer at the scene, sometimes buried or lodged in his victim's face.

His capture was not sophisticated police work. Sorry Wes........ Thor, or Chris Evans, was at the gay bar at the U. It appears he overindulged, and his judgment slipped. He followed a handsome young student into the can........thought the room was empty except for the kid he'd followed. The young guy was at the urinal. Thor swung at the kid who, of course, was facing the urinal wall.

About the same time, another student exits from one of the toilets and tackles Thor. In a matter of minutes, the noise attracts others; the public toilet fills with more students, and they pin Thor to the floor. Wes, you want to take it"

A subdued Wes took over. "Thanks Manuel, unfortunately, the student at the urinal died; the blow was too severe. But our friend Thor was prepared, like this was another step in his life. Once we got him to the station, he immediately shouted he would confess to everything but only to Judge Doug, Chief Kisashton, and Professor Carson. That was fine with me, saved us the cost of S1 truth serum interrogation.

I was surprised by the demand but contacted the Judge, the professor and set up the Chief to witness the confession. I looked up his record and found he was Chris Evans previously found innocent, about ten years ago, of a murder charge, using the S3 memory scan. The explosion came when, as you all know, he accused the Sector of turning him into killer and Dr. Max as the main culprit.

To continue, we searched his apartment and found a spectacular box set of hammers of more varieties than any of us ever knew existed, all with nameplates and their detail history: tack hammer for upholstery, antique blacksmith hammer, graphite flooring mallet, a jeweler's silversmith hammer, etc. Anyway, there were slots for 24 hammers, but seven slots were empty, and their nameplate description matches the hammers collected at the five unsolved murders. For the other two missing hammers: it meant there were two more killings and the bodies have not surfaced. This cooperative killer was prepared to take us to the burial sites. That's it, Charlie."

No one asked questions because they already knew most of the relevant facts. Charlie started again. "We have to get to know this guy. I mean in detail. We start at the beginning; Terry and I will go to the bar where he was first charged and then found innocent; Manuel do some more research Evan's background as far back as you can go, parents, friends, schools the works. Wes as you know you are only on call as required, so for the moment, I have nothing specific for you.

I will now bring forward the next angle in this bizarre situation. I want you to hear this recording. Remember, you'll have to treat this as confidential until we see what decisions are made.

We can't ignore this, but it is a helluva twist. You are aware of the Research Project set up to study serial killers like the Troll. My brother is part of the research group and had a few sessions with him. This recording is my brother and Professor Griffin, the Troll; it was part of their last meeting and here is where the Troll dropped the bomb."

Wes broke in. "I've seen it. You mind if I take off?"

"Best you stay..... I want an opinion....ok? You are about to see and hear a real scumbag." He pressed the button for a fast forward until the Troll came up with his surprise, debating with Charlie's brother Sam. It started with the Troll making an audacious announcement:

"I can tell you who the con artist is, but it will cost you."

"What? I don't follow. Who is the con artist?"

"He is the guy in the news who claims the S3 memory probe turned him into a killer. The guy with the hammers: Thor. I know who is, and he is not who he claims. He is not Chris Evans.

To name him: I want three more months of life. And this is not negotiable. Go tell that pompous Judge Doug he only has one option.

I can tell the police who this guy really is!"

"That is hard to believe."

"Well get this; the guy spouting off about the Sector turning him into a killer is the kid who was with me at the stockyards watching Bev get screwed."

"So after about 25 years,. you can recognize a kid you only spent about six months with, running around town. How is this possible?"

"A few clues: his face hasn't changed that much; his speech still has that occasional hesitation and a minor lisp. Finally, he has huge hands compared to the rest of his body."

"Come on Professor Griffin be serious. How the hell does a young teenager recognize what are unusually big hands and then remember a feature like this all these years? Too much to believe."

"Well Dr. Sam, in my first story there a few details I left out. I said as we watched Stan doing Bev, we were masturbating......what I didn't mention is: we were doing each other. He had his huge hand wrapped around my cock and got so excited he almost ripped the poor bugger off.

When I saw his TV interview and saw his hand wrapped around that mug of coffee, those long fingers, and big thumb, I almost screamed: that's him. No fucking doubt..."

Charlie stopped the recording. "This recording was sent to Judge Doug Brewster for a decision: will he give the Troll another three months? We can't touch him with an S1 because after his death sentence he was guaranteed three months and no more S1 or S3 if he talked openly with that Research Group. So the son of a bitch claims he knows the Thor, and he is not Chris Evans. Now, this is even more bizarre: if Thor is not Chris Evans then who the hell is he?"

Wes interrupted. "The general opinion is: Troll is lying, is trying to manipulate the situation for more months of life. Why not if we buy it? Judge Doug will have to decide if he gets three more months, based on a 25-year-old speech pattern and some teenage masturbation."

It was quiet, all stunned by the possibility to a mess getting more complex. Finally, Terry expressed the sentiments of the room. "Jesus H. Christ!"

CHAPTER 11: THE DECISION

As he listened to Judge Doug Brewster rant, Charlie thought: *I bet he remembers the time I offered to shove that pipe up his ass.*

The words escaped in between nervous puffs on his pipe. Judge Doug spoke so fast he almost slurred the words. "The son of a bitch is playing us…..a smart university prof trying to live a little longer….we are to give him another three months because 20 or 25 years ago some guy wrapped his big hand around his penis…..god damn I don't like this…..Chief care to comment?"

The Judge's chambers were large and lavishly furnished, but today there were only three occupants in the vast corner office. Across the desk from the Judge sat Chief Kisashton and Detective Charlie Taylor.

Chief Kisashton was a smart man with a long service record on the force but had never developed the instincts that Charlie, as a homicide detective, regularly demonstrated. The Chief's strength flashed in the administrative process and bureaucratic wrangling, not skills to endear him to the rank and file. He recognized his limitation; jealousy was one of the main reasons he hated Charlie.

Kisashton's answer was political, as were most of his other moves. "Judge, the President wants a comprehensive assessment and all bases covered. In fact, he has appointed two more scientists to be part of the assessment team, one from Germany and another from Japan. We have to demonstrate no avenue was ignored, no matter how thin the stream."

Another puff on the pipe and then, "I assume if two more scientists are coming they haven't started. Right?"

The Chief was current. "Right. Professor Carson and Wiek have been provided a large lab and office space over at the university chemistry building, and a few postgrads will serve as grunt men. The rumor is the man from Japan has been delayed…or more correctly may decline. My guess: it will be a couple of days before they start."

Charlie knew both professors had been publically humiliated by Max. In an academic presentation, they made the mistake of attacking his work, and he tore them to shreds. Both had followings and influential work in other fields, but they had stepped into the wrong arena, just once. This was probably why the President assigned two more men to the group; he wanted to ensure some objectivity. Good luck with that. Max's insults never stopped at a border.

An unhappy Judge looked at his other guest. "Detective, I'm sure you wish to add your comments."

Charlie was learning, no smirks, no smart-aleck reply. "One dimension we have to consider: Professor Griffin's request will probably become public knowledge. Oh, I don't mean this week but sometime, maybe even after this incident is over. This is too hot an issue; somewhere, somehow it will slip out: a man tried to give us a clue ……an extremely hot clue, and we chose to ignore it.

Someone will have to explain to the President why we ignored the clue. Me? I agree with you Judge; the guy is playing us …he wants the extra months of life…..I say let him get wheeled down the hall to the execution chamber."

Charlie's response jolted the Judge; Brewster hesitated and thought: *What the hell is this all about? He is here as Max's savior. He should be clutching at any straw.*

Become public knowledge? And I bet I know who will make sure it slips. The son of a bitch is painting me into a corner. The bastard is threatening to expose any decision to ignore the Troll.

The Judge glanced at the Chief who gave a short shake of his head, a negative, a disagreement with Charlie. Doug Brewster, another political animal, picked up his pen. "Well gentlemen that damn Troll has bought himself another three months. Charlie, I'll send copies to all the relevant offices, and here is your authorization to talk to him. Good luck and be sure to wash your hands after the interrogation. And remember: still no S1 serum......just old fashion grilling."

###

After Charlie left, the two men sat in silence for a few minutes then the Chief spoke: "Don't worry the Troll is a manipulator and a liar; he will lead Detective Taylor down a number of dubious paths and waste lots of time."

The Judge nodded and asked, "Is that Marcie Callay in the city? Has she arrived?"

"She'll be here in a couple of days and will bring her video of Evan's S3 brain probe. The Assessment Team should be up to speed by then and ready to talk to her. I've seen the recording; it will blow them right off their high academic chairs. God it is unreal, and the fact it was not made public at the time will enhance the explosion.

Marcie was worried about her position and secretly videotaped him for a few days as he was recovering. All the ugly scenes were recorded. Evans vacillates from a vegetable state to suddenly an angry, horny sailor, cursing at the top of his lungs, and menacing anyone who is close to his bed.

The video even captures a worried Dr. Kate hovering over his hospital bed. The good Dr. Kate will regret keeping this S3 interrogation from the public."

"Chief this is excellent. Sounds even better than we originally thought."

After the Chief left, the Judge smiled and thought about his revenge: *well smart ass detective……let's see how you feel when we shove this video up your ass.* The Judge always remembered when Charlie suggested he'd shoved the pipe up his ass to clear up his confused thinking; Doug had been a senior in the Legal Division, and the comment flew around the department with many laughs for the staff, from junior to senior staff they couldn't refrain.

At the time, one smart ass young lawyer, a natural-born mimic, went so far as to retell the scene perfectly imitating Charlie's firm suggestion and Doug's wimp response. His gross exaggeration produced tons more laughter, keeping the incident active for more weeks. The entertainer was a smart man but no longer in Legal; Judge Doug took care of him ages ago.

CHAPTER 12: THE HOLE

The planned illegal tactics made Charlie nervous; limited supply meant they had to be selective. And he repeated himself. "I'll doctor the drink of any witness. I'll decide who we dope; if I need a distraction, I'll give you the signal."

Detective Terry Patterson understood the situation and tried to reduce the tension: "Relax Charlie. It'll work. We've already covered this criminal process…a few times. Right?"

Charlie and Terry had returned to the club, where in 2018 Chris Evans had been charged with murder and later found not guilty with an S3 interrogation. They walked in the front door and without any hesitation introduced themselves to the owner.

"I have to admit 'THE HOLE' is a helluva a name for a bar." Charlie was smiling when he spoke the sentence; their visit didn't come as a surprise. Evans was prime news.

The owner, Scott Robinson, a pleasant young man, laughed with his response. "It was my dad's sense of humor; he died a few years ago, and I still try to follow along with his ideas. It has been successful for a long time. What you see around the perimeter was his innovation."

Along the outside walls were a series of booths; each booth had a large screen, a selection device, a printer, and a device to accept payments. The many stalls still left space for a small dance floor and a long bar for the heavy drinkers. The entire club was spotless, and although it was early and almost empty, it gave the impression of an orderly establishment and a well-run business.

Terry was impressed. "What selections are available at each booth?"

"So far we have: bar fights, amateur ladies stripping, comedy routines and documentaries. Yes, hard to believe, but documentaries are in there, for example, bar fights that make the news have been captured. You pay to watch a selection and have many options: close-ups, slow motion, rewind, freeze, and for an extra few bucks you can print out a high gloss picture of the screen.

The best part: a large piece of our inventory is customer driven. Women pay us to get their stuff on our network. They create the videos, and my sister, the techie, cleans them up, enhances and loads them. You should see the raw stuff we get; some women want to get recognized, and they don't give a shit about nudity. We get enough material so we can load a new set every two weeks …except for the bar fights. They are mostly history. I mean at one time the fights were more frequent, but not today, so we don't have as much new material."

Charlie took over. "It's the fights we are interested in. In particular, the one with Chris Evans when he was charged with murder."

"As soon as you phoned I thought it would be the fights. Sorry, you will be disappointed. The first fight took place about 10 or 12 years ago when Dad first started; the club was much smaller, with only one security camera, a cheapie near the entrance. Wait let me step explain.

Back then, for a short period of time, bar fights were all the rage. Why? I don't know. I think it started because of a movie which glorified barefisted combat; it was some sort of a macho thing, with women cheering. One wrong word and some idiot would start swinging. Dad was frightened they would wreck the place and hired a tough doorman and even a more massive bouncer. The intent was to get fighters out to the parking lot or just make them stop.

I wasn't around, but Dad told us the story many times; first, Chris was with a gang, or it might be better described as a group. In our club, there were two significant fights, started by this group. The first resulted in the murder charge; the second financed the club's current renovations.

The first fight was a real brawl, with dozens involved; that video is one of our selections, but the quality is inferior, so poor it couldn't be used at his trial. You can't see who threw the punches or where they were landing."

He stopped talking and waited for questions. The quietness of the bar was interrupted by the harsh sound of the shuffling of feet. A stout set man with huge boots, loosely tied, ambled his way to one of the far booths, a large sheepskin vest and faded jeans gave him the appearance of a rancher. He never made an effort to lift his feet, just lumbered his way across the dance floor.

The bar owner turned his head back to Charlie. "But better than the video: is that man."

"Who is he?"

"Eric Kyle comes in a couple times a week. Orders a sandwich and starts drinking, then by late afternoon he looks for a woman or just leaves. A closed mouth, mean bastard but doesn't bother anyone."

"Why should we be interested?"

"Remember I said: there was a group around Chris Evans? Well, Eric was a member of that group. He is cheap as hell; so if you buy him some drinks, I sure he will tell you about the group."

"What's he drink? Does he have a favorite?"

"A favorite? Are you kidding? All he drinks are Red Eyes. And in case you don't know what a Red Eye is: it's beer and tomato juice. My bartender can set it up for you, if you want to go to his booth."

"Good! Ask your bartender to fill up a tray. We're going to talk to the man, but I'll deliver the tray; Terry why don't you go over and introduce us?"

The owner went to talk to the bartender, and Terry left for the booth. Charlie watched the sheepskin react when Terry sat down; it was not going to be easy. The bartender was ready. "Here you are detective six beers and a big jug of tomato juice, and I threw in a few lemon slices. Oh, his mix is 2/3 beer and 1/3 tomato juice. Good luck."

After the bartender turned back to other patrons, Charlie reached into his pocket and retrieved the small bottle Max had given him; he generously sprayed the tomato juice and one empty glass. Next, he found out it was not easy to carry a full tray over to a booth.

As he walked across the floor, it suddenly occurred to him: *he had forgotten to test the strength of the solution on Manuel and Terry. Would he put his subject to sleep? Max said a couple of sprays in a drink. Or, was it one spray per cup?*

His target allowed him to sit and started. "I told your friend to fuck off. But since you are buying you can stay awhile." Charlie poured in the beer leaving enough room for the juice, which Eric carefully poured.

Eric downed the full glass and signaled Charlie for a second pour. This was the routine for three drinks; then the pseudo rancher started to smile. "So you want to know about Chris and our fights.

Well put some money in the slot, and we can see the first one, the murder scene.

You should understand: it was not this video which got him arrested. They tried to use it in court, but it was useless. I mean you could see Chris dance in and out of the fray but not strike the fatal blow."

"What do you mean?'

"First you have to understand Chris was a wannabe. Look he wore those huge orange plastic rim glasses, which he didn't need, because he thought it enhanced his image…..that and the long blond ponytail …. I mean, shit he wanted to stand out…be different. He sure as hell wasn't a fighter …..more of a cheerleader. Watch him prance around that mess of fighters, never really in the thick of things. Throw your money in the slot and hit fight number one. There we go. It loads real fast."

All three watched the fight: the orange frames made it easy to identify Chris but the rest of the video was poor quality, and other than bodies hitting the floor, it was of little entertainment value and useless as a legal tool. The result: no immediate arrests.

The tough beer drinker continued explaining. "It's the last few frames which made Chris the prime suspect. Watch closely, and I'll go into slow motion mode….there watch….see the swinging rebar coming down on the guy's head…..dead before he hit the floor….you'll not see who swung the bar but look who steps out of the melee……Chris steps right over the dead guy….and grins at the body. It's the damn glasses that ID him….otherwise, the video quality is too poor."

When it ended playing, Eric started again. "It was the second big brawl in this club that finished the group and led to Chris's arrest.

It happened within a couple of weeks of the first, and it was a monster affair, almost wrecking the bar; the news media put together a great video from two or three different sources; there is a clear shot of Chris yelling and pushing. For the police, this was the guy who was in two brawls, and they picked him up, with the hope he would cave and point fingers.

He kept his mouth shut. Then a bad break. That same night the police picked up another bar patron, a real low life. This guy was always trying to rub up against single women and follow them home. After multiple complaints, he was charged, but he was a slippery bugger and cut a deal. He knew the police considered him a small shit and wanted more. So he comes up with a story: swore it was Chris who used the steel bar on the first fight.

As you saw, the orange frames make it easy to see Chris in two brawls. Plus at that time, there is no S1 interrogation truth serum to contradict this low life. Net result: Chris spends years on death row."

Terry started to ask a question, but the beer drinker was impatient. "Shit give me the money, and I'll get the second fight up and running. The pace you two are going we will be here all night."

Almost as soon as the money was deposited the video was on their screen. The quality change was significant with sharp images and excellent lighting. One man was taking on three others, and he didn't need any help. It was apparent he had been trained and was enjoying each blow.

Eric continued his monologue, at times repetitive but always open and willing; the spray was working as Max said. "There is Chris standing on the edge of the action where he normally stood..... the guy was a hanger-on and scared to get in .....just wanted to watch.

He'd dyed his hair blond and wore it as one large ponytail and wore those stupid large orange plastic frames....he didn't need glasses...thought the frames looked good.... they only held plain glass....figure that one. That's me beside him. My vest still looks good."

"Is that woman part of your crowd? She looks like she is glued to you."

"Yes, that's Bea Sucart. Jimmy's wife or cousin. Never could figure which it was but she fucked everybody, so it didn't matter. God what a looker."

Charlie didn't want him to stop: "Eric let me pour you another. Who is the guy doing all the fighting?"

"That's Jimmy Sucart, our leader. The son of a bitch was as smart as he was tough, and he never told us how he learned to fight like that, half martial arts and half back-street style."

Sucart was a small man, lighting fast and well trained; his hair was a dark buzz cut, and he moved like a superior athlete. The fight worked all over the bar wrecking tables, smashing mirrors, glasses and bodies flew in all directions; Jimmy was jostling with three big men and laughing as he broke limbs and faces.

Eric enjoyed the replay and kept up his commentary. "Watch this wind-up. The oversized bouncer comes over to break it up."

The bouncer tried to turn Jimmy around and was immediately bent over from a karate kick to his stomach. Jimmy finished the man with a flying kick to the side of the jaw, and the man was down and out. The entire bar fell silent stunned by the performance; Jimmy gave a signal and the group, Bea, Eric and Chris, marched out of the bar.

Charlie thought more might help. "Another glass Eric?"

"Fill her up. Shit, that was the end of our group; as I said, they picked up Chris, and the others seemed to panic. It was a damn shame. We had a good thing going: Bea was a great artist and counterfeiter; Jimmy had the computer skill, and Chris and I did the menial shit. I lost count of the number of ATMs and accounts we cleaned out, sold phony debit cards etc...... the money rolled in."

"So what happened? What scared them off?"

"I don't know. Maybe they thought Chris would fold and talk about all our schemes. Anyway a few days after the fight, Bea shows up with a suitcase full of money about $90 K. She says they are leaving the city, and if I was smart I would too, and I did for about one year. You know that Bea for a good looking woman was a real slut."

"How so?"

"After she left, I started counting the money and found a photo; there she was: on her back, naked, legs widespread with a caption 'see what you missed.' Didn't matter...... never saw them again. When I got back to the city, this bar had undergone an unbelievable change. You should talk to the owner he knows more. I think Jimmy paid him off."

"Eric thank you. Terry is going to take your tray back and bring you a fresh set. OK?'

"Fine. You guys are really nice for cops, great guys."

Charlie smiled and thought: time to corner the owner. *Obviously, Max was right: the fine spray makes friends and loosens tongues.*

###

While the two detectives waited for the owner, they discussed what they had just heard. Terry was impressed. "That spray is better than any truth cocktail, no induced sleep and the guy couldn't stop talking."

"You're right. Except it won't work if we encounter someone who is guilty of a major crime; it won't induce him to confess and incriminate himself. Let's see how it works on the owner. I wish the guy would hurry up and get over here."

It took about 30 minutes to corner the owner, but this worked in their favor because it allowed them to take possession of a quiet corner, get a pot of fresh coffee and spray the coffee cup; the bartender said the owner only drank freshly brewed coffee and gave them the owner's favorite mug. As soon he sat down, Terry poured him a cup and Charlie started:

"It seems the last big fight involved a Jimmy Sucart and his crew."

"Excuse me for a second while I gulp this down. I love our brew at this temperature. A great jolt. Want a cup?" And with that, he drained the large mug which Charlie had sprayed.

"I wasn't here for the fight. I started a few weeks later, but Dad told me all about it. Jimmy and his crew had a reputation, lots of money, and I mean lots of money, smart and mean, but they were never convicted."

"Your dad ever talk about Chris Evans?"

"Not very much. He didn't understand the guy; Evans didn't seem to fit with others...not like Eric over there ...... I mean Eric was tough and street smart, not a guy you would challenge. And Dad said Bea was an extraordinarily beautiful, talented woman but had major issues; he thinks she screwed everyone in the bar, even... I think my dad, but he never admitted it. The other strange part was she only gave it out once.......seconds were reserved for Jimmy."

Terry asked. "You have another video or pictures of Chris?"

"No as I said, he was so vanilla, got lost in the crowd, the only thing that made him stand out were those crazy big plastic orange glass frames; what a shock when he was found guilty of murder. Excuse me I need more coffee. I told you I'm addicted. But, this morning I feel particularly friendly and at peace with the world."

Terry started to smirk and thought this spray might be good for his new troublesome girlfriend but quickly regained control when Charlie frowned and shook his head. "Eric tells us the gang broke up after the fight. You know what happened?"

"I think I do. Chris got arrested. This triggered the collapse. Dad said it scared Jimmy, and the tough guy started covering his tracks. The day after Chris's arrest Jimmy walks in here early in the morning. No one here but Dad and one patron at the bar. Jimmy hands Dad a lawyer created document which confirms dad will not press charges and that all damage has been paid for ...well Dad laughs.

Jimmy opens up the suitcase...full of money, $250 K. Dad signed and the renovation on this place takes place."

Charlie pressed. "That was a hell of a lot of money. Surely exceeding the damages, other than your bouncer."

"Yes Dad knew it was excessive, but he took it. At the same time, Bea visits our bouncer in the hospital. His jaw wasn't broken, but his face was marked up; he had facial fractures and a minor concussion; they had his face wired up and kept him in for observation. Of course, he is surprised to see her and her suitcase, even more surprised when she reaches under the covers and starts on his penis. Once she has his full attention she pulls out the paper he is to sign, it states: he has no claim, and all is fine. She puts the suitcase on his chest and opens it. There is a $100 K treat for him.

While he is signing, her hand is back under the covers; she gives him a handjob that has him screaming with pleasure. It also sets off all the alarms. I mean the alarms the doctors had ordered. She takes the signed paper and left. Jimmy and Bea leave the city, and no one presses charges; the police had Chris and no further interest in the group. This is the last we see of them."

Terry refilled his cup, and the young owner started on the fresh cup. The club was still quiet with only a few patrons, including a smiling Eric who gave the detectives a thumbs-up salute. Before Charlie could ask a question, Scott began again. "The mystery was: how did he get clearance to leave the Sector?

You see, Jimmy was under some psychiatric care for anger management; earlier in the year, he had been pulled in because of a street scuffle; he was under a restraining order of a judge, and until the psychiatrist released him, Jimmy was supposed to stay in the city.

Later we found out; it wasn't a minor street fight. About a month before our fight he kicked the shit out a different bar patron. It's a little confusing......bottom line is: Jimmy was attending an anger management course and under some legal constraint, when he came in here and started the big brawl. I think the court order was for both on them: Jimmy and Bea.

Our thinking was, he wanted to get away before the police started adding up all the incidents. He was in a hurry and pays us off or bribes us, along with the bouncer. Last move: the psychiatrist must have given both of them the green light, because as I said we never saw him or Bea again."

"You know the name of the doctor?"

"A Dr. Joe Luchart. Dad knew him because he was a regular and was always trying to connect with a woman. One night after some heavy drinking, he teased Dad by bragging how he had banged Bea so many times she was like a pet spaniel. Joe no longer practices; his health took a turn, and he resides in a facility for the elderly or the disabled. Dad was always surprised as to why Dr. Joe cleared Jimmy so quickly; within a couple of weeks he was cleared and disappeared from the city, with the doc's signature there was no holding him back."

Charlie knew there was little more to be gained from the club. With a nod to Terry, they said their thanks and headed for the door.

Back in the car, Terry started, "Shit we have a lot but really nothing. Everyone seems to confirm that Chris Evans was a soft man. It's like Willie said about him in prison. Shit now what? Maybe you should send me after the Bea; she might know ..."

Charlie interrupted, not in the mood. "Drop it."

"Right...dropped. But my question is how did Chris get convicted of first-degree murder on that amount of evidence?"

"On the surface you're right. However, thinking back.....there was tremendous pressure from all sides to end the bar fights. It was entirely out of hand; bars were getting wrecked, and injuries were becoming more serious. So when they had a suspect and a dead man, they were set to make an example of him. Of course he didn't help his case when he refused to take a lie detector test.

And before you ask, I think the reason he refused is that it would bring to light all the other crimes that the group had been into. Plus, apparently, his lawyer convinced him the verdict would be: not guilty!"

Terry replied. "I'll bet Jimmy paid for the lawyer and made sure the lawyer did what he was told. Then he skipped as soon as he could, just in case Chris caved and took the lie detector test. I still say: let's find that wild couple."

By the time they got back to the office, Charlie had made a decision. "Maybe you are on the right track; if we can find Jimmy and his Bea, there might be more to learn about Chris Evans. I know it is thin, but we don't have much else. Let's chase this thread. Chris might have done more behind closed doors than the face he presented to the public.

Next, I'll get Manuel to find out where this Dr. Luchart is housed and some other details about him."

Terry couldn't resist. "Sounds like, rather than spray, I should bring a hooker for the good Dr. Joe be more amenable to a conversation."

"Never mind hookers. The point is Jimmy was violent. What I don't understand: how the hell did he get Dr. Joe Luchart to give him a clearance? And why did Jimmy abandon his friend, Chris Evans, after his arrest?"

A couple of hours later all three members of the Cold Squad were back together, still struggling with the different events they had been encountering.

Manuel was ready with the results of his illegal searches. "I was right the blockage on Donna's history was because both women or girls were in the Juvenile Systems; Donna for 18 months for peddling drugs at the school and then ....get this.....beating up a competitor; she had a parole release but opted not to return to school until her sentence was finished.

Adela or Alice was at the same facility ....for a much shorter period...also drug-related...plus you'll love this.....in addition to drugs, they were hooking up with visiting businessmen at the downtown hotels...not sure if it was just prostitution or if it includes some blackmail. They were running a small group of girls."

Charlie was confused. "With that background how in the hell did she get to work with the Chief?"

"As I said when we started, the young offender stuff is all classified; you can't get access through usual challenges. Let me finish.

It appears neither one was a user ....just making money .....nothing in the records to identify inmates or friends ......definitely they were friends, but the official records don't mention any other friends. From what I can see both ladies have been clean for years.

Now Donna seems like the aggressive one; Adela has been focused entirely on her business ...a 24 hour seven day a week operation. She has a husband, a quad who is housed in a facility not at home.

My guess Donna forced the meeting with Wes, but I don't understand why Adela went along. Maybe it wasn't planned. Maybe it was random. Maybe we are too paranoid."

Charlie brushed that aside. "No Manuel there is too much here to be an accident. But I am puzzled. Why would they bother? What the hell do they want from Wes? We have two women with juvenile records, now connected via a horse ranch. Still doesn't explain why target Wes........what now?'

Terry was ready, "We have to push them. Why not get Wes to phone Adela and tell her he wants to hook up..............you know he can't forget her....needs to see her!"

Charlie walked around the small conference room. His team waited knowing he needed time. After completing a few circuits, he made the decision. "You're right we don't have time for a lengthy investigation. Manuel, you get on to all the phones registered to the ladies, for the ranch and all other lines of communication you can think of; we want to listen in to how the ladies react.

I'll have Wes call when you're ready. He'll have to put pressure on for a meeting; this will force Adela to call Donna. This should be enough to have them worry about a lovesick detective. Hopefully, we will learn more about what they are after and if there are others involved.

Manuel, I may not be around when it goes down so here it is: if they are to meet, get some of the parabolic mikes or listening devices to the ranch. I'm sure they will want to meet out in the open. Donna will feel safer than in a house ....thinking we can't bug a tree or the grass; you'll have to monitor the Barn yourself; we can't afford to assign anyone else."

Terry added: "My guess Donna will want to restrict the phone conversation and want to find a spot out in the open area of the horse ranch. So you will need some good equipment. Use our small van but don't get too close to the property line. Donna is damn smart. She'll be looking for surveillance."

Manuel didn't argue or let them know he had anticipated this move. He had all the required phone numbers and was well on the way to bugging most. "Not a problem. Some of the new technology means much smaller parabolic mikes with fantastic distances. I'll only need a few hours then Wes can call. The question is: will his call cause the ladies to panic? It's a dead end if they don't react."

"Listen closely Detective Taylor." After uttering that command Judge Doug stopped, glaring at Charlie, whom he deemed reckless and disobedient.

The Judge's revamped luxurious chambers didn't intimidate the detective. Heavy carpeting, expensive drapes, acres of polished wood did not change the fact that Doug was a sycophant, ready to bow to any Sector Board recommendation. So Charlie waited and thought: *what the hell is this all about? Was my spy right? Is he going to set a time limit?*

After a lengthy period of silence, Judge Doug started again. "We have a minor crime wave on our hands; it appears some our citizens believe we are vulnerable with Justice Reborn now suspended. Unfortunately, their assessment is correct. Besides being short staff, many staff are inexperienced in the interrogation of criminals without S1 or S3.

Our orders are to hold all suspects until this Thor issue is resolved but, of course, prisons have been decommissioned and are no longer available for storage. In summary, we have storage problems.

I've had all prisoners who have served two-thirds of their sentence released from our Farms; all bodily injury cases will now be stored in Sector 14 Farm-1. Less serious cases will be ankle cuffed with the special GPS monitoring and released on the streets. Obviously, this can't go on for much longer."

Charlie wanted time to think and asked. "How long will Carson's Assessment Team take?"

The Judge frowned. "We have a problem the distinguished gentleman from Germany is delayed due to a pregnant wife. The scientist from Japan refused to part of the panel, claims to believe in Max. I have asked the President to allow the team to proceed without those two. But that's not your problem.

You have this ludicrous assignment which the President has allowed to proceed. Besides making you a laughing stock, it will cause more delays. Therefore I have recommended to the Sector Board that your project be deemed concluded after another five days. You understand?"

"Sure I understand: you want to screw Dr. Max. If I haven't proven that Thor is a fake within five days, Max will be at the mercy of the biased Assessment Team."

The Judge was enjoying the discussion, although his face never revealed his happiness. *Time to slap this man down.* "Detective you always jump to conclusions which leads to rash acts. Let me explain something: if Max is found negligent and we have to revert to our original system of justice, it will take almost two months to be operational. Meaning many more criminals or suspects in limbo, Farms overflowing, the public in danger and screaming for resolution.

I've Judge Stephen working on a contingency plan. Creating a plan of action, if we have to revert to our original system of justice. We have to consider training staff to take on new roles, finding courtroom space and on it goes. The switch can't be accomplished in 24 hours. So I repeat we have to get this resolved quickly; and, I repeat you have five days. Now get out and get to work."

Charlie never responded. Within minutes he was out of the Judge's chambers and down the long hall. *Five days! One false path or distraction could eat up most of that time. Not even a clue to pursue, other than Thor is a lair. Shit!*

Sam was emphatic. "I'm embarrassed to admit it: but the bastard is getting to me."

Charlie was taking a small break; these short interruptions were a habit he started a couple of years ago; he recognized the value of allowing his mind to wander in a different direction. Even with the new time constraint, the breaks permitted his mind to clear, reenergized is what he called it. But his brother's declaration surprised him.

Sam Taylor. Charlie's brother and clinical psychologist, spoke louder than usual, another sign the interactions with the Troll remained an unpleasant experience. He and Charlie were in the off-leash area exercising Sam's large dog, Herbie. As Charlie threw the small ball and Herbie tore after the old piece of rubber, Sam continued. "You were right: the Troll is a piece of slime, but he is also extremely clever; he knows he is getting to me and relishes the idea. He deliberately selects words and phrases to see how I will react. Next, he follows with a self-satisfied smirk; thank god I am almost finished with him."

Charlie avoided the obvious: *I told you*. Herbie wanted more attention, bumped Sam until he rubbed his ears and threw a small branch. Sam changed the conversation, to what appeared to be an innocuous question. "I understand you and Monk have taken to swimming once a week."

Charlie guessed where this was going and decided to play it for all it was worth. "Sure. You know I try to avoid swimming, but I can't refuse Monk."

"How are you making out in the pool? From what I remember 50 yards was about your limit."

"Still is my limit but the rest periods between laps is getting shorter." Charlie thought: *I wonder when or how he is going to ask the question because I'm sure Monk told him what happened.*

Finally, Sam broke and went for the direct approach. "Well smart ass. Are you going to tell me? You know Monk reports to me."

Charlie decided to drag it out because he knew the brother was bursting to know the details. "I don't like to tell you the details because you will get upset."

"I promise not to get upset. Tell me the story."

Charlie smiled and knew his brother was lying. "I finished my laps and started to head for the men's showers. Monk is still in the pool. Our showers are down at the south end, and there are a number of other exits off the deck on the way to our lockers. Some exit into equipment storage, others into classrooms. Anyway I'm walking along, thinking about Chris Evans, the Stage 3 brain probe and what to do next. You know sometimes I get into my own world at times like this ....right?"

Sam just nodded and waved his hand, the signal to get on with it.

"OK, I am completely absorbed with my problems and make my turn into the shower. There is a bit of corridor with a big bend before you hit the main shower. Just as I get into the shower proper, the shit hits the fan. There are three women in the men's shower, two scream and take off, covering their vitals with their hands but the third one just looks at me. And I mean....a full frontal view, nothing left out ..... but she is not upset..... sort of smiles at me........ .she is a big woman not fat just tall and ...well you know......wow."

Sam moans and thinks: *shit not again.* "When did you realize you'd turned into the women's shower?"

"The tall one who is staring at me says, 'Don't you know: this is the no clothing zone? Why don't you take off those striped pajamas?"

"What is she talking about? Why were you wearing pajamas in the pool?"

"No, what happened I forgot my trunks, but Monk had a spare set with him. Unfortunately, they were an old style which were long on him, and they almost reached my ankles. They looked rather weird.

Anyway, I was going to turn and run out, but I look at her and thought...what the hell. I loosen the string and let the trunks fall onto the floor.......and this is the best part......one of my better lines. I say. '*Sorry, I thought the dress was formal; would you like me to do your back?*'

In the meantime from the ladies' locker room, I can hear the other two are still yelling...........boy are they upset...screaming as if there was a dead body in the place."

Sam lost it. He started stomping around the dirt trail, swearing and shaking his head in disbelief. Charlie was surprised at his vocabulary, must have learned that from his patients. After stomping around and waving his arms he started to slow down, "Son of a bitch! Charlie you have lost your goddamn mind. This is the dumbest thing you have pulled in years."

He was so intent on his lecture he failed to notice the grin forming on his brother's face. Next, the senior homicide detective burst into loud laughter and couldn't stop. The tension of the past few days evaporate as he roared; passersby on the trail stared but hurried on, afraid of the wild laughter.

Sam also stared for the longest time, and then it clicked. "You son of a bitch. You set me up."

Charlie doesn't respond immediately but finally was able to stop and catch his breath. "Yes, I did make a wrong turn, and two women went screaming out of the shower. The third one was tall and had a great build; she turned her back and said '*I believe you made a small error.*'

I just excused myself and got out, ran over to the pool manager who knows Monk. I told him what happened. He had a great laugh, along with Monk.......the son of a bitch. The pool manager talked to the ladies. After we got dressed, he got us out through the back door. Everything is good, except he doesn't want us to swim there for a few weeks. I knew Monk would tell you, so I thought I would get some laughs."

Sam was silent, thinking about the incident. "I don't know how you keep falling into it. Are you prepared for this complex case? You can't afford a wrong turn. No apology will work, if you get it wrong."

Charlie watched his brother run ahead to rescue a small woman who always kept treats in her large jacket pockets. The treats were for her dogs, but Herbie remembered her and was being a nuisance. The detective thought about his brother's comments: *how much does he know? Who's been talking? Does Sam know he'll be throwing the rule book out the window?*

CHAPTER 13: MANUEL'S FIRST REPORT

"Just horseshit! This is horseshit!"

Terry's outburst was like the chorus of a song; he kept repeating it, in one form or the other. He had changed his mind and was convinced a visit to Dr. Joe would prove useless, add to the pile of useless information they had already collected.

An edginess and anxiety were starting to creep into the team's spirit. The news media appeared to be in a competition to destroy Dr. Max Armstrong. Academic rivals and spurned women were all too eager to provide sound bites. One reporter dug up an ancient statutory rape accusation; the police knew it was a stupid teenage move and no charge was ever laid. Didn't matter it was titillating news, catering to an eager audience.

If not a Max story, Charlie's team was being analyzed or more accurately attacked. It appeared all his high profile success was forgotten in a rush to mock the group. They were subjected to daily ridicule, accused of a wild goose chase, of trying to smear Chris Evans and trying to save a friend, at any cost. The constant negative press and no substantial progress compounded the stress. The team members didn't speak about Judge Doug's time constraint, the extra pressure no help in this hopeless assignment.

While Terry debated with Charlie, Manuel continued with his Internet searches, smiling as he listened to his two friends. The trio's relationship had strengthened over years of working together, with Charlie regularly on the fringe of exceeding legal restrictions and ignoring any conventional protocol but never caught. The previous Chief rarely looked very hard as long as they got results; on occasion Manuel heard him yell 'you lucky bastard' as Charlie left his office and walked back to his desk after solving a difficult case.

Even with this unique assignment and Charlie's reinstatement, the team chose to stay in the Forensic Building: their home, as the Cold Squad, for the last six years. They were all more comfortable here rather than in the Justice Building where Chief Kisashton ruled. From the 25th floor Manuel usually had a great view; except today was different: there were dark skies, clouds, and tickles of rain hit his window.

The weather matched his mood, as he tried to shake the idea that his sister's daughter, Cara Gonzales, had been a victim of the Troll. The young teenager had been a top student and superb tennis player, not fitting the Troll's normal victim profile. Manuel never talked about her to the other detectives. Why was he silent? He knew he was keeping personal stuff to himself; it all started after his messy divorce from his wife of nine years; the bitch probably had been screwing around for eight of them. Terry was the only one who knew some of his misery.

Charlie shouted to get his attention. "Come Manuel, I can't hear those keys clicking."

Manuel laughed and was ready. "Yes boss man, I's a hurrying. You want any background on Jimmy and his wife?"

"No. Not now we'll get that we come back. Just find the Doc and whatever dirt there is on him."

Manuel was ready. "Bingo here we go; Dr. Joe is at the Professional Home, gets full service, whatever that means. His ex-wife says there is nothing wrong with him except he is a lazy bastard. The head nurse put a couple of notes on his file:

- First, don't bend down in front of him, unless you enjoy a scrawny hand up your crotch

• Have visitors bring him some of that expensive hard candy: Lemon Berry

• Most of the time he is miserable with lots of profanity.

Charlie sounds like you'll have a fun visit."

Terry started laughing. The ringing stopped them all. Charlie answered. "Hi Willie, did you find anything in the records before Chris's discharge?" Charlie never had the call on the speaker, so they had to wait for Willie's report; when Charlie hung up, they could see something had changed. Charlie relayed the news. "First the bad news: Dr. Kate was right everything in the way of identification was destroyed, no fingerprints, no DNA etc. Everything deleted when he was found innocent. But….."

Then he stopped and smiled. Terry burst. "Don't screw around Charlie. What else is there?"

"When Evans was released, our friend and mystery man Jimmy Sucart picked him up. Chris listed Jimmy's northern cabin as their residence for the next 12 months."

Terry was tired and hoping for a short trip. "How far north?"

Charlie ignored Terry's scowl. "A good half day's drive, one way; Manuel when Terry and I get back from our visit to Dr. Joe, you should be ready to review all you have on Jimmy and Bea.

I know it's only been a short time since we got the name from Troll but do you have anything? I mean on the kid the Troll says jerked him off. The name which Troll claims is Evans and which he used to buy himself three months."

Manuel already had some of the answers. "That kid is: Clyde J. Henderson, and yes, the Troll remains adamant this guy is pretending to be Chris Evans. Remember Charlie it was more than a hand around his penis. He claims the slow cadence and regular stops in his speech remain the same. I'll get pictures of Clyde and age them for comparison to Evans."

Terry was in a nasty mood. "The Troll bought three more months of life by swearing this kid, Clyde J. whatever, is presenting himself as Chris Evan. How in the hell do we prove that?

Jesus, this is getting complicated. We now know that Jimmy picked up his old friend Evans. It had to be the right Chris Evans because Jimmy knew him. But the Troll says this guy is not Evans. So where is the guy that Jimmy picked up? It's too bad we can't take that Troll and drop him off this building instead of giving him three more months of life."

Charlie, always impatient, was in a hurry. "Forget it. Let's go."

Manuel was thin and muscular, not the stereotypical view of a hacker as a sloppy fat, unshaven slob. He was a tight-lipped man, expending all his energy on the job and all it entailed. Since Charlie, in particular early in his career, was obsessive about unsolved cases, a 24/7 kind of detective, Manuel saw them as kindred spirits and worked hard to please and surprise him. Charlie was more than the boss to him, but this is how he usually addressed him: Boss.

With this obsession, it didn't take long before he was exceeding his privileged access and hacking whatever he thought was appropriate or required. No one on the squad had the knowledge or interest to question his results. There wasn't much he couldn't access.

He had found his niche. Unfortunately, this devotion had pushed him on to an edge, a condition he refused to recognize. He ignored any female relationships, avoided old friends, booze and the bar scene; his life was attached to a computer monitor.

Manuel continued with technical courses but soon found he was beyond the instructors. His detective status made software developers comfortable with sharing their code. He focused on security systems, reviewed new code releases and offered companies his opinion. Companies reciprocated with cash, thinking they had law enforcement as a partner.

This fascination with technology happened later in his career. When he first joined the homicide squad as a young partner to Terry, they formed a close team, often introducing raw humor to a meeting. And when his young son was born, he was very proud declaring for all who would listen the boy was exceptional even at one month.

The slide and change began gradually; first, the knife attack by the Five Star killer was slow to heal. Less than a year after the first attack, the Leprechaun struck him with a large cleaver; the two injuries shook his confidence; he struggled in coping with the physical pain, forcing a need for heavy painkillers

But given all that, his behavior changes still didn't make sense, at least to Charlie. Once the new Cold Squad was established Manuel enrolled in an evening program and got an IT degree, in fact, soared to the top of the class. The faculty recommended he continue to a Ph.D. path, but he refused.

A series of abrupt moves followed: he divorced his wife, never even asked for visitation rights for his son, and ignored the boy.

The extended drive to the Professional Home took longer than anticipated because of the search for the Lemon Berry candy, which turned out to expensive as well as hard to find. As they stopped and started in the traffic, Charlie asked. "Terry, what is going on with Manuel? The divorce is long gone; he has a new IT degree, makes good money, and still I'm worried. Come on time to let me know.'

They drove a few more blocks before Terry opened up amidst the honking horns and the roar of the trucks. "He made me swear to tell no one...... I haven't until now.

The divorce and everything associated with it was a heart breaker for him. His ex-wife was fooling around. I'm not sure how many she screwed, but there was certainly more than one; I think she is mental.

Sorry. Look I jumped right into the middle of this mess, but it was ugly. Let me go back. After that damn Irish Leprechaun slashed him with the cleaver, he went to the same hospital where his wife was working as a dietitian. After he was discharged, I picked Manuel up; we tried to hurry out. But when we got to the elevators there was a shit load of people waiting; we decided to take the stairs; there was a sign which said 'stair closed', which we ignored.

Christ, we got down one floor, turned a corner for the next set of steps and below us was a couple going at it; they were standing up in dark corner, lots of noise as they went at each other. The woman back was to us and her pantsuit down on the concrete floor. I yelled at them and when the woman turned. For Christ's sake: it was Manuel's wife. He never said a word, walked up and slapped her face. We kept going without a word spoken. In the car, I promised to keep my mouth shut.

During the divorce, she went wild, started screaming that the son wasn't even his ...he never made enough money and on, and on it went."

Terry stopped, his emotional recall drained. A stunned Charlie blurted. "Jesus Christ Terry.............you should have told me ......at one point I was even bugging him not to divorce."

"Charlie it gets worse. The guy was a doctor she knew through her work at the hospital and looks like they'd been going at it for some time. Manuel was so pissed he insisted on a DNA for his son. Here is where the bottom falls out........the kid is not his!"

Charlie was so stunned he couldn't comment and thought back to all his previous conversations with Manuel and Manuel's avoiding any comments about family, now making sense.

"From that point on he wants nothing to do with her or the boy. I know her, and she turns to me, trying to bullshit her way out of this. According to her, it was a onetime thing…one time in a hotel room and never again…the pregnancy a pure accident…..the incident in the stairway…..she claims the doctor caught her and was so aggressive she couldn't get out of his grasp.

She claims she loves Manuel and wants him back, saying the price is too high for one bad decision. I didn't believe her, and neither did Manuel. We found out later she was lying.......only turned back to Manuel because the doctor transferred out of the city."

"Jesus, no wonder he is so quiet."

"I'll cut it short; he turned away from most people, except for us……. won't see his son…shit, I still see him as Manuel's, they were always so close…of course, you know about his success in the evening degree courses ……..always working or in class…this way he doesn't have to think about it."

Terry stopped to recover, and Charlie was shocked to the point of speechless; he understood how hurt this passionate man must have felt.

"Charlie we have to cautious because I feel he is starting to get too close to the edge. He has infiltrated a hacker group with a false ID. I'm not sure what activities he's been into and what he has shared with you. I think you have to talk to him. If his membership is official like an undercover agent, then he is ok, but this freelancing could destroy his police career."

"Anything else?"

"Not that I am aware of, but he has been abnormally closed mouth recently. I'm sure there is something else bothering him, but every time I try to reach him, he clams up and brushes me off. Damn rights I'm worried. It's almost like each day the cynicism deepens."

"You're right. I'll talk to Manuel, and I understand it has to be done without giving you away."

###

They reached the parking lot of the Professional Home, stayed in the car while Charlie explained how he wanted to hand the Lemon Berries. "Terry, I have this cheap plastic bowl and want to use it to pour in most of the candies. I'll keep the other half of the Lemon Berries in their original plastic bag."

"What the hell is this all about? Some kind of candy game?"

"Just wait. Here I have the truth spray. Ok pour half the candies into the bowl. Hold steady while I spray....careful keep your hands below the bowl....I don't want any spray on you. Good. Now shake them a bit to get a new layer of candies on the top. There hold. One more spray should do it."

"Got it. What about the original bag? It's still half full of candies."

"We can't leave a bowl full of doctored candies. Jesus, any nurse or other patient sucking on the candies might start something......you know some candid comments which would not be appreciated."

Terry laughed, this appealed to his sense of humor. "I understand, but it might be funny to have some very outspoken opinions flying around."

"Forget it. We work like this: when I am satisfied, and it's time to leave, I'll nod to you and distract Dr. Joe again. This time you pretend to stumble and pour your coffee into the bowl. I'll apologize, clean it out and pour in the new candies."

"Charlie, the old Chief always said you were a lucky bastard. But I am beginning to appreciate your crazy moves are more than luck."

Charlie laughed and said, "Well cowboy lets ride."

The Professional Home was immaculate like a mission control center and redecorated in the latest fashion, the well- to- do being its target audience.

The nurse in charge guided them down a long hall. "I see you men have some sour hard lemons. Good move. He is better when he's in a good mood. He isn't sick just an asshole most of the time. He was in the garden under the shade of the large elm tree but now ran back to his room. I told him two detectives were coming; he said 'piss on 'em'."

Terry smiled and thought: this should be interesting. *An obscene old fart under the influence of a truth serum.*

The nurse led the way, and the detectives followed, down a long hall, past many open doors. Suddenly an older man in a loose-fitting gray sweatsuit confronted the nurse; he was angry and loud. "Hi Nursie, come to spank me?"

"Ike, I understand the staff had to drag you out of Hilda's bed. You snuck in in the middle of the night and were buck naked."

"Another case of an overactive night staff; two consulting adults, and they have to interfere. Jesus, Hilda likes me and has been flashing me signals all week."

"That's not how the staff tell it. It was her screaming that alerted them, and when they got to her room, Hilda was putting up a vigorous defense."

"Shit that was all a mistake; I should have turned the table lamp on; it was dark, and she didn't know it was me."

"I understand she was screaming for Stan to come; Stan is her former husband."

"Another mistake. She only screamed for him because ….. well it's like a nightmare, and she spent many years in his bed and woke up confused……………you know an automatic reaction when you are asleep…it was dark…..she's had enough of that bastard. You can see it in her eyes. Jesus, I'm not stupid."

"Ok Ike, here is the situation: the staff will be monitoring your nighttime travels, and if anything happens to Stan, you will be the prime suspect."

"Nursie, you know how much I care? I'll drop my pants right here in the hall, and you and the entire nursing staff can take turns planting some juicy ones." With that, he turned strode into his room and slammed the door.

The two detectives thought the incident priceless; the experienced nurse was calm and continued down the hall without a comment. Within seconds she stopped and pointed to an open doorway. Charlie dismissed her. "Thanks, we'll take it from here."

Charlie held the bowl of shiny candies in both hands, and with a short knock, they marched in to see their man. "Good afternoon Dr. Latcher"

Dr. Joe Latcher after years of preferential treatment and submissive staff still saw himself as the prime candidate, top man on the ladder. The bean pole, with a few strands of hair left on his skull, quickly let them know his attitude: "Piss off boys!"

Charlie was ready and held out the bowl. "We thought you might be interested in sharing some candy with us. Those hard sour lemon berries."

"You two are smarter than you look…come on give me a handful."

Charlie stretched out his hand holding the small bowl of candies. Latcher grabbed a handful and popped four into his mouth, sucking hard. "Oh, good stuff…………so what do I have to do to deserve more?"

They game him time to suck and swallow and sigh. Latcher was not concerned with the slobber rolling down his chin, just signaled for Charlie to bring the bowl over for more. Dr. Max had told him the truth spray would absorb abnormally fast, and with a compliant man it would become effective within seconds; but, Charlie gave the man time to suck and swallow, trying to hide his disgust at this greedy leach.

Then the detective tried a soft probe. "Dr. Latcher we want to talk to you about two of your patients…. Jimmy Sucart and Bea…….."

Dr. Joe wiped off his chin and almost exploded. "Oh those two nuts, mean bastards, wish I never had them as clients. Jimmy at least tried to fake it and pretend to behave, but Bea allowed her true character to flash. Before I got them into group therapy, I thought it best to hold some individual sessions. He came on Thursday and every few days after the start." He continued to suck and sigh as the sour flavor (and the S1 truth serum) filled his mouth. Every few seconds he swallowed another mouthful of juice.

"You didn't like her?"

"That's not what I said; she always came as the last appointment on Friday, my secretary left and locked the front door as she went out. I had a couch in my office…it wasn't mandatory, but some patients liked to lie on it. Well on the very first visit she is on her back, and I'm on the side of the couch……goddamn if she doesn't lift her skirt to her chin, and of course, no underwear…and says something like *'it would best if you threw one into me before we start.'*

Honest that is how she talked *'throw one into me… throw one into me'*. I'll never forget those words. God, she was so good looking."

I stood looking down at her naked body, my chin, as they say in the books, dropped to my chest and my mouth agape. She reached up, grabbed my crotch, gave it a good rub and said, 'It appears part of you understands and is willing.' In my practice, I've come across all sorts and weird behavior, but she was in a league of her own. Goddamn woman. A nymphomaniac with a psychopath's personality. Son of a bitch.....I never had sex like that in my life."

"Does that mean you had an affair with her?"

"An affair! That's a laugh. That word conveys too much dignity and class to our encounters. It was animal lust, and she was the master ....even now there are nights when I wake up and look around the room, afraid she might be here."

"Afraid? What happened?"

"On her second appointment she brought handcuffs.....said she wanted to play tough prisoner, and I had to smack her a few times.

After we were both naked, she gave all the commands. Once I handcuffed her, the beating started, a smack in the face, smashed her breasts and then she got on all fours and wanted me to use a narrow hard belt, almost like a whip, she'd brought with her. Bea kept up a running set of commands; hit the back, harder, more on the ass, doesn't matter if it is bleeding. Always threw her head back and yelled. Damn, it was a workout, I was tiring, but she seemed to thrive on it, her nose was bleeding, one eye was almost shut, there were small whip lashes across her ass, now these thin marks began to bleed slowly.

She must have sensed I was done, because she screamed *'throw one into me.'* I had to get down because she was on the floor, on all fours and that is how it ended. In this finale, she insisted I pull her long hair back, really hard, like it was a halter for a horse. And I mean pull hard. I was afraid I would dislocate her neck, but she continued to yell for more. After a harsh climax, I was wasted and collapsed on the floor where I stayed for the next full hour. She got up wiped her face, got dressed and walked out without another word spoken.

At the third session, she lowered the boom. Our entire rough play episode had been tapped; she'd hidden one camera in her oversized purse; the other she set up across the room where she piled her clothing. It was well done, and with the sound suppressed, her yelling of commands looked like screams of anguish and fear.

My first reaction was to fight back; I thought a good lip reader would be able to confirm she was in command. However, Bea did a great editing job, and there were no close-ups of her mouth. Plus, and this is the embarrassing part, she had a close-up of my face; my face was in full view when she commanded me to mount her. There I was: each hand pulling on to her hair, grinning like I won the lottery and screaming obscenities. Anyone would be able to read my lips as I thrust and shouted '*you fucking cunt,*' along with other related phrases.

That 20-second clip would be all she needed to prove: I was the master.

I was told there were three copies. I now had a choice: first, my wife and the professional association would get copies of my slapping her around and then me forcing her into some wild sex. Second, of course, I could have all copies, if I created a report stating that Jimmy and Bea were fine and could stop coming.

She waited while I created the report and sent it, then she slapped me with some type of club, the slapping continued until I was crawling on the floor crying; the warning was plain for me to understand....no more games with these two....they play for keeps."

"Do you have any contact info? Any idea where they went?"

"No, and I never tried. Here is what I will say; no matter where they go, Jimmy has to kill and he will; Bea has to screw a stranger and she will. But here is the strangest part: once they were free of me, a compact suitcase arrived, full of money plus a lewd picture of Bea….. legs spread and text message written on the photo: **see what you're missing**."

Charlie called out. "Dr. Joe look out the window, the woman beside that large flower bed; isn't that best rack in the complex?'

The good doctor was out of the chair and over at the window in a second. "Shit no. Wait until you see the big blond…. tits like basketballs."

Terry moved to see and stumbled into Charlie. "Oh shit! Sorry, my coffee splashed and your candies are all wet."

A furious Latcher yelled at Terry. "You dumb shit! Damn. All my candies are soaked in your fucking coffee."

Charlie came to the rescue. "Not to worry I have more; let me clean the bowl and get a refill."

The senior detective dumped the candy into a spare bag, rinsed the bowl at Joe's bathroom sink and wiped it dry. From his outside pocket, he retrieved the untainted candy and refilled the bowl.

A placated Latcher praised him. "Detective you are a genius, but if I were you, I'd leave this partner at home."

Back in the car, both men laughed at the incident. But both knew: again lots of information, leading not very far. With the video and money, Jimmy had tied Dr. Latcher into a knot, and there was no way this psychiatrist would ever change his diagnosis of Jimmy.

"Terry this incident with Dr. Joe Latcher happened while Chris was still on death row and appealing his sentence but not found innocent yet."

"So what the hell were these two playing at?"

"It appears they wanted a release and a get-out-of-town card. They were worried about something and wanted out fast. What? I don't know nor can I guess."

Terry tried to summarize. "So this reinforces: they had money; Bea is a slut; Jimmy is a smart guy and ruthless. What else? Oh yes, our ex-warden, Uncle Willie, tells us: as soon as Chris is free, Jimmy signs out Chris and takes him up to the cabin cottage somewhere up north."

Charlie starts the car and ends the conversation. "Well let's go find out what Manuel has for us. What a hell of a trio: a slut, a smart, violent thug and a passive follower who claims the system turned him into a serial killer. Unfortunately, since they are friends, I can't see Jimmy giving us anything on Chris."

###

The drive back to the Forensic Building took longer than the trip out; it was late and getting dark before they arrived. Manuel was upstairs rushing from one work station to the other. "Hi guys, give a few minutes; I've been running since you left. I hope I've captured everything; it all happened so fast."

Charlie smiled at his frantic pace. "Jesus, Manuel slow down. We aren't going anywhere."

Manuel stopped and started to explain. "I know you wanted all the detail on Jimmy and friends. But Wes made the call, as you asked, to shake up Adela and Donna. Well shit, I had to drop everything to go in another direction to get all my recording gear in place. Damn it Boss; this is almost too much too fast. Wes should have given me more time. We were lucky.

Thank god I had started preparations and had all the appropriate numbers captured. This recording comes right after Wes calls Adela and requests a meeting.

What you are going to hear first is a brief phone conversation. By the way Boss, you were right: Donna didn't want to talk. Here we go: the first voice is Donna responding to Adela's call:

Adela love, what's the problem? You seem upset?"

"Donna we have a problem. Wes found me. He wants to see me again ...he says he...."

"I will be riding this afternoon. I'll be out, right after work and we can talk. Right?'

"Good see you then."

"Not much to hear on this call. So I hurried back to the ranch. I already had an aerial video of the Barn and saw where most of the riders went...there seemed to be two trails which attracted them........along each path was a sort of natural resting spot...not that far apart. I parked outside the property line, behind some massive bush.

I had to use two parabolic mikes. One location was close to the maximum distance for this gear. ......the first mike was easy to camouflage ......the second mike was a little more exposed... I was out of time and took a chance the second mike wouldn't be seen. The last location was close to the maximum distance for this gear. I was lucky; they selected the first spot.

After all the rushing to get set up, I was ready; I knew Donna would be there within the hour. You know nothing we have is legal and not admissible."

Charlie responded. "I know. I just hope we can figure out what the hell this is all about."

Manuel's presentation was disjointed, but they understood he was still recovering from his frantic attempt to capture the clandestine meeting. "Ok, so as I said, I hurried out to the ranch and made it before Donna. I'd guessed right. The two rode to the one spot which was deserted. Donna had a good look around but was eventually confident, and she gave Adela a nod to speak; here we go:

"How in the hell did Wes find me?'

"Adela, don't panic...tell him your husband is recovering and is to be discharged from the nursing home, and you can't see him.......What? Goddamnit. You want to see him?"

"What's the harm?"

"No stay away ....I don't want him near you......later in the week, I'll corner him, and I'll make our pitch."

"God it seems a helluva way to get cooperation from one detective. You can tell Streak this is my last one."

"You forget if it wasn't for Streak, we might have done some hard time; she kept her mouth shut under lots of pressure."

"I don't give a shit...... this is the last one.........you tell her no fucking more.......I'm happy with the Ranch...... don't need her."

Manuel shut off the recording. "Adela was pissed, turned her horse and just took off for the stables; Donna wasn't happy, screamed after Adela. Then she calms down, just finished her ride across the ridge; she is one hard customer; you'll have a tough time with her."

"I gather you haven't found out who Streak is."

"I'll get on it as soon as you two leave; my guess she has a record; maybe a juvenile record. I'm convinced it was in the juvenile system that these two had contact with the criminal element. It shouldn't be too hard.

Listen I need some recovery time. I feel like I've been running around in big circles. You now have the recordings from Donna. I need to sit back and think about my next move. I had started on the Jimmy search but didn't get very far. I had to chase those two women.

I'm not tired. Just need some space. So Boss why don't you two call it a day and leave this evening to get reorganized?"

Across the room, Terry rocked back and forth on his chair and declared, "I need a fucking drink! This is worse than some type of kid's alphabet soup. What do we have: Jimmy, Bea, Streak, Donna, Chris and now Clyde? Shit did I leave someone out?

Charlie recognized that everyone needed some time to absorb all the players and twists that were occurring. He tried to summarize.

"Let's not lose our focus. We are after one Chris Evans who I am convinced is running some type of scan. Jimmy and Bea are his old friends who have known him for years; they pick him up after the

S3 brain probe. They take him home. To look after him? These are the central characters. Everything revolves around these three.

Now it appears the Chief's admin assistant Donna is involved. How? I don't understand, but she wants to pressure Wes; again I am sure it is about this case. And Adela is just her old teenage friend. It's hard to believe that Evans would have that long a reach to be able to get to Donna, but that is what I think. Yes, I haven't forgotten the ladies mentioned someone they called: Streak. Maybe she is the missing link and will help make all the connections make sense.

Unfortunately, we do have an unnecessary complication. The convicted killer, the Troll, claims the man presenting himself as Chris Evans is not Chris Evans. He states the man we see on TV making all the accusations against the S3 brain probe is a Clyde J Henderson who jacked him off when they were both in their early teens. My brother has been working with the Troll; he loathes the man but asserts this killer has an exceptionally high IQ with an excellent memory. So my brother, Sam, the top paid psychologist is inclined to believe him.

I know it sounds crazy. But as people age, facial features mature and underlying bone structure starts to dominate.... and now years later there is recognition! I think this Troll is trying to buy more time before his execution; he has already manipulated one delay with that government-sponsored research project and is now working for more. Given how grim Evan's accusation is: we can't afford to ignore the Troll's claim. This killer understands we are all desperate and will chase any clue which might save Dr. Max.

My guess: he will drag this out as long as possible. Giving us one small clue after the other so we have to chase this false identification. If it wasn't so dangerous, I could almost laugh at this soap opera playing out in front of us.

Manuel, you are right it is time to take a break. One last thing: don't tell Wes. I'll talk to him."

As he walked to the exit, Charlie thought about his colleague, Wes. *The senior detective understood his friend, and all his instincts told him: this woman, Adela, had made an impact; Wes would not let it go. The man had deprived himself of any substantial female companionship for a long time; he was vulnerable. He was lonely.*

Adela's facial appearance was the clincher; she bore a striking resemblance to Wes's lover who had been murdered a few years ago. This was going to difficult to unravel and keep Wes away from a married woman with a questionable background.

CHAPTER 14: SECOND REPORT

"Nice tits!"

Terry roared with laughter after he delivered the punch line; Manuel screwed up his face and looked confused. Terry recognized the situation. "Shit! You still don't get it. Pay attention: I'm creating an alternative scenario. Suppose: when Charlie and I left Dr. Latcher, we left the bowl filled with candies soaked by the truth serum. The bowl sits on a table near the main hallway; anyone walking past can snitch a candy or two.

Suppose a tired, young intern grabs a couple and starts sucking and chewing, not realizing he is being drugged. A few minutes later he is at the front reception where a small group of staff have surrounded the female receptionist. It's her birthday, and she is wearing a bright new sweater which everyone is impressed with and letting her know. She turns and asks the young intern what he thinks. He, under the influence of the serum, has to be honest and let them know what is on his mind and out comes: 'Nice tits!'

What a riot. Every time the intern is asked, he has to give an honest answer. He is aware he is damaging his image but can't stop himself. If this particular morning he is in a horny mood, the poor bugger could be fired before the end of his shift.

Funny? Jesus man, laugh."

Manuel forced a weak smile, shrugged and trotted off to his desk. For Terry this is another sign that his partner was a troubled man; the scenario was not uncontrollably funny, but with a little imagination one could see others sucking the candy and creating a riotous morning. This was their kind of humor. Manuel never responded to the situation.

###

It was another day, back at their offices, each detective was occupied: two working and one, Terry, wandering in and out of the small conference room.

Later in the day Charlie and Terry were to drive north to Jimmy's cabin and confront him and maybe Bea; there was no firm plan, other than hoping they got an opportunity to spray Jimmy's drinks. Finally, Charlie finished his phone calls, and Manuel shoved his chair back from his computer.

Manuel was prepared, and by the smile on his face, Charlie guessed he had something of interest. The two detectives barely got seated, and Manuel started; he stood in the front of the big wall screen used to display his supporting material. His delivery was rapid:

"As I tried to say yesterday, my primary research has been Clyde J. Henderson who the Troll claims is now trying to pass himself off as Chris Evans. Clyde was the kid at the stockyards with the Troll. That teenage sexual Peeping Tom incident happened many years ago, but Professor Griffin, our Troll, is adamant: Clyde is the one who we see being interviewed and claiming the State turned him into a killer.

There are gaps in Henderson's history. I started with the old school records which are adequate, but Clyde's family like the Troll's moved around frequently. Clyde came in the later part of Grade 7, was in the community during that summer and got a couple of months into Grade 8 and then moved away. The written comments in his record indicate a smart kid whose grades could vault him to the top, if he decided to work at his studies. A small kid but an excellent athlete. Baseball pitcher with large hands which allowed him to put stuff on a ball.

The Troll is right: their contact was only for a few months.

After he moved away from the Troll.........at the new school: the same pattern...passing but mediocre grades...spent his time with baseball and football, now a receiver with soft hands. Then a family shake-up: his dad died very young from a heart attack. Mom remarries rather quickly, but it seems to be a good move for Clyde. He and his stepdad bond over sports and camping.

His stepdad is an ex-Marine, specialist in close quarters combat; he trained Clyde which caused problems at school, as Clyde started to kick the shit out of anyone he didn't like. He and his new dad became very close .... so good the stepdad officially adopts him....about this time Clyde who never liked his name starts using his middle name and that goes on the adoption papers. We have an official name change."

Charlie was about to leave. "Manuel all very interesting but not relevant, as I'm sure you know. So why waste our time?"

"Boss, slow down.... always in a hurry. Alright the good stuff. You noticed his middle initial was J. So what do you think his full middle name was?"

Terry started laughing. "The son of a bitch took the name Jimmy. Right?"

"Yes you are right: J turned into Jimmy, but you should have stopped and asked about the full name."

"Meaning?"

Manuel explained. "His step dad's last name was Sucart!"

"Holy shit...Jimmy Sucart....could there be two of them?'

"I asked myself the same question. The best picture I had of Jimmy was at age 14. I used my system to age Jimmy's image, added a blond ponytail and threw in the orange plastic frames. Here we are. Gentlemen, look at the screen."

Terry was off his chair. "Son of a bitch! There he is: Chris Evan, but it is really Jimmy?....the guy the Troll said is trying to pass himself off as Chris Evan..... let's go Charlie, we have a northern cabin to visit."

Charlie was ready. "Wait. Wait. You're saying the childhood friend of Professor Griffin's: Clyde J. Henderson changed his name to Jimmy Sucart when he was officially adopted. Then for some reason with a few minor changes in appearance turned himself into Chris Evans. Claims he is Evans, for some damn reason.

We have a problem.........too many Chris Evans........did Jimmy bury one? If this Jimmy Sucart is trying to pass himself off as Chris Evans, then did he kill the real Evans? Or is Chris still around and allowing all this to go down?

Last, why wouldn't someone recognize him as phony? Lots of criminals knew Chris and should be able to identify him."

Manuel had an answer. "I wrestled with the same question. I went back to the fight video where there were excellent pictures of both men. The facial recognition software had them as a very close match; but I could see this without the software analysis....take away the difference in hairstyles and the crazy glasses, they could be twins.

Superimpose the maturing process where the underlying facial bone architecture starts to dominate; there will be other changes. This group was somewhat insular and didn't have a wide circle of friends; I mean if someone never saw them for five or ten years, I think it would be easy for Jimmy to take on the role. Bea would be the only one close enough to both of them, the only one who stayed with the team. My conclusion: Jimmy has taken on the Chris Evans ID. Boss, I bet my car on it."

Charlie laughed. "You can keep the car; I'm convinced. Great job. Come on Terry let's get the son of a bitch."

After the two detectives left to find Jimmy Sucart and possibly Chris Evan's body, Manuel started pacing; in the quiet of the vacant office area, he tried to find some peace. Each day he struggled to keep his focus on his job and maintain an even keel. Two features of his life helped him keep stable: the IT world which he saw as the only factor in his life he could trust, and Charlie whom he often addressed as 'boss', but knew he had his unquestionable support.

He tried to avoid thinking about his childhood, with the hard climb out of the cellar. As a child, he lived in an extensive one-room basement accommodation on a busy urban street, along with an older sister and his parents. His father was a legitimate immigrant from Mexico who struggled with the language which, in turn, held him to low paying jobs; his mother, although not an immigrant, was also poorly educated, the result of an improvised rural, single-parent upbringing.

For the first eight years of his life, he and his sister had a nightly view of the outside world via two narrow windows; the small windows hung just below the room's ceiling. Numerous evenings they watched a parade of footwear and shin wear, the window became that narrow restricted view. They turned it into a game; who could guess the age, sex, and remainder of the dress. If his sister pressed her face hard against the wall below the window, she was tall enough to be able to catch a glimpse, if her target wasn't moving too fast. On occasion when the debate got heated, they raced up the stairs, out the front door and down the street to catch the quarry. His sister invariably won, but her good-natured laughter compensated for the loss.

Their concrete world revolved around the narrow rectangular room with the view. It was crowded but adequate, because they had no large appliances, just beds, a kitchen table and chairs, and a two-burner hot plate, no refrigerator, no oven, and no TV. Adjacent was a large common area which the family could use, but its primary purpose was to allow the other apartment tenants space for odds and ends their rented rooms could not accommodate. A flimsy wall, part wood part plastic, separated this room from any tenants wanting access.

A tin tub sat on their side of the wall; a bath became an ordeal because the only hot water had to be drained from the big boiler one pail full at a time. Then another issue was timing: that is, only a rickety door kept tenants from bursting in to retrieve their storied property. Bathing was not a daily event.

On the other side of the flimsy partition was the boiler, furnace, a coal hopper and a single toilet, no sink. His mother and dad did all the maintenance and janitorial duties, with dad always trying to work a second job.

Neither parent understood the big city culture, the associated sports opportunities, libraries, the art world, and social services. The result: the two children were always behind their peers, always learning from the other kids at school. His sister's artistic abilities almost carried her beyond the childhood poverty; unfortunately, a greedy, unscrupulous music agent took advantage of her naïve temperament destroying her career and ambition.

The result was an unwanted pregnancy and a hard life as a waitress for a restaurant chain. When Manuel thought about her failure, he fumed at the austere upbringing, but then as his marriage fell apart, he began to resent his young naivety.

This bitterness festered under the surface and only occasionally flashed with some of the black humor he and Terry used to practice. His wife's infidelity shattered all his hard-earned stability and left him with an extremely narrow set of friends. Now he found with IT he could give everything, was challenged, and rewarded with high praise, peer recognition, and financial rewards.

Manuel knew Terry, his long-time partner, was worried about his behavior. Terry was the only one to witness the most embarrassing moment of his life, but he had kept his promise and not a word had surfaced in the gossipy police community. Terry attributed his attitude on this incident because Manuel had never shared his anguished history, nor the truth about Cara.

If Dr. Sam Taylor had known this development, Manuel would no longer be on active duty. Intense suppressed anger and irrepressible self-pity would be considered a dangerous combination for a homicide detective with training and access to weapons.

Manuel rationalized by thinking: *his feelings only surfaced when he looked back.*

CHAPTER 15: AT THE CABIN

Charlie spoke the obvious: "Damn it. Looks more like an explosion, than a fire. There's almost nothing left."

After a hard six-hour drive, they arrived at the northern cabin: a large white sandy beach fronted the cottage; a dense growth of various evergreens stood about 30 yards behind, some trees reduced to black stumps. Both detectives walked the perimeter of what used to be Jimmy Sucart's cabin. Part of the front deck was the only large fragment of the cabin that survived. Terry shuffled through the remains, kicking burnt debris out of his way, a fine ash soon covering his shoes. He turned his head at the sound of an approaching vehicle. "Charlie looks like Sheriff Bob Austin has decided to pay us a visit."

A big truck, with all the police trappings, braked hard and a smiling uniform came out and reintroduced himself. "Guys, I'm not sure what else I can add, but I thought I'd come out and see if there more questions about Jimmy and his cabin. You can see this is an isolated location, and the fire was intense. You can see there is about a ten-foot border around the entire perimeter where the sand had turned black, no walls just stumps like a dentist had pulled a tooth and was left with parts still stuck in the gums.

You've probably noticed the large lot sizes and the isolation with these cabins; this is an expensive subdivision with 100-yard frontage and various bushes at the property boundaries. Not that any neighbor could have helped, one in town shopping, the other out of the country.

This isolation was ideal for Jimmy's habits and lifestyle. I liked the guy.... a good bull shitter."

"Sheriff, how was he identified? The body must have been all carbon."

The Sheriff was fast to answer: "Here is how we think it played out: he was inside his cabin, baseballing with his back next to his large front window. He had the cocaine-ether mixture in a large spoon, heating it with a propane torch....... once that small mixture exploded and started burning he never stood a chance; the son of a bitch stored ether in different containers all over the cabin. Shit, he treated ether like bottled water.

I'm also guessing: he must have a moonshine still someplace around here, because there were gallons of white lightning in the back room. The place was like a fuel storage dump, all that homemade alcohol, in addition to extra tanks of propane in the kitchen area. So when the propane flame touched the ether, as the saying goes: all hell broke loose. There was a series of different of explosions as the fire reached a different particular inflammable storage space: first the ether, then the moonshine, and last the extra propane tanks, damn near tore out those big trees.

He must have been bending over to inhale the fumes when the explosion took place. The detonation blew him backward right through his big front window on to his large front deck, the glass cuts were substantial, almost took his head off, and some body parts were ripped off and blown across the yard.

I think the only reason the deck didn't completely burn was that one of the last explosions caused a massive downdraft and blew out the flames on the deck.

The result was a bizarre-looking corpse. He landed on his back. The upshot was his entire front was a crispy black critter; his back against the porch floor was relatively untouched; I could even recognize the checkered shirt he was wearing the day before. His wallet deep in his back pocket was a little scorched, but we were able to retrieve a driver's license and some credit cards."

Charlie wanted more. "With the burnt face how did you identify him?"

"His sister, Brenda, insisted she recognized the scars on his left ear, came from a bar fight, some guy tried to tear it off. However, we're able to do better; one hand was severely burnt, like a crunchy piece of bacon, except two fingers looked promising, so we tried them. What remained of the little finger was an 80% match, and the finger next to it was a 100% match. It was Jimmy, no doubt. We had Brenda's identification of one ear, a bundle of personal ID in his wallet and the two fingerprints.

His sister claims she tried to warn him about the habit, but he couldn't stop."

Charlie needed more. "Bob, we understand; what happened to the body?"

"Brenda had it cremated, even included the two fingers. Just finished the job the fire started."

Terry thought he knew who the sister was. "Was his sister a tall, dark-haired woman.......extremely attractive?"

The Sheriff smiled. "Yes, that's Brenda."

Charlie shook his head and wondered how many roles this Bea woman played: the wife, sister, and cousin. But there had to be more. Charlie was still optimistic. "If we can get at the burial site, it is possible to double check the ashes with DNA analysis."

Bob laughed at Charlie's tenacity. "You don't give up. That's good. I wasn't clear on the burial. There certainly is a headstone in the cemetery. Unfortunately for you, his ashes were scattered on the lake where he used to fish."

"Shit!"

Later in the day, the three men were enjoying a small lunch. Charlie asked. "You said he liked to baseball; you mean freebasing?"

"Yes that's it. I never caught him, just heard all the rumors. He heated up the powdered cocaine dissolved in ether...and inhaled the vapors. I warned him he was inviting disaster when using a propane torch with ether.......biggest dangers are explosions and fires. But he never admitted he was doing it. He went up like that old comedian, Richard Pryor."

Terry made his contribution "The effects of freebasing are almost immediate, into the brain in 10 to 15 seconds. We know the sensation it produces is the attraction: a 30-second rush followed by a two minute euphoric high gets into the brain for a maximum high."

Sheriff Bob continued. "Jimmy was alone.....no one knows how much he had to drink. My guess he must have been plastered; the bugger loved his moonshine, and his blood alcohol was sky-high. Again like Richard Pryor. A drunk handling ether and a propane torch, great combination."

Charlie kept probing. "When did the cabin explode? And, was Chris Evans not nearby to help him?'

"First, I can't remember the exact date, but it was one, no... more like two years before Chris got arrested on campus, at the gay bar.

Second question: no one was around. Chris and Brenda were out fishing. When they heard the explosion, they rushed back to shore; they were a long way out, and it took some time. Wouldn't have mattered. With all the ether, moonshine and propane the fire was fast and furious.

By the time they hit the shore, it was all over. Just burning embers scattered around the property. Chris panicked and ran up the beach to the site, tripped on a root and went down on to the hot embers. He twisted enough to save his face but burnt up his left hand and knee on the hot remnants. Brenda was able to bandage him up using the boat first aid kit. I could see he was in pain. Burns hurt, and he only got limited medical treatment."

"Does his sister live in the area?"

"No. After they scattered the ashes, she and Chris jumped in his car and took off. Chris, all bandaged up, was suffering, and they wanted to get to a bigger center for better treatment; he said his hand was infected and oozing shit. I saw his bandages had turned a yellowish color. Not a pretty picture. They didn't say where they were going, and have never been back."

Charlie wasn't happy. "Sheriff is it standard practice to allow a full cremation so quickly after an explosion and fire. Don't insurance investigators have to provide the clearance?"

Sheriff Bob turned his head away and looked out the restaurant window; suddenly the man was uncomfortable, a straight shooter, not use to deception. Charlie's instincts took over, and he took a chance. "How often did you screw Brenda before you released the body?"

Bob bowed his head and avoided eye contact. "After the fingerprint results came in, she called and asked me to come to her motel room to discuss the process. The wine was cold, and the damn woman was in the shortest skirt I have ever seen."

He hesitated. Terry gave him a boost. "No need to feel bad. She's an exception and has seduced the most sophisticated pros."

The Sheriff, although embarrassed continued. "Well, no need to go into details. We went at it all night. I've never encountered anyone like her and don't think I will ever again. When I was getting dressed to leave, she asked to have the body released; she wanted to get the estate settled. I was in a good mood. I wasn't concerned and thought this should be ok. The fingerprints were reliable, and I did recognize his clothing. Plus, I do represent the insurance company on most fires, so I am authorized.

Are you suspicious? Why are you concerned?"

Charlie took pity on the man. "No, it is ok. I'm a bit paranoid and tend to push hard. I agree the fingerprint was solid and good enough. No need to go beyond this. We will leave you now Sheriff. Thanks for being so open with us."

Terry decided to end the lunch with a mundane comment. "To end all this let me pass on a little-known detail: the term 'moonshine' derives from the fact that the spirit was illicitly produced outdoors, under the light of the moon."

They drove for a number of miles in complete silence, both men knowing their theory had been crushed. Terry finally voiced his frustration. "That bloody Troll got an extra three months and wasted our time; his old schoolyard buddy is dead. The damn Chris Evans is solid. And according to the sheriff, after the cabin exploded, he had a couple of years hunting in the gay crowd and killing."

"Let it go Terry. We had an idea, and it's finished; time to move on. Regardless, my gut tells me that Evans is a liar, as well as a killer. We have to look in another direction."

The rest of the way home was mostly silence. Both detectives knew Charlie was right. They knew they were running out of time. There was no new direction to chase. They were dry. Terry finally spoke what they were both thinking. "This cut into our time. Goddamnit we only have two days left. That damn Judge Doug won't give an inch; he'll shut us down in two days......."

Charlie interrupted. "I know. I know. Two damn days. God, we need a break."

###

The drive was just as boring on the way back. Both men had difficulty staying awake; the harsh ring phone jarred them into the present. Manuel was on the phone, and Charlie put him on the car's speaker.

Manuel asked, "What did Wes say?'

Charlie and Wes had discussed Donna's request before this trip north to the cabin. It was time to update the rest of the team. "Donna wants a daily debriefing on all Cold Squad active cases. She already sees Wes' progress reports because he answers to Chief Kissass, but our Cold Squad reports aren't going through her. I decided to let him go ahead, even if I have to fabricate. We'll see where she goes with it."

Manuel provided more detail. "I did trace Streak. When our two girls were in a half-way house, there was a girl that earned the nickname Streak; she was an older girl, and she provided them an alibi. I can't tell what Donna and Adela were up to, maybe back to pedaling. In any case, they both got charged again; what saved them was Streak testified: she was with them in the barracks the entire night. No doubt they owed her. Here is the interesting part of this: her real name is or was Bea Justik."

"What the hell! You mean Streak is Bea! That has to be Bea Sucart. The woman who is Jimmy's wife or cousin or sister or bed partner."

Manuel laughed at the excitement her name generated. "You're right. I'll show you her teenage photo when you get back. She's a match."

"Why the hell is Bea interested in our progress?'

Charlie summarized. "Bea started all this before the fire. Now whatever they were planning is no longer an issue, with Jimmy dead; he was certainly the leader and probably ordered this surveillance. I've changed my mind: no more monitoring that damn Donna. I'm going to challenge Donna and get this fixed. Enough of this bullshit."

Manuel hesitated; he could sense the extreme frustration in the two men, but then he went on. "Listen, I also analyzed Adela's face, using the new 20 point analysis tool to.."

Charlie was abrupt, never let him finish; he'd already guessed. "Damn it. I don't need a bloody computer to tell me she looks like Pameela. Drop it. It probably explains Wes's instant attraction but adds nothing to the rest of this case. Just drop it. I don't want to hear any more about this Adela woman. See you in about an hour."

After he hung up, there was more silence. All three detectives had known Pameela Sharma. Some years ago the Robin Hood killer had mutilated and killed her. In the process, her death sent Wes into a deep depression. Their love affair had been the talk of the Division, an upper-class woman and a homicide detective. Charlie felt Wes had never fully recovered from her death. On occasion, he did date other women, but no long term relationships ever developed.

Charlie thought about the various relationships he had seen develop, from patrol people to those at the top of the chain; *all those founded on lust were doomed to failure.* Wes was firm Adela's attraction was more than lust; Charlie had his doubts about the woman, particular with Manuel's report about her history, a flighty bird with a craving for excitement.

###

There were only two old friends in the oval office. The Vice President put down his cup and started, "Mr. President it appears every scientist Max has insulted has found a way to get some press, either on the late night news or on some damn talk show. Thank god, Max has not tried to respond."

The President forced a smile and responded. "I'm worried about our Attorney General; he could be close to a nervous breakdown. Every damn lawyer in the country is trying to getting into the action; all smell big money, and once greed starts to dominate I know the rules will go out the window.

Goddamnit, even Europe and Asia are acting as if we are responsible for all the lawsuits they are facing for illegal executions. Did you hear me? I've started swearing in front of staff and family. Look at my hands. Jesus, I'm shaking."

The VP tried to calm his friend. "Bill don't look out your window and ignore all the crazies and their marching placards. This will get resolved. I'm beginning to think we might have to sacrifice

Dr. Max at least that way this is all over, and we can deal with the fallout.

Your election is coming up. We don't want this to crest just before the voting starts. If we make a decision this week, we have time to massage the news. May not be fair to Max, but there are decisions to be made."

The President rose from his chair and paced the floor. The VP sat and waited; he understood his friend but had never seen him under so much pressure: a system of justice ready to blow up and the President without a resolution.

Finally, the President stopped. "I know you are right. I think that Professor Carson would be willing to do anything we ask. He and his colleague hate Max so intensely they are not ready to accept anything but a guilty verdict for our good Dr."

He started pacing again, and the VP, used to his friend's habits, drank his coffee and waited. In a short period of time, it might become too late to save the re-election. All the turmoil would land on the President's desk; at least that is how the opposition would force it.

Was it time to call Professor Carson?

CHAPTER 16: DISASTER

"Turn on the box to channel 15. This shit is going to bury us."

Manuel's outburst brought both detectives to their feet. The long return trip had exhausted Charlie and Terry; the unexpected cabin discovery had depressed them. The two detectives had returned to the office, dejected because of the surprising results. For the last 30 minutes, each man had sat, slumped at his desk, silent and brooding.

Terry was first to the TV set, turned it on and tuned into channel 15. A handsome mature announcer was part way into his presentation:

"This is exclusive footage we received from an anonymous source, but it has been confirmed. This is part of a report being prepared for the President. The first two men you will see are Professor Carson and Professor Wiek. They have been studying the after-effects of an S3 interrogation and the allegations of Chris Evan."

There was a short delay, and then both scientists came on the screen while in the background a video displayed a man, Chris Evans, in a hospital bed. At times the footage focused on Chris, with only the academic voices in the background, discussing his condition. At other times both men filled the screen, and the bed was a minor object in the background. Carson did most of the talking with Wiek throwing in whenever there was an opening:

"Professor Wiek and I have always maintained that there has never been proper follow up on these S3 brain probes. As you see Mr. Evan's condition, there can be no doubt he is suffering. These pictures we are showing are the actual video captured immediately after his interrogation. The severity of his reaction

was never made public; Dr. Max Armstrong and the woman supervising the interrogation, Dr. Kate Martinez now married to Judge Stephen Miller, should be made to explain.

Look at the man in that bed. There is no doubt a significant transformation has occurred during that excessive 55-minute brain probe. It is no wonder he turned into a killing machine with urges he could not control."

The rest of the commentary was, in one form or another, a repeat of their conclusion. Most of the time the cameras focused on the Chris, large leather straps holding him on to a bed, drool rolling down his chin, eyes rolled back in his head; at random intervals, he would try to get off the bed and scream a stream of obscenity at his attendants. The wet yellow stain on the crotch of his white khakis capped off the image. The voices of the articulate academics superimposed over the pictures of a wild man were great TV but a disaster for Max and his work.

The finale of the video showed Dr. Kate leaning over the shrieking patient; she turned, and the camera captured her face, full of concern and doubt. She shook her head and walked out of the room.

Charlie jumped out of the chair. "I have to go. When Max sees this, he'll explode."

####

While driving over, a couple of concerns lingered. Charlie thought: *an unauthorized release but how and who? Is someone just looking for glory or something deeper? Trying to destroy Max? Hurt Kate? Wreck my investigation?*

He rushed from his car to the main entrance of the Research Center. The massive front door flew open at his touch, nearly bowling over Max's young wife, Sally Armstrong. The words escaped from his mouth. "I thought you'd left Max. Did you forget something?"

The young wife grinned and softly spoke. "I assume you came to cheer him up. No need...... that's my job. Don't look so surprised. He has never admitted needing this type of support, but today he'll gladly accept it. I always wanted this role. A role he was never prepared to accept. Today will be different; besides I bring other good news."

And with that, she pointed to her belly. One glance was all Charlie needed. The distinct small bump said everything. The detective didn't hesitate. "He's all yours. I wish you the best. Tell him I was here and will be back tomorrow."

He walked out and thought: *Max will be floored; first a career in the toilet and now a baby. This will rock him to the core. But Sally will be staying which is good news. The two were still in love: unbelievable.*

But how did that damn video get out? This was deliberate. To hurt more than Max? Dr. Kate will be sick when she sees the program. Is someone after Judge Stephen and hope to smear him by association with Kate? Next news release might cover Kate's original conviction.

Before her marriage to the Judge, she made a serious mistake, in an attempt to assist her daughter. Her actions were accepted as a mother's love for a daughter and the resulting guilty verdict a minimum sentence. The fact that the mistake happened years ago will be irrelevant. Someone wanted to smear her or possibly Judge Stephen. The type of news report was an illegal move but who will stop it?

My investigation is going nowhere. But does anyone know that? Or is the mystery source still worried I might turn something up? No, they are not concerned with my investigation; they are after Max, to destroy his scientific reputation. Also, it reinforces the idea that my team and investigation is a joke, a waste of time and at best an attempted cover-up.

Best turn Manuel on to this. Maybe he can find out who released the damn report and video. He's prepared to do whatever it takes.

It was near the end of an uneasy morning.

His frustration was reflected in his posture as he strode up the steps of the Hall of Justice. Usually, Chief Kisashton's presence was enough to make him hesitate before entering, hesitation not from fear but disgust. The morning he didn't care. The Chief was fortunate to be out of the building.

Charlie walked straight up to the Chief's office and to Donna's desk; she gave him her superior business smile. "Have you come to arrest me? Or do you want to put me under some rough interrogation." With that, she laughed, utterly oblivious to the look on Charlie's face.

He stared at her for a long time, stern and ugly. Finally, she lowered her eyes and understood this was serious, and she was not in charge. Charlie didn't waste any time. "Give me the pictures. Every bloody one. Next, let me see you erase them from all your systems. Don't fuck with me or I will destroy you, Adela and Bea; the bunch of you are lucky I feel generous today."

She started to protest. "You can't.."

"What did I say? Are you stupid? It's over. Now give me what I want."

Donna wasn't sure what he had for evidence. But did understand she had too much to lose. Her position was well-paid, with benefits and pension. Bea wasn't worth a gamble. She went into her desk, pulled out a small package, and then signaled Charlie to come over and watch her delete dozens of photos.

Charlie took the hard copy photos and walked, stopped at her door and turned. "If I find you have more or anything shows up on Internet, you had best resign and start running."

He walked away, down the hall and started to smile, almost laughed out loud. All he had would never be accepted as evidence, all illegally collected. But he'd guessed Donna loved her high profile job and deceived her into cooperating.

The reckless Bea had forced some old friends to track Charlie's progress on the Chris Evan case. A stupid move which could have resulted in criminal charges. This campaign of hers started before the cabin fire; with Jimmy dead, the wild and sloppy Bea didn't even to bother calling the women to cancel. Charlie guessed the women would never hear from Bea again.

Charlie walked back to the Forensic Building. It was more a march in a dream mode; his team would have recognized his state and left him alone. Some many questions whirled around his mind:

Why would Bea be interested in his progress? Did that mean Chris Evans was vulnerable? Is there a weakness in Evan's story? There had to be. Why else would this group of miscreants rush through with this stupid plan? Trying to blackmail a detective is a desperate move. Has to mean Evans is worried. About what? We have nothing. Or what are we missing?

Although he never spoke this last thought to his team, it stuck with him. The detective became convinced they or he had overlooked something. As always, it meant he couldn't let go; it was with him all the time.

CHAPTER 17: DEAD END...

Depression permeated everything.

Even Emma was depressed, sorry for Max and Dr. Kate, as well as Charlie. The unauthorized news release and the leaked report had the President fuming, but it was out and so were numerous enemies of Max. Anyone who wanted was given air time: Max and Kate were the primary targets, but Charlie didn't escape. Some mocked his attempt to help Max, equating it to a Don Quixote run, chasing an impossible solution. But the thrust of the criticism spoke of a detective who had allowed his earlier successes to skew his judgment; this was not a serial killer, but cold hard science and the facts were undeniable.

Most of the last few hours had been spent reviewing all the data they had collected. Each detective took a turn studying the other man's work or collection of material. Whenever the time permitted, Charlie turned to the physical with vigorous workouts; he was down to the last 24 hours, but he found it impossible to think clearly, tension and emotions keeping a tight grip. That damn Judge Doug would not bend. It appeared he already had a recommendation, with detailed analysis, for re-establishing the old system of justice. Unless Detective Taylor could find some answers there was little the Sector Board or the President could do; even Charlie could not shake the image of Thor screaming on the hospital bed, strapped and drooling.

Charlie had to get out. The other two detectives were not surprised when he abruptly left the Cold Squad offices. His favorite spot was Monk's current residence, the Abbey, which had undergone numerous upgrades, its gym, pool and work out facilities; these renovations coupled with miles of jogging trails, far from the smoke of the city, made it an ideal amenity for the serious athlete. The

Abbey was a good 90-minute drive on a winding road which climbed out of the valley to the top of a series of tall hills

Monk set the pace, led the way and controlled the work out; about every 400 yards he would stop and start a ground routine. No words were spoken, Charlie understood: 40 push-ups and then a full out sprint for 200 yards followed by 200 yards of medium speed, stop now sit-ups and on it went; interval training to an extreme. Charlie thought he needed to clear his mind, soon forgot about clearing his mind and started worrying about his heart and lungs.

Finally, they popped out of the wooded area, with a flat 400 yards to the club entrance. For the first time, Monk spoke. "Charlie we race for the door and no holding back" and he was off. Charlie charged after. Somehow around the last 100 yards, he got a second wind; as they raced down the stretch, to the surprise of both men, Charlie pulled away for the final 25 yards.

At the club entrance, Charlie bent over the bike rake, unable to talk, exhausted. Monk watched, impressed with his friend's endurance and stubbornness, always able to pull the last ounces out of his body, just like pursuing a killer he never gave up. "Charlie you are a piece of work, but today I can't stay. The Bishop has called a meeting for the entire company, so it's a fast shower. I'm off."

Charlie was finally able to utter a sentence. "Hold it. Remember you are coming for a BBQ supper on Saturday and don't bring the kids any more gifts. We catch Paul up late so he can search the skies with the telescope and star book you bought. I can't control the kid."

"I understand, but I have an even-up present for Ellie."

"You're spoiling them."

"Listen Mr. Detective; you had better accept the fact that both kids are exceptional…two five years olds with vocabularies and maturity of 13-year-olds. You are going to have to deal with them."

"Yes, we know. So far we haven't devised a plan. Go, I know you're in a hurry. Wait a minute, hold it. I need the key to the downstairs exercise room, the one with the hardwood floor."

"Ask at the front desk, I'll vouch for you. Bye."

Charlie tried to stand tall and take in all the fresh air he could. He looked around the complex while recovering and it seemed deserted; it appeared the Bishop's talk had pulled in the entire Abbey staff. When he improved, he entered, stopped at the front desk to get the key he wanted, went down the back stairs, opened the large workout room, turned on only one bank of lights, closed the door, and sat on the floor in the semi-darkness with his back against the wall.

It was time; he started the methodical Yoga breathing Max has taught him, eyes partially closed, his back supported by the wall. The near exhaustion from the workout made it easier for him to relax. There were no more anxious moments, no underlying force driving him to keep moving. Everything slowed down as he continued to allow the breathing process to control his mind.

After about 15 minutes his mind moved on to his core concern. He always needed a firm starting point to use as a base of reference as he assessed incidents. First, even with all the evidence, he assumed Max was right; Chris was a liar, a killer, and a phony. With this assumption burnt into his brain he began. He started at the beginning and mentally reviewed every interview, every video, every photo, every expert's opinion, every facet of the case.

His unusual strength was that he would not deviate, would not be distracted by other possibilities, each event was scrutinized as if

Max was correct; what was false in these events? What didn't make sense? Suppose Troll is telling the truth: Jimmy is Chris Evans. That means Jimmy is not dead. How the hell is that possible?

His other asset: for crime scenes and criminals he had a photographic memory. He could replay old videos in detail, review photos of criminals as if he had the picture in front of him. Unfortunately, this talent only applied to the criminal world and not the rest of his life.

At a leisurely pace he recalled Dr. Kate's description of the disastrous S3 brain probe; watched Chris explain how the probe changed his personality; listened to Manuel describe Jimmy's history; and on it went, each segment dissected and analyzed.

He was fully relaxed; it felt good. There was an anomaly; something wasn't right, an aberration. He was close. Relax. A little more time and it would reappear. Suddenly there was key in the lock, and a young woman, in work-out clothing, walked in; Charlie's presence temporarily confused her. "Hi, I'm Ann the Tia Chi instructor; I have to get the room ready."

"No problem I'm done." And with that, he was up, down the hall, to his locker, and with a few steps into the steam room. It was a short steam; he wanted the hot tub. The Bishop's talk meant the tub was vacant, the way Charlie liked it, no need to converse with a stranger. He leaned back his head resting on the edge of the tub, the rest of his body entirely covered by the hot water, pummelled by the water jets. It was a male locker room and no need to worry about strong jets tearing off a swimsuit. Not a sound in the adjacent locker room, maybe everyone did go to the Bishop's talk; didn't matter. Eyes closed. Breathing slowly. The only sound in the room was the water pounding his body and his slow breathing

He kept his eyes shut. Without any conscious effort on his part, various scenarios began to resurface. If this was his unconscious mind at work, it wasn't revealing any answers. Surprisingly, some of the scenes were not directly related to the problem: the kids running around the kitchen, cursing each other; then the photo of the Bishop and Monk. However, most images related to the issue: a burnt cabin, a chastised Sheriff, a fight at the HOLE, and so on.

But a few scenarios did repeat, as if he was being forced to look again: up popped the photo of the Monk and the Bishop, with Monk complaining. He was able to remain relaxed and not pressured for an answer. Finally, an idea surfaced. Not eureka, not even a loose end. A coincidence which he didn't like. A long shot, but not impossible. The anomaly, he almost had in the exercise room before the instructor wanted the place, surfaced.

No rush. A good shower and a fresh set of clothes. As he dressed, the idea took shape. A call home and a long-distance goodnight to the kids and Emma. Last the vital call to Manuel.

"Manuel I need you to get some photos set up. Plus we will need your best digital analysis software. Ready? First, get the first interview tapes of Chris Evans. Trim out the best shot of his left hand and blow it up. Next, when I hang up I'll send my photo of Monk and the Bishop; you can trim out the Bishop. I need Monk's head. Then set up Monk and Chris for comparative analysis. I mean just the trimmed sections, not the original full photos. Last, if Terry isn't in the building call him. I'll be there in about 30 minutes."

It took more than 30 minutes, and as the others sat waiting and listening, Charlie had Sheriff Bob on the speaker. "Bob one short question. The fingers used to obtain the fingerprints were they attached to the hand or had they been blown off?"

The Sheriff responded, now familiar with Charlie's insistence on detail. "No, they're no longer attached. It was just the stub of a thumb left on that hand. We found those two fingers about a foot away from the hand; it's good the fingers were that close otherwise it would have been easy to treat them as just another smoldering pile of carbon. As I said those two fingers although burnt and black with layers of carbon were good enough for a match."

Charlie ended the call. "Thanks Bob, I'm sure there were no mistakes on the prints. Bye."

On the near wall, Manuel had projected the two images Charlie had requested. The three detectives sat in the dark room staring at the close-ups of Chris Evans, left hand and the Monk's head. Terry was baffled. "Charlie, what the hell is this? You back into the bottle?'

Charlie ignored his frustrated friend. "Manuel I need you to narrow down on two sections and blow them up. First Monk's ears, one ear and part of his face will do. Second, Chris's left hand. Get those two images side by side and blow them up as far as possible."

Within minutes the two images were side by side on the big screen. Charlie was ready. "Look closely. Look at Monk's ear or rather the prosthesis. It looks exactly like Chris' two little fingers. Those fingers don't look like the rest of the hand; the new prosthesis material doesn't photograph correctly; I mean for some reason it shows up darker than human skin. This Evans is missing two fingers!"

Terry was tired. "Shit Charlie, why is that a surprise? Remember Sheriff Bob said he fell on his left side and burnt his hand, ended up with an infection, and Bea was in a hurry to get him to better health facility; they were worried he would lose his hand with the infection."

The senior detective wasn't upset. "It's a coincidence.......Jimmy lost two fingers in the explosion, and this guy is missing the same two. I don't like the coincidence. Why was Bea in such a big hurry to cremate the body? I know she is a nymphomaniac, but why screw Sheriff Bob all damn night? She was desperate. Why?"

Manuel tried to bring some sanity to the discussion. "Charlie you are saying: you think Jimmy cut off two of his fingers and roasted them as evidence he was dead? Then he took over Chris Evan's identity; he is pretending to be Chris Evans!"

"Yes!"

"Jesus man. Look at the rest of Chris's hand the middle finger, and the index finger have both lost the first knuckle from the fall into the smoking embers. Did he lob those off too?"

"I don't know. Shit, I don't know. But you're not answering me: why did Bea make sure no DNA was possible? The entire scene from the cabin explosion to the scattering of ashes in the lake doesn't make sense to me.....too much haste. Sheriff Bob never saw Evan's hand. It was all bandaged up. So if fingers were missing, he wouldn't have known."

"Dammit Charlie, Bea would screw a spruce tree; her time with the Sheriff is no mystery. And her running out of town was because they had to get to a good doctor. And last, why the hell would he want to do it?"

That ended the debate. Charlie walked the room; Terry went for more coffee; Manuel played with his keyboard. Terry returned with fresh coffee, the entire pot, all filled up. Not a word was spoken. The process was not unusual for the team. They had worked together through major crimes and understood each other; all the arguments have been expressed, now was the time for the ideas to percolate and a conclusion to be reached; this was usually the time for Charlie to make a decision; the others knew it and waited.

Charlie put down his coffee and smiled at the pair. "Gentlemen I know this is not strong. Yet I think the bastard did cut off two of his fingers; I don't understand the entire process, but I have to move. We have nothing else. As it sits Max is ruined and Kate disgraced.

I'm going to move on my theory...... Jimmy is still alive and posing as Chris Evans. Why I don't know. But again, due to time constraints and other restrictions, the rule book is going out the window; I'll say no more...... I think you can fill in the gaps. So now is your chance to bow out of the investigation."

Manuel and Terry laughed. Terry spoke for them. "Thanks for the opportunity, but you forgot to ask when we were spraying beer and candy! We are in. Do you have enough of the spray?"

Charlie was prepared. "The regular spray is too weak for a hardened lying criminal. Maybe we'll have to revert to the original fluid concoction. I'll go to Max and get him to mix a specific cocktail for Chris, I mean Jimmy. I have his height, age, and weight: Max will need that at a minimum. At the meeting with Jimmy, I'll carry one container, and Terry you'll have to handle the other one. Hold it. Hold it. That sounds stupid and confusing. Let's think about it. We might have to play as it unfolds. I think we can set it up, so either one of us will have the opportunity to spike his coffee.

While I get the S1 truth spray from Max, Terry you get on to Campus and scout the Lounge entrance and seating. Sorry…. I don't mean spray. I just told you it wouldn't work on this guy. I need the standard original truth serum, properly mixed and calibrated to Jimmy's age and weight.

This still doesn't feel right. I need time to think."

Charlie was almost in a rant and running words together; his mind ahead of his mouth. Manuel struggled with Charlie's confusing instructions and was concerned. "Charlie this won't work. A confession like you are planning, when an unauthorized S1 truth serum is used, will not be accepted as evidence. Instead, you will be charged with conducting an illegal interrogation. It'll all be for nothing."

"I know. I plan to get it spread on the Internet …get it out fast and wide. Once the entire world sees him, it will be impossible to allow him to walk.

Second, you know Judge Doug has his Discretionary Clause. He can use it once a year to allow this type of interrogation…….convict the man and forgive the interrogator."

Terry added. "A couple of problems. First, you are guessing as to what Jimmy, or Chris, will say or confess to …might not be what you hope. But worse Judge Doug hates you and is always looking for ways to bury you. And he also detests Max. Why the hell would he allow you to walk?"

Charlie bowed his head and bopped from side to side: "You're right, but I owe Max and Kate. We have to roll the dice. I'll try and minimize your involvement. Manuel, what do we have for the last five days….what was Chris' routine? Damn it I mean Jimmy. It is Jimmy from here on, right."

Manuel was ready, "Well, the good news is: he has a habit, follows it every day. Jimmy is living on campus. The Assessment Team got him a single room in the male residence. I think he is free most of the afternoon; he meets with the Profs in the morning and is free in the afternoon when they do their analysis.

After lunch around 1:30 pm he goes to the large cafe on campus, called The Lounge. Here he orders his large, full strength Brazilian coffee, black, and no sugar, always sits in the middle section, right up to the front railing looking over the University Square. He never varies."

It didn't take Charlie long. "Terry you set it up. Tell him I want to meet in a friendly setting. This means the University Lounge. Terry take some photos of the entrance and the coffee bar, send them to me; I want to see the layout before I get there.

Let see; try to set the meeting for tomorrow that should give us enough time to get the place ready. Manuel, can you get his spot wired up by then?"

"No problem boss. Full-color video. Hope he talks."

Charlie wanted to wrap it up. "I'll leave now to get what we need from Max. I have Jimmy's physical stats; this will allow Max to customize the mix we need. And Terry, walk through the process of ordering and paying for coffee at the Lounge. I want those details and send me the pictures of that front entrance and the coffee counter. Then we can decide on the best way to spike his drink."

Before Charlie could leave, Manuel spoke. "Charlie I'm not sure this will work. Chris is a helluva smart guy; the Profs will know about the meeting and probably brief him. You have a reputation for trying to use unauthorized S1 truth serums on suspects. I know: never proven, but the Profs may have heard the rumors. And if they know, then Chris will know. Shit I mean Jimmy.

He may be a killer, but he is damn smart. If he cut off his fingers as you think, I can't see him meekly walking into an interview with a detective with your reputation. He will be prepared."

###

As the preparations were being made, Wes made an unexpected visit.

Charlie, unfortunately, was not in a sympathetic mood. "Well Wes, when are you going on your first horse riding lesson? The case is closed, and she just got a slap on the wrist.............Jesus, stay away ...she is married and too damn loose."

"Charlie I know you all think it was just a drunken encounter in a public place, but there was a helluva a strong connection, and I have to see what happens in a sober setting. Her husband is bedridden or a quad and lives in a nursing home; the only reason there are not divorced is the prenuptial agreement which would mean she loses the ranch."

"Jesus Christ you have been out there seeking true love. Goddamnit stay away. Manuel says she has been screwing a number of different guys; one was her hot lover for a few years. You're not in her league; she'll walk as soon as the novelty of a homicide detective wears off."

"I told you it's not that simple."

"Ok! Consider yourself warned."

Charlie watched his friend walk down the hall and out of the building. He was worried. Wes rarely fell in love, but when he did it was fast and hard, but he always seemed to strike out for one reason or another.

That damn Robin Hood killer nearly destroyed Wes, when he killed Pameela; Wes still struggled with her memory. Charlies strongly believed this Adela was trouble, and she could wreck his career, eventually making Wes an unhappy man.

###

As Charlie listened to Max he sensed the concern; he wasn't shouting into the phone, but his voice seemed near the breaking point. "Charlie before I complete this S1 for Chris or Jimmy, I have to confirm the numbers you gave me. His height and weight mean he is a small man. Not my picture of a ruthless killer."

"Max don't worry about his name; we are calling him Jimmy at least until it all unravels. And yes the numbers are right he is a small man but he is all muscle, and he is ruthless. Go ahead mix on those numbers. You seem worried. We've done this before. Why the concern?

"I'm on a fine line: enough meds to get him to open up but not too much so he becomes a blabbermouth and won't shut up, then it becomes obvious you have drugged him. I'm going to err on the side of caution and assume he will want to brag. You OK with this or do you want to go with a stronger mix?"

"I agree. With only the two of us present, I think I can get him going. He is very confident, and I think he wants to flaunt his intelligence."

After ending the phone conversation, Charlie wondered about the decision. *The meds for Jimmy would be far from maximum strength. A poor choice? Would the bastard open up, if his doctored coffee only provide a gentle push? Too late to change the decision.*

CHAPTER 18: THE CONFESSION

"Charlie get ready. He is about 10 seconds away from the front door."

Terry was outside monitoring Chris Evans as the suspect strolled toward the Lounge entrance. The entire Cold Squad was back on campus. It was about 20 minutes after the standard lunch hour, most students back in class, a sparse crowd lingered on the grounds.

Once entering the Lounge, a patron, immediately encountered an elaborate coffee bar, with all the offerings of any high-end service. Charlie had already ordered two cups of the Brazilian variety, black and strong. His timing was almost perfect as he lifted a lid and emptied the small vial into it. Unfortunately, 'almost perfect' meant not good enough.

He turned and greeted Chris. Previously the two had endured brief discussions about the case, and there was no need for introductions. They shook hands and welcomed each other as if they were old friends; each man had his reason for the manufactured friendliness. Evans was not extremely short but was a small man, around 150 pounds; the large orange glass frames made him appear bigger and more impressive. After the handshaking routine, Charlie tried to direct the process. "Chris, why don't you select a table? We need to sit. Have a short discussion.''

Chris Evans was a suspicious man. "Before we walk any further, I want to scan you. I have to make sure you're not wired. You know I've been living on campus; surprisingly, many academics are sympathetic to my cause. In any case, a couple of young physics students tell me their homemade device will locate any recorder. May I?"

"Go ahead use your scanner but be careful. I don't want to spill the coffee."

The killer turned on a small electronic device, definitely a product from a post-grad physics lab, and ran it across Charlie's body; nothing buzzed, the detective was not wired. The domestic device was turned off and shoved back into Chris' pocket. They walked out of the reception area, down a couple of steps and into the dining area. Chris walked straight down the middle aisle to his favorite spot looking over the Square. The surprise came when he abruptly turned and walked to the farthest table at the edge of the dining area.

A stunned Charlie hustled to keep up. "Jesus, Chris where are you going? You can stop any time."

Evans kept walking to the far end of the dining area. The table still looked down on the Square, but there were no occupants on any tables surrounding it. The location was an isolated setting, far from the target area, certainly good for any secretive discussions. Both men sat, one satisfied, the other concerned, with the location. The detective struggled to control his emotions, wondering about the quality or range of Manuel's technology this far away from the wired favorite table.

As soon as the lids came off the coffee cups, Chris poured a portion of his coffee into a small container and sealed the unit. "Just a tiny sample. Charlie, look to your left, up to the very top. There is a student who is witnessing my taking the sample. He is recording the pour and documenting the sample extracted. It's not much, but I'm sure it is enough to test for drugs.

You look confused. Allow me to continue. You have a reputation, yes I know all about the rumors of you making illegal use of the S1 drug cocktail. Hence, I have to be vigilant. For my final request: I would now like to switch cups. Here you take mine. I'll drink from your cup."

Charlie immediately refused. "Oh shit, that's ridiculous; you've become paranoid. There's no need for this switch."

"Let me make myself clear. Either you allow the switch, or I walk, and within 30 minutes this sample I took ends up in a lab. The intent will be to determine if it contains the S1 truth serum. If it does, your detective career is over, along with your partners' profession and Dr. Max's reputation.

Charlie knew his smile must look like a pained version of a tooth extraction, but he had to retain his composure. He thought: *the only way he would ever get another shot at this killer was if he cooperated. How strong was the solution? Max had customized it for Chris who was about 40 pounds lighter and possibly had a slower metabolic rate. Could he fight the drugs? Could he control most of the impact? In the past, there had been other incidents where doctors had to use a larger than the standard dose of painkillers on him. His system seemed to filter the impact of tranquilizers. Could his body handle this batch of S1 truth serum which was specially tailored for Evans' smaller anatomy?*

Then with no choice, a hell-with-it decision was made: "Jesus! If it is that important, here is my cup. Pass your coffee over."

Chris was delighted and lifted his exchanged cup for a toast. "Good here we go. Best to drink up; they don't serve their coffee very hot, and it cools quickly." With that, he drained most of his cup. "That was good. I love their coffee. Go ahead see if you can drain yours!"

Charlie did as he was told and drained most of his exchanged coffee. Charlie was thinking: *God I've lost control of this interview.* Surprisingly both men found enough to keep a steady stream of small talk; within minutes Charlie felt the impact: this is going to be harder than I assumed. Max was right this was a fast-acting drug cocktail.

His opponent grinned. "I should confess I have been planning this for some time. Once the Profs debriefed me, I started developing alternate scenarios. Hope you are not angry with me for insisting on the switch."

Charlie now under the influence, projected a warm, cooperative mood. "No, I understand. It's not a problem; you've every right to be suspicious."

"Well, you seem rather mellow, not like your normal disposition. Interesting. And you look a bit tired. Not getting much sleep?"

Charlie never responded, and Chris continued. "I'd like you to confirm my understanding of how the S1 drugs, the truth serum, impacts a person: first, it results in the drugged person being very cooperative, impossible to lie…then often gets very tired…..doesn't fall asleep but is fatigued. When the session is over, the other strange side effect is that the drugged person cannot recall any of the conversations which took place. He is astonished when the video is played for him…….he can't remember a word of what was said. Is this all true?"

"Yes, it is all true…fatigue, memory loss and the inability to lie."

"Detective you look like you need a nap. I have one question: did you drug my drink?"

Charlie never hesitated. "Yes, I did." Then his head nodded; he looked like a young baby trying to fight off sleep. His head would drop. Then with a sudden jerk, he would bring it back upright.

"I gather you also wired my favorite table. Yes?"

"Yes, we wired that table and the three adjacent as well."

"Well aren't you a real bastard. Too bad you are so full of Max's drug cocktail that you will never remember this conversation. Here drink all of it." He took out the sample he had captured and poured it into Charlie's cup. "Might as well drink the rest. Now we are going to play a game. First, I ask a question, and then you get to ask one. Goddammit, this will be fun.....two honest men without a care. You can't lie; I can be honest, and you won't remember any of it. This is the best. Right? Ready? Me first: why did you suspect I was a phony?"

"I believed the Troll."

"What? You believe that little bastard when the entire nation took it as a con job."

"Let me explain. At first, I was convinced it was a lie.... bullshit to buy him more time before his execution, and believe me, I was firm. But my brother Sam, a clinical psychologist, conducted a series of interviews with him; and, the interchanges disgusted Sam so much he continued to turn to me for some consolation or a sympathetic shoulder..... to share the brutality.

Listen there is no doubt the Troll is a vicious predator, but the more I listened to his history something became apparent. For lack of a better word let me say he had a string of unparalleled successes. Think about it: how does one select a victim? A victim who will not report you, who will obey your instructions, who will break school rules to see you. He was able to make selections with what I assume was minimum one on one contact time."

Jimmy held up his hand for Charlie to stop: "Detective you had best step back and give me some details."

"Yes sorry. This killer is a tenured academic; his specialty is educating the handicapped, primarily low IQ kids who don't fit in a regular classroom. On a regular basis, institutions which train the kids and in many cases board the kids ……..they contract him for a variety of different jobs. Sometimes all he does is audit their classroom work; other times he develops a complete education program for a particular stream.

This is where he selected his victims. At times he assessed kids with individual interviews….always watched them as they participated in activities….he was a hawk, and as I said with a minimum of contact, he was very successful in choosing and grooming a vulnerable young girl.

The more I thought about it, the more my instinct started to move toward believing the Troll. He is a slimy bastard; however, he is also observant and smart in his way. He went into numerous institutions, able to select the girls who would cooperate with his scheme. I don't think he even understood how he did it. What did he see in a girl to make him know she would do his bidding? I don't think even he understands how he can pick the right one. This made it hard for him to explain how he knew the image on TV was not Chris Evans; so when he struggled to try to explain his reasons, there were many doubters.

But the more I reviewed his history I concluded: he had a special talent. Whether it was face recognition, body language or some combination, he was a near genius, able to assess a young girl in minutes, without even knowing her history. The only reason he got caught: he got greedy and hunted in his classroom. When he said: that man was not Chris Evans but was his old school mate, my gut told me: he could be right. He had been observing and watching people for a long time. He saw something."

"Good very good. As I said, I am a fair man: your turn."

"Jimmy, when did you get the idea of imitating Chris Evans?"

"First, some background. Both Chris and I were amateur actors; an enjoyable hobby for thieves who want to con people. He was much better than me, much better. Often at the end of a dull day, he would entertain us by imitating some of the people we encountered that week. He could do the whole package, voice, facial, and posture. I sometimes thought he should have been a performer; he was that good. Enough.

You know we picked him up at the prison, after he was finally released and found innocent. Bea and I had him in the back seat of the truck. Then as we're driving to the cabin, he started bragging about his last performance. In the recovery room, he heard Dr. Kate whining about the extended S3 brain probe; she was agitated and worried sick that permanent brain damage had occurred. The support staff were not aware of the fact that he was conscious and listening to the discussion, even absorbing all the details of what they might expect from a diminished brain.

Chris decided he should have some fun. His decision? To wake up as the village idiot.....slur his speech, slobber on his food, roll his eyes, and stagger around; he thought they would catch on within the hour. But he was so good it went on for a few days. He felt his wild profanity screaming might give him away, but it just added to their stress. Finally, he got tired of the charade and ended it.

Of course, when they tested him he was fine, but he deliberately gave some wrong answers on the IQ tests; he wasn't sure how he would score, just wanted to make sure it wasn't too high. He bragged and laughed at how he had fooled the experts, even those who analyzed the close-up photo shots.

As we drove along, an idea formed. What if I became Chris? Would I be able to claim the brain probe made me a killer? You look confused. Let me back up; the situation was I had been killing at a solid pace and knew I wouldn't stop; this meant soon, or later I might get caught. I needed an excuse to avoid the death penalty.

Now I had the answer: it was performing in the back seat, still laughing and bragging. Growing my hair and changing the color was easy. I had to reduce my exercise routine and allow some muscles to go soft….that was the difficult part.

This week I had a difficult time not laughing as I watched that Assessment Team of imminent scientists review the video that dumb bitch, Marcie Callay brought. Those scientists could barely control themselves, replaying Chris's performance over and over again. Bea and I had watched Chris perform many times. It was easy for us to see the show for what it was. The scientists on the other hand: their hate or envy for Dr. Max blinded them. So much for an objective evaluation. I feel like talking. Ask me another."

Charlie struggled with his posture, finally able to utter a question "Why all the killing? All the gays. When did all this start?"

"This is my most painful memory. My mother remarried to a finishing carpenter who was able to charge top dollar for his skills. Life was good for us; he became my biggest cheerleader, came to all the games, practiced with me in the backyard, and even officially adopted me; that was when the name change occurred.

On my fourteenth birthday, my stepfather planned a wilderness camping trip for the two of us. On the second night out, my feet were aching; he gave me a couple of pills. I passed out, and when I woke we were both naked, his hairy body on top of me. Well, I won't go into details other than the rape, and physical pain was intense. In the morning he acted as if nothing happened, but I was no longer the same kid; I'd aged ten years that night.

Next day, we had a long day on a hiking trail that almost went straight up, very difficult and very isolated, no one on the trail at mid-week. Late in the afternoon, we stopped to camp. The early sunset excited my pedophile stepdad; he ran to the edge and yelled for me to come and catch the view. I ran real hard and hit his back full force; he lost control.... went down the rocky drop.........a vertical drop over 100 feet to a pile of boulders....the impact on one of the rocks almost tore his head off..........I stood at the top and felt damn good.

I was surprised my mother recovered so fast. It took a little while before she confided in me: after the marriage, he confessed he was gay ...not a pedophile.....just gay. She went with it because of the convenience but then started worrying about his relationship with me.

No one doubted my story that he slipped. A surprise: I inherited his hammer collection, all first-class hammers with a detailed history on each, stored in a great carrying case. There were 24 different hammers; today there are only seventeen left.

I started hunting gays when I turned 20 and was able to move freely at night......it was like hunting wild game....search their hunting grounds ..... hunting the hunters....after some kills, I started leaving a hammer at the scene....never wanted to see that killing hammer again.

Enough. My turn: you seemed satisfied when you left the burnt up cabin. What changed your mind?"

Charlie didn't hesitate. "I didn't like the way Bea rushed everything, no DNA, the way the two fingers were separated from the hand and still in good enough condition for prints. Sometimes, I can't explain it….some crime scenes stay with me…it appeared convenient …hand burnt beyond recognition but fingers far enough away to allow fingerprints.

A friend of mine has the latest prosthesis, for his ears; the material is top quality, with one minor quirk. For some reason on a photo, the prosthesis doesn't show the same as natural skin. Looking at your interview photos, I realized you had lost two fingers. That was too much of a coincidence. Both you and the body had lost two fingers…….it started to fail the smell test.

I am curious: why the hell cut off two fingers when one would have done the job?"

"It was that bitch Bea. She used the pruning shears for the little finger of my left hand. Yes, it hurt like hell. When she was roasting it over a campfire to get the burns and carbon, she got into the weed and burnt the hell out of that finger. That's why an only 80% match. We had to take a second finger to be sure of a good print; she is lucky to be alive, but I needed her to complete the plan.

This time I did the campfire roasting; you don't know how strange it feels to be roasting your own body part."

Charlie couldn't wait. "You're such a detail planner; you couldn't leave it to chance to have the left hand survive and be found. You understand my question?"

The killer laughed enjoying the question and the opportunity to brag. "Very good. I had to be sure, and it was easy. Chris had turned into an alcoholic and grabbed any drugs available; it was a simple process to have him overdose.

The large ax in the shed, now a burnt pile of boards, allowed me to separate the left hand from his body. I took part of the forearm because I wanted a piece of that ugly flannel shirt of his. The rest was tedious: use the pruning shears to remove some fingers and then roast the partial forearm and hand with the help of some of my moonshine. Well, it wasn't that easy, some parts had to turn to carbon, others just burnt, and there was no practice run. Last the strategic placement of my burnt fingers near the hand and the job was done."

Jimmy tilted his head back, staring at the ceiling, his confession slow and powerful, almost like a formal recital; he was reliving the thrill, proud of his performance, glad to have an audience to appreciate his brilliance. This was much better than two biased academics.

As Charlie listened to the gruesome story, he thought: *the man is almost glowing....the murder of his best friend treated like a game, and Chris lost the toss... chopped off a forearm as if he was slicing off a piece of cheese.....roasted his own fingers as if they were wieners for a campfire hot dog cookout...a true psycho.....no remorse....Bea had better start running because if he ever was released, she would be next.............Jesus, we have to stop him.*

Jimmy decided to wrap it up: "We used the ether and moonshine to saturate the cabin, set Chris on his chair next to the window. The problem to solve was: how do we set it off without burning up. The solution, which I never tried to understand, was a trick Bea learned from an arsonist she had been entertaining a few years back. You know she gets around and is damn smart but also reckless. This remote timer trick allowed us to get out before the explosion. Impressed?"

"Yes, I am. You and Bea did one helluva of a job. I think the bandaged hand was the crowning touch."

"The other complication. I couldn't walk around with two missing fingers. I couldn't go to the hospital for treatment......in a small community word would spread within the hour. The story we were going to use: I was to trip onto some warm embers; this would allow Bea to bandage me and hide my missing fingers. All good except: instead of a fast roll in some ashes, I had to remove all evidence of the remote timing device. Once I got into the shell of a cabin everything was hot as hell; in my rush, I wasn't careful and got burnt. So the part about a burnt hand was the truth. Ironic!

She didn't clean the hand correctly, plus we were late getting to a major hospital; we had to drive far enough to ensure word would not get back. An infection set in, and I ended up losing the first couple knuckles of some other fingers ....a goddamn mess.........as I said, she only lives because I need her."

The killer was winding down, and the detective began to remember some words his brother had almost preached to him: *power is nothing unless it's manifested and felt, showed off.*

There was a vital issue Jimmy needed reassurance on: "Still my turn: without the info from this conversation do you have enough evidence to get authorization from the Judge to conduct legal S1 Interrogation on me?"

"No. Not a chance ....it is all speculation on my part. The Judge has already been clear about his feelings for Max......he hates him and will not bend to help him. You're safe.

One more question: why did you have Bea screw the Sheriff? You needed to get out of the city?"

"Yes my hand was throbbing, burns hurt. Also, I was worried some insurance agent might show up and demand a DNA test. I could see Bea eyeing Sheriff Bob....the damn woman would screw a snake...... I knew she had to blow off steam ....too much tension for her ....so the tumble would serve two purposes .... I knew she would give him the ride of his life."

When Jimmy finished, he started laughing and waving his arm as if signaling a victory. "I watched for a while from the adjunct motel room but soon fell asleep....there is only so much porno anyone can stand. Detective, is there anything else?'

Charlie wasn't finished. "Yes, the video of Chris after the S3 brain probe, tied down on that bed, putting on his act, yelling obscenities, spitting at staff......who did you send the video to? That was the key part of the Assessment Team's report to the President."

Thor grinned. "Good. Very good. You guessed I sent it ....damn good guess. I knew it had to be someone with authority otherwise the news media wouldn't touch it. Also had to be someone who would like to screw Max and you. Rumour has it: your boss fits both criteria."

"Jesus you sent it to Chief Kisashton. Shit, he released it to the news media? The unauthorized release? An illegal act?

"He's the man. The guy is a nasty piece of work.

Now to wind this up, for the record, which will never become public: I'm Jimmy Sucart and not Chris Evan. I freely confess to Detective Charlie Taylor; I'm not under the influence of any drugs. It is too bad the Detective will not remember a single word of this conversation and failed to record it. I hope he finds another satisfying career. Goodbye Charlie." With that, he shoved his chair back and stood up from the table.

Before he could take more than three steps, Terry was on one side of him and Manuel on the other side. Jimmy exploded. "Detective Taylor, what the hell is this?"

"Jimmy you will now be taken in and charged with first-degree murder; you have given us enough to execute you many times."

"You smart bastard had this taped. How? Doesn't matter you used an S1 solution illegally, and this is all not admissible. Not so smart."

"Actually Jimmy, no S1 was used. What you saw me pour into your drink was just more coffee. All the discussion was just two guys confessing our sins, but I was not truthful and was setting you up to brag about your plan."

"Bullshit! I saw your reaction; you're not that good an actor."

"Thanks. I thought I did a good job; you should know I practiced a number of hours. The hardest piece was imitating a baby trying to ward off sleep."

"I want these cups as evidence."

"I thought you might. Here is a pen. Be sure to initial and date each one sample. Manuel has the large plastic evidence collector you may use. Even call your student to be a witness, if you wish. In any case, all samples will go to the Forensic lab."

The student came down to the table and added his signature to the sample cups; Charlie sealed the cups in an evidence bag, and the journey was over.

As Terry walked Jimmy out of the University Lounge, another facet of the interrogation was underway. Charlie had Manuel run the confession tape over to their news contact, and within 20 minutes it would make the late afternoon news and within another 20 minutes would be played all over the world.

Two university academics and a chief of police would have to go into hiding.

Charlie thought: *best call Max.*

CHAPTER 19: THE CELEBRATION

"Higher Daddy, higher."

It was mid-afternoon: Emma working in the kitchen, Charlie working the backyard swing set with the twins screaming. Next, it was a grass wrestle with his son on top of Charlie; even Ella sat on him. "Daddy what are you going to do when there are three of us on top of you? You will not be able to win."

"Not to worry that's not going to happen."

Paul spoke with authority. "Dad it appears we know more than you."

"What does that mean?"

Ella laughed. "Oh boy, mommy will be upset. It was a secret she wanted to tell you after that last case was closed and all done."

Charlie got up and started to the back door. "Come on you two. Time to talk to mommy."

Emma started to laugh when he came in. "The window was open, and I heard.....they're right I'm pregnant. "

Charlie hugged her, and the twins joined the huddle. Charlie broke the spell. "Enough, we have about 30 minutes to get to the Judge's place; he has become an excellent cook, and Kate is so happy she's invited everyone remotely associated with the case."

Emma teased Charlie. "Paul, daddy will be the big hero tonight!"

The doorbell rang to announce the arrival of the babysitter; the excited twins ran to greet her. The resolution of the case resulted in an exuberant mood; tension dissipated, smiles and laughter the order of the day. The newly charged atmosphere filled the house like an intoxicating miasma, even the serious Paul allowed his emotions to flare.

It wasn't until this moment that Charlie, and Emma, understood how much tension and stress the case had caused in their family. The two adults felt light-headed, the weight lifted from their persons, their friends safe. Emma couldn't remember when she had seen Charlie so happy and loose. It made her wonder what else had been going on that she was not aware of, and Charlie, as usual, never volunteered the extras.

Judge Stephen's yard had never accommodated such a large, raucous crowd. Charlie was right: an ecstatic Dr. Kate had invited anyone remotely associated with the destruction of the Chris Evans or Jimmy Sucart case. With anxiety no longer an issue and beer and wine in abundance it meant the crowd was getting louder by the minute.

One surprise was Sonja, Steve and Kate's daughter, and her immediate attraction to Manuel. The silent man didn't know how to react to a young woman who was open and free with her comments and feelings. An embarrassed Manuel moved from one location to another, hoping she would leave him. Instead, she followed him around the yard and peppered him with a string of questions about the case and his work. Terry thought it was funny and whenever the couple passed close, he threw in some advice: "Come on Manuel be nice. Don't be humble! Sonja, this man is a genius."

Charlie had to go over and cool Terry off; the last week of little sleep and his fast beer consumption had pushed him over the top.

Charlie quietly got him into a back bedroom for a quick, short but necessary nap.

Dr. Max and Sally were last to arrive; both in excellent spirits. Max, surprisingly, gave Charlie a big hug. "Master detective you keep saving me. We have to stop this; my system can't take it, and neither can my pregnant wife." With that, he ran over to hug Dr. Kate.

Charlie, a little stunned, by the comment and behavior, looked at Sally. She smiled at him. "He is right; I'm three months; it was a strange way to announce it, but he so happy I don't think he is even aware of what he is doing. Thanks Charlie, we owe you. I mean it. Thanks."

"It looks like you are also very pleased."

"I'm ecstatic ....your surprised I can see. Well so am I. But am beginning to think I will have to control Max; otherwise, he will spoil the child." She laughed and walked across the lawn to Emma.

Charlie thought: *two people he never believed would even want children...now they are extremely happy; I hope Emma announces her status.*

The steaks and corn had been demolished, the crowd a little more settled, Sonja almost on Manuel's lap and Terry, now stabilized, up and around. Uncle Willie took center stage, a position he appeared to enjoy. "Since we are all friends I think it is only fitting that our master detective shares a few secrets." The crowd cheered, and Charlie thought: *Shit....not now!*

"First I want to know: how the hell you knew Jimmy would select that table in the Lounge's large dining room? The room holds

40 to 50 tables. You and Manuel had it wired and rigged for a full video. How in the hell did you know he would select that spot?"

Charlie grinned. This one was going to be easy; he looked at Max who shook his head with a negative sign. "The President gave Max a very generous budget. This is the money I used it to hire as many techs as Manuel could supervise. We wired every table in the place....it didn't matter where he wanted to sit..... we wired every spot....the guys worked all night, and it was close, but we finished before the place opened."

"Unbelievable you wired almost 50 locations! Alright, what about the drinks and the confession."

Again Charlie looked over at Max who again gave him the second negative sign; no one noticed except Emma. The detective thought for a few minutes then he started a slow delivery. "I had to make some assumptions, but I was confident. He'd been around the prison population, and the two professors had briefed him on all the background issues and potential traps; one of the professors, Dr. Carson, even called me and warned me not to try and trick him to drink a drugged coffee. This meant I needed a more complex plan than doctoring a drink with S1 drugs".

Charlie stopped for a sip of beer and time to think.

"Come on Charlie don't stop now." the crowd wanted more. The ringing phone provided a welcome interruption, and all stopped as Kate answered. She was very subdued. "It's the President, and he wants to talk to Charlie!"

With the phone in his sweating hand, surrounded by friends, he started a remarkable conversation. "Good afternoon Mr. President" was all Charlie was able to say except for "Thank you." and then "Goodbye."

Charlie hung up walked over to Emma and hugged her and whispered in her ear. Willie pushed. "God damn it …..Charlie speak."

Emma answered for him. "Charlie has to go to the Capital on Friday. The President is going to present him with the Presidential Medal of Freedom, for saving our system of justice. It's the supreme civilian decoration. I am so ….."

She never finished; the crowd exploded with screams, handshakes, hugs and back clapping. Even stoic Judge Stephen was high fiving one person after the other. Terry and Manuel grabbed Charlie, and with one lift carried him around the barbecue pit and tables. It was the highest civilian honor possible out of the President's office. An honor bestowed on a man who only days ago was subjected to some cruel commentary: accused of trying to play super cop with a hopeless case.

Willie's questions were almost forgotten. But almost means it was still active and within a few minutes, Uncle Willie was back. "Now to return……you knew or thought they had your tactics figured out…….so you then had to develop a different strategy."

Charlie understood he had to answer. "I knew with that prof's phone call, I'd have to roll the dice. Jimmy is a brilliant man plus he had the profs feeding him…….so I thought Jimmy is very confident …………everything he presented had been accepted……I thought he doesn't have any respect for me or any of the police…he almost laughed in Terry's face when he set up the meeting….he didn't have any doubt that we were an inferior class.

The tricky part was dumping the small container into his drink and making sure Jimmy saw me, without me being aware that he saw me. You with me? It had to look like I was not aware of the fact that he could see me.

It went like this: Terry was outside and gave me a heads up; we had practiced the move. I was ready, with my back to the front door when he walked in and started in my direction. The Lounge has a large ceiling mirror over the coffee bar; it was the ceiling mirror which allowed Chris to see me pour a small vial into his coffee. But the trick was: I only poured more coffee into his cup."

Willie had been celebrating and was loud. "You crazy bastard! You guessed he would force a switch. You had the drugged drink! Your coffee was loaded!"

Charlie smiled and lied, as everyone expected: "No. You know the unauthorized use of the S1 drug mix is illegal."

As the group listened to every word, Emma stopped watching her husband; her gaze alternated between Terry and Max. These two men, in different ways, were sending unintentional messages, at least that was Emma's conclusion. Terry was trying to suppress a know-it-all grin. He was always an emotional man with a quick temper, albeit short-lived. Under Emma's close scrutiny his suppression was not good enough.

Max, the genius, couldn't take his eyes off Charlie. It was if no one else was present. To Emma, this was beyond tense; he was afraid. Of what? Damn it; she was sure something had taken place. Something this tight set would not likely share with this party assembly.

Charlie continued. "I was sure Evans had convinced himself that he was the smartest man in the Sector. He oozed arrogance. Why not? He had fooled the academic community, the best legal could throw at him, and the news media ate up his story."

Brother Sam interrupted: "I probably provided an unintentional assist by quoting from an old book I'm reading. The author, Cositca Bradaton claims *'power is intrinsically erotic: it is nothing unless it's manifested and felt, showed off and taken in. Power doesn't truly exist until it leaves a mark on the minds and bodies of others.'.*"

Charlie laughed and confirmed, "Yes that quotation stuck with me, and I was convinced it fit this killer. But I had to be careful.

After Professor Carson warned me not to try and drug his drinks, I knew Evans would be expecting it. He'd come to the interview to play with me, mock us and have fun. There were two risks to be considered: Would he take the bait and switch the drinks? Second, would my acting be good enough to fool him? I had to convince him I was completely under the influence of the S1 truth serum and never remember his bragging."

Willie was impressed. "So when he saw you pour something into his cup, it was just another example of sloppy police work, an inferior adversary. Here was his chance to turn the tables and force you to drink the doctored coffee, because Jimmy was convinced you had poured the S1 truth serum into his cup. He had you.

Last, your acting was supreme. You must have watched a lot of S1 interrogations."

Charlie continued. "I did. Still, it all depended on how overconfident he was; but we all thought he was ripe. He wanted to brag to someone. Why not a drugged detective?"

"If he doesn't insist on the switch."

"Yes, it might have happened. Then all I could do was push, insist on a detailed analysis of his hand and fingers, so forth. I doubt anything would have worked."

The crowd was impressed, except Emma who shook her head, always surprised at how far her husband would go and how many men had probably assisted. Again the phone rang; this time Judge Stephen answered, waved the crowd to be quiet and spoke in a low voice, so no one heard; he hung up and started laughing.

Stephen relayed the call: "Charlie come over here; this is a day most of us will never forget. That was Judge Doug Brewster he thought you might enjoy the news coming from me. The new announcement: Chief Kisashton has resigned, and Judge Doug wants Charlie in his office tomorrow at 11 am. There will be a press conference so he can announce Charlie as the new Chief of Police!"

For the second time, the backyard erupted. Terry almost doubled over with laughter. Then Judge Stephen broke them up once more by uttering. "Jesus H. Christ!"

The second phone call had been fortuitous, making everyone forget a key point: Charlie's lie didn't explain everything.

Much later the happy couple was finally alone in bed, and Charlie reached for Emma. She decided to find out the truth, no more willing bed time partner. "Charlie I saw that wave off Max gave you. There is more to this story than you are telling. I want to know. This night will not have a happy ending unless you are honest with me."

Charlie got out of the bed and walked around the bedroom; he trusted Emma and thought if the secret is to be safe, she is the only one he and Max would trust. He sat on the edge of the bed, the only light the moon shining through the window, the entire house still, kids sleeping.

"I'm serious when I say this is state secret, but I'll share because I know you will keep it. I think Max will accept this one time revelation."

"Thanks for the confidence. Now talk."

"Max has made a series of improvements; the first one: the new S1 solution no longer has the side effects of making you sleepy nor is there a memory loss; also, it can be used as a fine spray, for minor cases. And we did use it throughout the investigation, mainly on reluctant witnesses.

But for Jimmy's session, I needed the full strength solution, and Max mixed a batch to fit Jimmy's profile. As I said, the revised S1 means no drowsiness and no memory loss. Second, after about a 30-minute exposure to the air, it is impossible to detect. This means put it in a drink and leave the remainder or dregs exposed to the air. Bingo, the cup tests negative for S1.

I had Terry purchase two of the Lounge's franchised mugs, with their prominent fluorescent crest. I needed to control the cups; I didn't have to wait for the serving staff to select a cup. I dumped the customized S1 into both mugs: Max had tailored the strength for Jimmy's size and weight.

This was before the server filled the cups. Timing was critical: I had to get the drugs in before the coffee but not too soon, otherwise it would degrade in the air. Terry was outside keeping me informed of Jimmy's location. Once the cups were full, I waited until he was through the front door and my image was on the ceiling mirror; Terry and I practiced this move a couple of times. I mean making the bogus pour into his coffee. It didn't matter, but the ideal would be for Jimmy to see me dump something into his cup, believe he has overturned our plan, outsmart us and then gloat with his success.

The Profs had been stroking his ego for days. In addition, the favorable news reporting, made the guy think he was on a roll, arrogant and unstoppable. I was sure he couldn't resist. Why fool the entire world and not be able to brag about it? I was presenting the idea of a priest confessor.

Last, the most significant breakthrough: Dr. Max has developed a blocker. I mean: take the pill about 20 minutes before an S1, and it blocks the impact; you are not compelled to tell the truth."

Charlie never gave Emma a chance to ask questions. It seemed he, too, wanted to talk about the process, tell the truth to someone he trusted. "Last little confession: we never wired all the dining room tables; we couldn't get that done without the staff knowing and possibly telling friends or other students. The solution? Manuel has invented a unique parabolic receiver, or whatever it is; it picks up ....gathers everything....sound and video, with an unbelievable range. Didn't matter where the bastard wanted to sit. We had him, even if moved across the street. Manuel wants it kept under wraps until his patent is finalized."

"My God! Your team pulled a real fast one."

"It worked like this: I took the blocker and then doctored both drinks. If Jimmy didn't see the doctoring and didn't ask for the switch, it didn't matter. As long as he drank up, he was drugged up. With the blocker, I had to act the part. I mean I was drinking a doctored coffee but was in control of the conversation. Did a good job right?"

"I knew it. Terry and Max will have to practice a better poker face. Now get into bed, and we can have a private celebration. And, by the way, forget about an acting career."

"Yes Ma'am."

They had agreed to meet in the back parking lot of the small church. As soon as Monk drove in, he saw Wes's car in the back corner in the shade of a big evergreen. After parking, he strolled to the solitary car. Before knocking on a window Monk stopped and listened to the music blaring from the interior; it was screeching lament: an ancient hit song, sung by David Bowie: Cat People (Putting out Fire).

Even standing outside the car, the keywords were easy to hear: **putting out the fire with**. And then, as Wes must have turned up the volume, an ear-shattering note: **GASOLINE.** Monk was sure Wes had it on a loop or repeat play; this would match his disposition. The one line of the song continued to be played and rock the car, as Wes had the words screaming from the speakers.

Monk thought about a recent advance seminar he attended, dealing with people suffering from emotional distress. For some reason, a few paragraphs attracted his attention and were reread many times. Was it because of all the loud music Wes preferred? Monk could reproduce the words at will:

The social, emotional, and psychological rewards for listening to loud music have not been studied in detail, in part, because such studies would expose listeners to be sound intensities that would damage their inner ear. Even without a definitive conclusion, it is clear that loud music changes the mood and behavior of listeners, often in a pleasurable way.

There may not be consistency among individuals with different temperaments and values, but the seductive attraction of loud music has a simple explanation: it does something pleasurable for listeners even if the details are not known or vary among individuals.

But like all forms of pleasure, excess produces damage, and everyone must balance the risk versus reward. While the physiological properties of damaged hearing have been documented, there is less discussion about the social and emotional consequences resulting from this hearing disability.

Zimbardo et al (1981) demonstrated that simulated deafness in normal individuals produced symptoms of paranoia.

Before he could knock on a window, Wes popped a lock and waved him in to sit on the cold leather front bucket seat, and stopped the music. Wes started immediately. "I've been so goddamn lonely and never really understood how lonely until Adela touched me." He tried to retain control, but each word was an effort, his voice nearly breaking with each word. "Charlie should understand; we all helped him for almost two years when his family was killed."

Monk didn't hesitate, "Charlie understands; he also knows how vulnerable you are and wants to protect you, wants you to be cautious. Let me ask you something: do you see the resemblance to Pameela?"

Monk's question hung in the air, threatening to block the dialogue, because Pameela had been Wes's lover before her brutal murder. But they were alone, and Wes was comfortable with the big man. "Monk it's a bit of a stretch. She is physically the same size and skin tone …ok, yes there is a resemblance."

"Good I think it is important for you to accept the resemblance and be aware of what is happening."

Some years ago, Pameela Sharma and Wes had been deeply in love when she was brutally murdered by the Robin Hood killer. Since then Wes rarely dated and stayed away from bars and clubs; just occasionally sharing a drink with Monk who allowed him to rattle on and at times whine about life. Monk continued. "How bad is it? Can you stay away from her?"

"It's bad. I've tried physical exhaustion….running miles, heavy weights, karate workouts but within an hour she's back in mind. Do I love her? Shit, I don't think so. Do I want her? Yes, I do. I know Charlie and the team are pissed with me, but I can't shake her."

"You know you're vulnerable. You've been lonely….without a female for a long time and then the booze, at the Polish Hall, set the stage."

"Sure I understand. I'd been guzzling beer, plus an hour of close hot dancing with a woman, but for some damn reason she fits….. whatever that means, …………….then when her skirt fell onto the floor, I almost lost it and was seconds away from public fornication. I'm completely helpless …………….God, I understand horny………….but Monk it's more than that. I have to see her when we are both cold stone sober. Just the two of us. Straight talk."

"Wes is it safe to open up to her? Remember she is married; her husband may be in institutional care, doesn't matter, she is still married. If she trapped you once, can you trust her?"

"I'll be careful and go one step at a time. I have to do it. She is not Pameela …..believe me, I know that but ….but she …but she……Jesus Monk I can't explain it without sounding like a naïve teenager…..all I end up saying is 'she fits'…..I "

"No need to explain any further.....let's talk before you make contact and review a strategy." With that Monk started to make his way out of the car, his colossal size didn't make exiting the vehicle easy. He hoped Wes would call before he tried to see the woman.

"Thanks Monk."

Wes knew his career was on the line, if this woman was still tied to Bea. Was he fantasying? But it appeared in the early part of that evening she looked at him with what he thought was a plea; was this good looking woman also lonely? She projected physical strength and energy, but her touch was light and her voice a whisper in his ear. He knew he was going to see her and would open up and see how she responded. If he was just one of many and she was playing a game, it would get ugly and maybe a career issue if she was still tied to the criminal Bea. Could Monk help? Would Charlie cut him some slack?

CHAPTER 20: A BAND OF BROTHERS

It was the start of a new week, the last week ending with the shocking confession. This Monday, the three detectives set out on independent paths: for Charlie one mundane task, for Wes an embarrassing undertaking, and for Manuel a life-changing mission.

In the late 18th century, at the Battle of the Nile, the then Rear-Admiral, Horatio Nelson referred to the 15 captains serving with him as "a band of brothers." Although Charlie never used the phrase, this is how he thought of his close-knit group of detectives: Wes Krause, Terry Patterson, Manuel Moreno and himself.

Although they were not military, the team had fought numerous dangerous street clashes, wrestled with killers, faced psychopaths, and under Charlie's direction bent the rules in pursuit of maniacs. Sam Taylor, a clinical psychologist, often wondered how they achieved their extraordinary success. They all, at one time or another, had been tested by him or had been under his care. He knew their personalities, intelligence, and normal behavior patterns.

Theory predicted: they should be in constant chaos instead of a focused set of men. His only conclusion was that Charlie was so fixated on success, he allowed, or maybe encouraged, an extensive set of diverse behavior and never let himself or the team get sidetracked by irrelevant issues. The normal chain of command was, although not openly treated with contempt, generally ignored; Charlie was always on the edge of disobedience and set a strong example.

On some hard-backed chairs, Charlie and his son remained in a crowded room, an adjunct to the main Emergency Department waiting area. Emma had gone, with Ella, to the x-ray unit; the young girl had fallen out of a tree and tore a few branches off the main trunk on her way down. She landed on her back, knocked the wind out of herself and created a panic in the household; the entire family traveled to the hospital.

The harassed intern believed there were no broken bones or other complications but did order a series of x-rays. It was quiet in the small waiting room jammed with about 20 people, mostly just staring into space, hoping they would next to be called for treatment. Charlie could sense Paul was upset.

"Listen Paulie it's going to be ok."

"Dad please don't call me Paulie......I ask you before."

"Sorry, you're right. My fault."

"And I don't think you understand."

In the quiet of the small waiting room their conversation was clear for all to hear, and it did relieve the boredom, a father and son under stress with an honest interchange, the young boy articulate and not afraid of his dad.

"What do you mean Paul? What don't I understand?"

"I worry, not only because she is my sister, but because I love the little fucker."

It seemed to take a few seconds before the incredulous comments from the five-year-old sunk in. But then the entire room erupted with laughter, except Charlie.

The embarrassed detective studied his young son. Years of interviewing criminals and hours of studying liars allowed him to see what others had missed: a very slight self-satisfied smile on his son's face. Charlie thought: *Oh my god, he is punishing me for calling him 'Paulie'. Monk was right: his son's growth was going to be one helluva of a ride.*

Thank God Emma is not here.

Wes knew the other detectives believed lust was the compelling force; they thought his feelings were a raw basic need, understandable but still not a rational motive.

He pulled into the parking lot of the Barn, as Adela's ranch was called, turned off the motor, sat in the car and thought: *idiot.* He got out of the car and stood beside his front door, more hesitation. The parking lot was empty, as he planned when waiting on the ridge.

Earlier in the day when he drove out, it seemed like the right move; now he wasn't sure. Rejection was one thing, but humiliation was another dimension, and surely the rest of the crew would eventually find out about this trip. Charlie had been angry with him or maybe more worried about him. Monk had cautioned him and also saw the resemblance to Pameela. Were they all right?

He trudged up the sidewalk to the side entrance. There was a large raised wooden deck, full of outdoor furniture, probably used for meeting customers; it was a good 25 feet long and about 15 feet wide. Wes walked up the four stairs and took a few steps toward the door. Then stopped midway across the deck and turned; his resolve had evaporated, best to slip away.

Before he could go down the small set of stairs, a voice called out. "Wes where are you going?"

He turned and saw Adela in the doorway; she walked across the deck and stood in front of him, nearly touching him. Her closeness was almost too much; for a few minutes, he closed his eyes and concentrated on her voice. She never gave him a chance to speak but started on her confession. "I'm sorry.......I thought it was important to help Donna...it wasn't supposed to happen like that....it had been months since I had been out, and there was an immediate magnetism...well, I was attracted, nervous, and soon drunk ... Jesus, I mean really drunk.....I don't ..."

Wes pressed his finger against her lips. "No more. There is nothing more to say. I want you to be absolutely honest with me, no more games. Yes? Good.

I'm going to give you two choices. One: you say something along the lines of 'Wes it was nice but time to wrap it up.' Second option: you invite me in, and we lock the door and get to know each other."

Adela stared at him and reached for his hand. "Wes, you best come in; it's too hot to be standing out here."

It was an unusual Monday morning for the Judge; there were two appointments he could not avoid; to add to the confusion, his secretary vacated her position in an effort to replenish their coffee supplies. First, on his agenda, Brewster had to deal with a man whose actions revolted the entire country. Later, he would have the job of formally swearing Charlie in as the new Chief and confirming Terry as the new second-in-command; both detectives understood his dislike, and of course, he knew the feelings were reciprocated.

Before he could give it more thought, the Troll arrived with, surprisingly, only one armed guard. The Troll was in Judge Doug's office to make a deal for another month. His assertion: his interrogators had been in a hurry and once a few killings were declared they stopped the mind probe. The Troll claimed when he first started he did two street kids, years ago, maybe the parents would like to know where the bodies were located. This he also held back from the Research Team, headed by Sam Taylor.

Judge Doug was in a terrible mood: after firing his sycophant, Chief Kisashton, the Regional Executive Board forced him to appoint Charlie as the new Chief. He tore into the Troll. He reverted to a prosecuting attorney he used to be. "Listen you son of a bitch your deals are finished. I'm booking you another S3 Interrogation which will be good enough to verify your claim and find the bodies. Might wipe out a few brain cells, so be it. Get out!"

"Wait a fucking minute I was promised no more of this interrogation shit."

"The provision was: you would be straight and confess to the Research Team. It appears you didn't tell them about your early start with the street kids, so the deal is off and get back to the Farm and get ready."

"Ok Judge, Jesus no need to get excited. Drop the S3; it was a long shot; I thought since the first story worked, you might bite on another one. No, I didn't work the street …no interest ….not an exciting group …so screw more mind probes…it will gain nothing."

Before he could finish his protest, Manuel barged in with his gun drawn. The armed guard hadn't moved, completely taken by surprise. Manuel spoke with authority. "Put your weapon on the floor, turn and get out." The man never hesitated, within seconds was out of the office and hustling down the long hall away from the office, stopping long enough to call for a SWAT team.

Manuel never spoke a word. Both men shouted at him and were ignored; the detective first handcuffed the Judge to his oversized desk and the Troll to the other side of the massive piece of furniture.

In many ways, the setting resembled an old fashion opera, two men wailing and screaming at their assailant. Their opponent silently went about his business with only an occasional grunt or a swipe at the head of the Troll. All this took place in one of the most ostentatiously decorated offices in the Sector. All furnishing reflected the exalted status of the Judge: heavy drapes to block the sun, thick carpet to assist with the subdued ambiance and heavy oak furniture which the Judge liked and had demanded.

Then the scene escalated one more dimension; in his hurry to gain access to the office, Manuel had failed to lock the door. To his surprise in walked Sonja; she was working as special research assistance for the Judge. Within seconds she understood what was happening; last night, after too much alcohol, Manuel spoke about his murdered niece, his failed marriage and the boy who was not his son. It had been more than the beer and whiskey; Sonja connected with him and drew him out as no one had been able to do. The sex had been hot and intense; Manuel was gone when she woke, but she was convinced they would be meeting later in the day but not like this.

She turned, locked the door and walked to Manuel: "I'm staying with you."

Manuel tried to get her to leave. "Sonja, please go; this is a family matter. I have to take care of this scum."

At this point, the Troll started laughing. "I know who you are. Cara used to speak about her Uncle Manuel, a star detective. Come for revenge? First, let me tell you she was delicious. God ....I wanted to keep her for a month....not often I get a smart one…God… her little breasts were unbelievable….." He then started to smack his lips and grabbed his crotch with vigorous rubbing. " and then her beautiful ass …". He started to moan and wiggle his hips simulating intercourse.

A strange scene started to unfold: the Troll bragged about how he tortured and loved Cara's body; this boasting took place in competition with the conversation occurring between Manuel and Sonja. Even in his terrified state, the Judge found the dual dialogue intriguing as he tried to listen to both at the same time; a raving maniac going to lurid details of his assault on the girl competing with what appeared to an evolving declaration of love. Sonja was trying to speak louder and louder to drown out the maniac who wanted to enrage Manuel. The bizarre scene with overlapping dialogues captured Judge Doug's attention; he almost forgot his danger.

Sonja tried to make her case. "Manuel, it's not often I bond with anyone. You and I connected fast and were tied together the entire night…..you know it was special……..don't throw it away."

"Sonja you're too young. It was my mistake; I should've walked away."

"No! No! I'm a woman, young but not a girl. I knew what I was doing."

Manuel gently pushed her aside and walked up to the desk. "Don't worry Judge I just want this scumbag."

Even the Judge tried. "Manuel he isn't worth it. He'll be executed within the week. Just stop now, and all is forgiven. He just wants to take you with him. Wants you executed for first-degree murder."

Manuel crouched down in front of the Troll and smiled at him, then delivered a series of cuffs with the gun; blood and other fluids splattered across the carpet. For the first time, the killer was silent and recognized the naked hatred in Manuel's face.

Marching down the hall towards the Judge's chambers was a content trio. Terry was flirting with Janet, the Judge's secretary with an armful of coffee supplies; she was pretending to ignore him, but her giggling gave her away. Charlie trailed behind them smiling at the game in front of him.

When they turned a sharp corner, the running guard almost bowled them over. Within minutes, Charlie understood what was going on and gave the runner instructions. "At this moment, there is probably a SWAT team outside the front entrance; they will be reviewing all exits and entrances into this building. Go to them. We were in before they assembled. Tell them I'm at the scene, repeat the Chief is at the scene and will be in the reception area with Terry. Go!"

Janet immediately ran to her monitor and with a few keystrokes had the images she wanted and called Terry. "Detective, this is the Judge's chambers; he had this recording equipment installed as soon as he was appointed."

Terry knew what had to be done. "Janet leave. Get out of the building. I'll call when it is all over."

She hesitated for a few minutes then started to run. Terry called Charlie over. "I have the feed camera from inside the Judge's chamber; Janet activated it, and we are live."

Both men watched the unfolding scene. Both desperately trying to think about the best way to resolve the situation. Then they heard pounding boots coming down the hall. "Good, it's the SWAT group. Shit! That hard-nosed Captain Biller is running the squad. Better grab him. His team always manages to shot first."

It was a crowded hallway with only the small reception area outside the Chambers. Charlie introduced himself. "Captain Biller, I'm the new Chief, and I want you to understand that I'm calling the shots on this."

A stubborn captain remained firm, and his reputation flashed. "As I understand the Sector protocol: in hostage situations, the SWAT commander is in charge until the issue is defused."

Charlie knew he could not afford to give this man an inch. "Those are general guidelines and not rigid or set in stone. As Chief of the Investigative

Division for the Sector, I'm giving you a direct command. If you or any of your men chose to ignore it, I will make sure this will be your last day of employment. I will make it my life's obsession to get you kicked out, and during the time it takes me, you will get every shit job in the Sector.

If you doubt me, remember my nickname and reputation; it hasn't changed because of my new title."

Some of the SWAT members close enough to hear tried to pull the Captain back; the tenacious man stared at Charlie. He was not used to being challenged and didn't want to step down in front of his troop.

Terry stepped in, looked at the second in command, he spoke loud enough for the entire hallway to hear. "Lieutenant, the Chief just gave your Captain a direct order. Are you guys dumb? Or hard of hearing? One more minute and your careers are over."

Slowly the SWAT group lowered their weapons. The Captain knew he had lost and just nodded at Charlie. What he didn't understand: by next Monday his career was over; there was no way a Chief could allow this type of lack of respect for his office to become public knowledge, without a strong response.

"Captain, contact you snipers in the high ground. No one shoots without my command."

While the Captain spread the word, Charlie and Terry discussed how to best proceed. "Charlie you know he has the door locked so we can't walk in. I'll try and phone him. Are you ready to talk to Manuel?"

Manuel continued to whisper to the Troll in a soft voice. "I plan to kill you in pieces. I mean I will shot various parts of your body, one at a time I think one knee is a good start. It hurts like hell. "

To everyone's surprise, including those watching on camera, Troll shut his mouth and seemed terrified. Since his arrest, he had continued to brag about his superiority and his prowess with young girls. Something in Manuel had petrified him. At last, he understood: within minutes it could all end for him, the ending not to be a painless exit.

Sonja never tried to pull Manuel away from the Troll but continued to stare at him and talk. "You know we are special to each other. Why throw it away? I commit to you right here without any reservations. Doesn't matter what might result because of this. Look at me! Look at me!"

In the reception area, still watching via the feed camera, Charlie was impressed. "Terry, Judge Stephen and Dr. Kate have one helluva a daughter. .....smart and tough ....some lady."

Terry was ready. "You want this on speaker phone?"

"Yes just keep the volume down a low as you can and have the SWAT group move down the hall."

Within a few rings, Manuel picked up; he guessed who was on the other end. "Boss, just let me do this. You know what a creature this is; a needle in the arm is too easy."

"You know I agree. Even my brother has nightmares from having to speak to him. But let's face it: dead is dead. That is the big loss for him. It doesn't matter how he goes. Cara is gone, and nothing you can do will change that reality. Look there is an extraordinary woman beside you. I mean very special, and you know I'm an expert on the female sex."

Even in the ridiculous tense atmosphere, this last comment brought a laugh because of Charlie's mess with relationships. Sonja spoke next. "Chief Taylor, will Manuel be kicked out of the force because of this incident?'

It felt strange hearing someone address him by his official title. "Not if I can help it. The Troll has deliberately egged him on and has pissed off everyone, including all the convicts at the Farm. His murdering so abhorrent I can't believe anyone will be prepared to speak for him. We can try to get his confession made public.

Judge Doug what is your opinion because you will be included in the decision. Even if you are not on the Disciplinary Panel, you can influence them. Care to comment?"

The Judge rubbed his wrist, for some reason he felt safer with Charlie on the phone. "I will do everything in my power to see that Manuel gets the minimum disciplinary action. The murder of a relative has always been a special case...... if we can end this without a killing......it will be treated as a minor indiscretion."

Charlie managed to suppress a smile but thought: *old Dougie must be scared shitless.*

Then Terry was waving the spare key he found in the secretary's desk. Charlie didn't hesitate. "Manuel listen we are coming in. Terry is unlocking the door and coming in. Don't shot Terry....... he cries real easy."

At what appeared to be his rescue, the Troll recovered his courage, leered at Manuel and bragged. "Cara began to love it. I used to lick her entire body from toes to the forehead, never skipped a square inch until she begged for more. The best was when I turned her over, and she screamed 'shove it in' ...."

The Troll never finished the sentence. Terry already had one step into the office. Manuel gave his old partner the briefest of smiles; then bent over his victim. He held the weapon between Troll's eyes and pulled the trigger. The blood and brain matter splattered Judge Doug's face.

As the door was now fully opened, Terry was in first, followed by Charlie. Sonja ignored both of them, never screamed, walked up to Manuel, hugged him and took the gun out of his hand. Within seconds Terry was beside them, followed by Charlie. Again within a few more seconds, there was a four-way hug as the Troll bled all over the carpet.

Judge Doug's throat was entirely dehydrated, making it difficult to speak. The various fragments of the Troll's brain splattered over the Judge's face and what didn't stick rolled down his face, but most disturbing he realized he had wet his pants, and a yellow pool was gathering on the carpet. After a few tries, he was able to utter a few words.

"You're all crazy. Now we have to prepare to execute a detective!"

THE END

NEXT BOOK: **SAY HELLO TO JESUS**

THE PROLOGUE

The tall detective was subjected to the universal anguish of the rejected; the intensity of his love for the woman magnified the pain. Although in time he would forget the words exchanged, the scene itself replayed in his mind at regular intervals.

It started after he finished his morning coffee and was about to leave, when he saw his meager set of belongs, all packaged in his large duffel bag, beside the kitchen exit. Before he could start his questions, the woman, standing by the sink with arms crossed against her chest, "We have to end it; It can't go on. Andy is coming back to the ranch by the end of the week. His physio has progressed to a point where he can walk with those two short canes....whatever they are called...it's awkward but it works."

Wes tried to be composed but was losing control with each second. "I thought we talked about this and had a plan of action: you would help him readjust and then demand a divorce."

"Well I thought about it, and this is best."

"You are a real piece of work; last night it was all hot passion and then this morning 'see you around'. What the hell is this?"

Adela knew it was going to be difficult, but she had been through this scene before. "You are not listening to me..."

BOOK 1: **KILL MOST OF THE MISCREANTS**

BOOK 2: **KILL SOME OF THE PRIVILEGED**

BOOK 3: **KILL ALL OF THEM**

www.ingramcontent.com/pod-product-compliance
Lightning Source LLC
Chambersburg PA
CBHW022159170626
46807CB00005B/2270